In the winter of the heart, spring is not far behind...

THE SWEET STING
OF FIRST LOVE

"I know what you're about to say," Maggie told him. "And I do not wish to hear it."

Hunter laughed shortly and stepped back a pace. "And what am I about to say?"

"That I am just a silly girl and you are a *man*."

He smiled at the small pout formed by her mouth. "You are not a silly girl, little one. You are a delightful young woman."

"But too young," she offered forthrightly, squinting up at him, for the sun was at his back.

"Yes, too young for some things." He cupped her elbow in one hand and led her toward a fallen tree.

When they were seated side by side, Hunter leaned forward, bracing his elbows on his knees and lacing his fingers loosely together.

"I shall wait for you, you know," she said.

She was staring out over the pond, and Hunter could feel her sudden sadness. "You will soon be meeting many, many young men, Maggie. You'll soon forget me."

She turned her head abruptly, and he could see moisture gathering in those bright blue eyes. "I will never forget you," she said firmly. "You must promise to come back."

This book also contains a preview of another exciting new Diamond Homespun Romance, **Golden Chances** *by Rebecca Hagan Lee.*

SPRING BLOSSOM

JILL METCALF

DIAMOND BOOKS, NEW YORK

SPRING BLOSSOM

A Diamond Book / published by arrangement with
the author

PRINTING HISTORY
Diamond edition / August 1992

ISBN: 1-55773-751-7

Diamond Books are published by The Berkley Publishing Group,
200 Madison Avenue, New York, New York 10016.
The name ''DIAMOND'' and its logo are trademarks
belonging to Charter Communications, Inc.

PRINTED IN THE UNITED STATES OF AMERICA

10 9 8 7 6 5 4 3 2 1

*In memory of my dad,
a quiet man
with a great capacity to love*

To Bea and Ric, Barb and Mike, Eric, B.J., Maureen, Nancy, Pauline, and a very terrific lady, Betty! My own special support network.

Thank you all for being there, and not only for the writing of this book!

With love always!

SPRING BLOSSOM

CHAPTER

❧ 1 ❧

**Treemont Farm,
Virginia, 1880**

Maggie Downing frowned at her sister. "Denise! Not on my bed!" she wailed as a slim body catapulted into the center of the narrow bed.

Denise giggled, not in the least put out by her sister's tone. "Tell her, Florence," Denise called eagerly as ten-year-old Florence entered the room in a more subdued fashion. "Tell her."

Maggie looked from one sister to the other and then fixed her attention on Florence, who was always more coopera-tive. "Tell me what?" she asked.

Florence moved to her oldest sister's side and whispered in awe, "We've seen him."

Maggie frowned. "He is a friend of Papa's, Florence, not the President. And you hardly have to whisper."

"But he is *beautiful*, Maggie," Florence whispered again, and Maggie felt her impatience growing.

1

"He's big!" Denise piped up, scrambling to her knees on the bed.

"Please get off the bed, Dennie," Maggie said reasonably and then turned back to face the shy, retiring Florence. "More beautiful than Chad Moran?"

Florence nodded with enthusiasm, but it was her thirteen-year-old sister who responded to the question. "Much more," Denise said. "And he smiled at me. He has a very beautiful smile."

Maggie whirled on her. "Get off my bed, you little wretch!"

"Denise is mushy!" Florence said in unison with Maggie's comment.

Denise scrambled down to stand a safe distance away while Maggie smoothed out the flowered counterpane.

"Don't call me names," Denise said self-righteously. "'Wretch' is not a nice name."

"Well, Anna will think I messed my bed up, and she'll fuss at me." Her calf-length skirts swayed as Maggie straightened up and flung a thick blond braid over her shoulder. "Did he speak to you, Florence? Is he impressive?"

"He didn't even see her!" Denise giggled again and earned a fierce look from the quiet sister. "Florence was hiding behind a tree."

"I am talking," Florence said. "Go away."

"I think he's beautiful," Denise put in. "But he's old."

Maggie moved across the pretty room, decorated in yellow and white chintz, and perched demurely on the edge of a small boudoir chair.

"Is he fierce-looking, Flo?" Maggie asked anxiously.

Her sister raised patient brown eyes to her. "Oh, no. He is big, and he is very pretty, and he has a nice smile. I don't think he's fierce at all."

"Men aren't pretty!" Denise insisted, but her sisters ignored her.

Maggie frowned thoughtfully at the youngest girl. "But you didn't speak to him."

Florence could only shake her head.

Denise snorted from a corner of the room. "She was afraid."

Maggie shot her a brief glare. "Florence is polite," she said. "You might take a lesson." Having acted as the mother since their own mother's death, Maggie had become peacemaker, teacher, and adviser. Now, giving her attention to the girl who had come to sit in the opposite chair, she asked, "Does he look savage?"

Florence looked surprised by the question. "What a mean thing to say!"

Frowning more intensely, Maggie leaned forward. "You mean he was dressed like a gentleman?"

Frowning now also, Florence asked, "What did you expect?"

Maggie straightened up, puzzled. "Well," she drawled, "he *is* an Indian."

"He doesn't even carry a knife," Denise replied, obviously disappointed.

"Not that you could see," Maggie said sagely.

Florence's doelike eyes widened. "Oh, Mag—"

Maggie waved an impatient hand. "Now, don't get all upset, Florence," she ordered and then fell into silence.

The bright-eyed Denise crossed the room and plunked herself down on the edge of the bed. She had a round, almost cherubic face and thick auburn hair that always seemed to defy her braids, and she positively worshiped Maggie. "Whatcha thinking, Mag?" She grinned when her older sister gave her a smile.

"I thought he would be fierce and exciting." Maggie sounded disappointed by her sisters' report.

"I think he just looks ordinary," Florence offered.

Maggie smiled. "That's because you're only a baby."

Affronted, Florence straightened abruptly. "I am not, and I think boys are stupid anyway!" Glaring fiercely, she mumbled, "My pony is friendlier," and she raced out of the room.

Denise looked unhappy that Florence had stomped off in anger. "You know she hates being called a baby," she said softly.

Maggie nodded. "I simply meant she's too young to appreciate men."

Denise smiled at that. "So are you."

Maggie took her turn looking affronted. "I'm sixteen."

Almost gasping at the falsehood, Denise shot back, "You're fifteen, Maggie."

"Well, not much longer. I have to think of my future."

Denise could only stare at her, obviously confused by her last comment.

Maggie provided the solution. "I won't stay at Treemont forever, Dennie. I have to think about finding a suitable husband."

Husband?

Denise looked thunderstruck. "But, Maggie," she breathed. "Why?"

Maggie took on the role of senior adviser as if born to it. "None of us will stay here forever, silly. We must all find husbands eventually."

"But Papa will be lonely without us," she added frantically.

"We'll find rich husbands and live in grand mansions," Maggie added dreamily, oblivious to her younger sister's growing fears.

Denise attempted to absorb all these thoughts and added with confidence, "But you won't live far away, Mag. Chad will surely ask for you."

Maggie waved a hand airily as if to brush away the thought. "Chad Moran is boring," she said, getting to her feet and shaking out her skirts. "I'll find a handsome man who is fiercely exciting." Leaving her younger sister staring at her back as she moved quickly toward her bedroom door, she threw back over her shoulder, "And I believe I'll go see what this Hunter Maguire is like."

Gasping, Denise raced after her. "You can't, Maggie," she called as she followed her slim, long-legged sister down the wide corridor of the second floor. "You have to wait till Papa calls us down to meet him."

"I simply want a little peek, silly," and she grinned, rushing on. "He's with Papa, then?" She didn't wait for an answer as she raced headlong down the narrow stairs.

Denise stopped dead, shaking her head, firmly convinced that Maggie was growing stranger with each passing day.

Hunter Maguire opened the French doors that led to the small second-story terrace off the blue guest room. He stepped out and took a deep breath of the fresh, sweet air as he admired the rolling green landscape before him. This certainly was lush, rich country, this Virginia. Beautiful and pleasing to the eyes and all one's other senses. He had been born to this land, on a small farm a few days distant from this grand old house. And while the scale of his mother's farm did not compare with this ancient establishment, Hunter had plans for the future. His mother prospered with crops, but he was about to increase the diversity of the farm by purchasing some good bloodstock and raising fine saddle horses. And he knew that some of the best animals in the state could be found in the stables belonging to his father's old friend, Alastair Downing.

He turned back to the room, stripping off his shirt and flexing his shoulders, easing out the stiffness. The room had no bath, but the housekeeper, a crusty woman by the name of Anna, had filled a large copper tub that sat before a small fireplace at one end of the large room.

He was looking forward to a long hot soak after his ride from the coast. Now he could relax and enjoy a bit of freedom after being confined on that miserable ship. He was not very tolerant of confinement. He chuckled at his own thought; he had absolutely *no* tolerance for confinement, and he had prolonged his own personal torture by stopping in New York before coming to Virginia, keeping himself mummified in high-collared shirts, straight-legged trousers, and long coats. God, he looked forward to getting into his soft, comfortable britches and an open-necked shirt.

Hunter struggled out of his high boots, then peeled off his fawn-colored trousers. With a sigh he lowered himself into the hot water and leaned back, closing his eyes and smiling as his thoughts drifted to his own home. The home he had not seen for fifteen years.

He could still envision the tightly masked expression of his mother as she said farewell to her twelve-year-old son. But his father had been adamant that Hunter receive a formal English education and there was no place in England for Rebecca, Hunter's mother. His father had been recalled to London to assume his family responsibilities and a full-blooded Cherokee woman would never have been accepted in such a place back then. Additionally, Hunter still remembered how much she loved the land, and he firmly believed the woman would have withered and died had she been taken away from her home.

Now, at the age of twenty-seven, he would see his mother and his birthplace once again.

Suddenly all his senses became alert as he detected a rustling noise out on the terrace. Too much noise for the breeze that would disturb the vines on the trellis there. His body tensed but remained motionless in the water as he opened his eyes and watched the area of the open French doors.

A halo of blond hair, so fair as to be almost white, appeared above the balcony railing, followed by a youthful face, which was frowning in concentration as the girl looked down and to her left.

Hunter watched in utter disbelief as she gained her footing, swung her stockinged legs over the railing in a flurry of white petticoats, and stood up, adjusting her skirts around her. She uttered a soft expletive when she discovered a small rent in her dress, and despite himself, Hunter smiled. This had to be one of the Downing girls—the eldest, he assumed, since she appeared to be in mid-adolescence. His thoughts flashed back to a comment Alastair Downing had made during their earlier conversation, something about a male trying to survive in a houseful of females. Well, there must be constant surprises, at least.

The girl stepped to one side of the open doors and peeked into the room. Her eyes traveled to where he sat in the tub. Realizing that he had been studying her, she stared at him in confusion for a moment before shrugging in resignation and taking a single step into the room.

Hunter forced a serious countenance. As an adult, he felt he should deal with this intrusion in a firm manner, but in the face of the girl's impish grin, that was difficult.

"I wasn't sure I'd make it," she commented with a wave of her hand in the direction of the balcony.

"Perhaps it's unfortunate that you did," he offered seriously.

She did have the grace to flush slightly. "Yes, well . . . it appears I've arrived at an inopportune moment."

"I should say," he returned dryly, but he was inwardly surprised as he realized the girl spoke as if she were fifty years old. An old soul, he thought. Alastair's influence, no doubt.

Now her smile disappeared, but her eyes maintained contact with his. "Well, I had to come and see what all the fuss was about." She blushed and looked as if she could have bitten her tongue.

"Fuss?" He raised his eyebrows questioningly."

"Denise and Florence are all excited about a guest in the house," she explained.

"I see." He smiled, not really seeing at all. He retrieved his cheroot from the small table beside the tub, but he kept his eyes on her as he drew deeply on the tobacco. Hunter was fascinated to see that the girl was not at all intimidated by the situation. "And you came to investigate this . . . curiosity for yourself?"

"Oh! Not a *curiosity*!" she hastened to reassure him. "They both thought you were beautiful!" Maggie had the grace to blush again at her own ineptitude while Hunter threw back his head and laughed. "Mind you, I don't judge people by their appearance," she added, deepening the hole into which she wanted to fling herself.

"No?" He was still amused.

"Well, no. You could be the most handsome man in the world and be an ogre deep down inside."

"Very astute," he commented with a wry drawl.

She hurried foolishly on, afraid she had offended him. "Although I am certain you are not an ogre, you understand."

"How can you be so sure?" he asked with feigned seriousness.

She looked confused and cocked her head to one side. "Are you?"

"Only when young ladies invade the solitude of my bath."

"Oh." She flushed slightly again. "I suppose I should leave. I don't wish to make you uncomfortable." But in truth, Maggie was having difficulty tearing her eyes away from the man seated in the tub. His eyes were so dark she felt they must be black, and he had much more hair than her father. Thick hair that shone in the light of the room like sun rays reflected off the blue-black of a raven's wing. His chest was wide and more muscled than any Maggie had seen, and she found that staring at him was a delightful experience.

"My dear, you do not make me uncomfortable, but I surmise you will be made to feel more than *uncomfortable* if your father discovers where you've been."

To his surprise she giggled in the face of the threat.

"Oh, Papa would absolutely fly into a rage if he knew I had disturbed you, and Anna would be forced to lecture me about the impropriety of entering a gentleman's room." Obviously the girl felt she could cope with both of these situations.

"Anna is quite correct, you know."

Maggie felt he was taking on an adult role in chastising her, and stiffened her spine. Raising her chin in what she felt was a completely alluring pose, she said, "Yes, well, I simply wanted to welcome you to Treemont, Mr. Maguire. I shall see you at supper." With that she turned toward the terrace doors.

"Miss Downing?" he called, choking back the desire to laugh with delight.

She turned to look at him.

"I suggest you become familiar with the quaint but civilized custom of entering and leaving rooms through the doors."

"Oh!" she breathed with girlish humor and then half curtsied before turning to her right as her blond braids flew with the abruptness of her movements.

He waited and listened as she darted behind him. When he heard no sound of the door opening, he looked over his shoulder to see her hesitating, one hand on the doorknob.

"May I ask you one question, Mr. Maguire?"

He sighed for dramatic effect, then turned so she would not see his smile. "Quickly, then."

"Papa said you have recently traveled in Europe. Will you tell me about the places you have seen?"

"I shall give the matter some thought, Miss Downing."

"Will you tell Papa I was here?" she asked quietly, but he was not entirely convinced of any serious concern on her part.

"That, too, will require some thought," he said softly. "Now scoot!"

With a giggle she was gone.

CHAPTER

2

Dressed in a fresh white shirt, a dark green coat, and buff trousers, Hunter returned, refreshed, to the main floor of the house. The dark color of the coat complemented his black hair and eyes, and he cut such a tall, elegant figure that no one would have dreamed he did not consider a fine house and fine clothes his natural state. Some considered him confident almost to the point of arrogance, casual almost to the point of aloofness, intelligent almost to the point of genius, and complementing all these traits was a fine sense of humor. But this was not quite accurate. He was a man of strength and fortitude who was comfortable displaying his gentler side.

Tonight he was shown to the wide parlor doors by the frowning Anna. Stepping inside the large, airy room, Hunter first noted a life-sized portrait hanging above the elegant marble mantel over the fireplace. The subject was a woman gowned in soft blue, with eyes to match and hair so fair as to be almost white. The glorious curls cascaded over one shoulder and covered one breast as if to protect it from artist and viewer alike.

11

She was, without a doubt, the most beautiful woman Hunter had ever seen.

"My wife, Margaret," Alastair offered.

Only then did Hunter realize that the man had stepped to his side. He glanced briefly at his host before his eyes drifted back to the portrait. "She was lovely, Alastair."

"Aye," the man said. "I miss her." Then as if shaking off a morose mood, Alastair Downing clapped a firm hand on the younger man's shoulder. "Come and meet my girls," he said lightly. "They are anxiously awaiting you."

Hunter smiled then, looking at the area before the wide fireplace. Two plump upholstered sofas faced each other across a low, rectangular table, and three well-groomed young women sat quietly, staring in his direction. When they noticed Hunter's attention focused on them, all three rose in well-rehearsed unison to stand perfectly still, lacing their fingers together before them. Hunter felt as if he was expected to inspect the king's guard.

"Come along." Alastair took a few steps across the room. "Jennifer, my youngest, is only six. She is with her nurse, but I would like to present my older girls," he said proudly.

Extending his hand, Alastair acknowledged the first girl, who dipped into a respectful curtsy. "This is Florence," he said, frowning as the timid girl seemed to wilt under the scrutiny of the two men.

Smiling, Hunter repeated her name, but the girl ducked her head and refused to look at him. Alastair gave her a reassuring pat on the shoulder.

Turning then, the men faced the two oldest girls; the first, Alastair introduced as Denise, a pretty girl of perhaps thirteen or so who possessed the same creamy ivory skin that all three of these children seemed to have inherited.

And then his bedroom visitor was dropping into a low,

graceful curtsy and rising to smile up at him like someone who shared a confidence.

"And Maggie is my eldest," Alastair said with pride.

It was clear to Hunter that this one was a miniature of her mother.

Hunter found it difficult not to laugh, knowing this elegant figure had a distinct mischievous streak. "Maggie, is it?" he said softly. She looked a bit concerned when he failed to smile. "We have met before, of course," he said. Alastair looked startled, and the girl's complexion seemed to pinken. Hunter saw the girl take in a deep breath and hold it, obviously fearing the worst. "Perhaps not," he added thoughtfully, and then chuckled when Maggie breathed a soft sigh. "I believe I saw you on the landing when I first arrived?"

"Yes." Looking relieved, Maggie added, "On the landing."

But Hunter knew exactly what she was thinking and laughed softly as he reached out and lightly touched her cheek before turning away.

"Your daughters are lovely, Alastair," he said, facing his host once again and giving Maggie a much needed moment to recover.

Alastair nodded, bowing slightly in acknowledgment of the compliment. "Off to your supper now, girls," he said, then smiled as they filed out obediently. When he turned back to his guest, Alastair offered, "A light libation, perhaps?"

Hunter caught a last look from Maggie as she whirled to close the parlor doors before joining her sisters. He smiled and nodded, reassuring her that he would keep her secret.

Alastair took the nod as assent and asked, "Brandy or wine?"

"Brandy. Thank you." Then, seating himself in a large

wing chair, he asked, "Your daughters don't join you for suppers?"

Firmly shaking his head, Alastair turned from the rosewood table in the corner and handed his guest a snifter of brandy before taking a chair. "They are a bit young yet, although I did promise Maggie she could serve as hostess in the dining room for her birthday supper in a few months' time."

Hunter was not surprised by this situation. Seldom had his own father allowed the younger children to join him for meals in his own formal dining room. But while Hunter was aware of this custom, he was not particularly in favor of it. However, he merely held his glass aloft in silent toast before inhaling the brandy's fragrant bouquet and sipping its smooth fire.

Maggie could hear the distant drone of male voices and thought her father and Hunter Maguire were surely going to talk in the parlor all night. Meanwhile she could detect the fragrant odors of their supper from the far side of the dining room doors and was dying of starvation! If they did not soon move she just knew she would swoon and they would find her in a heap on the floor outside the doors to the dining room. It was true that nervous flutters, as well as hunger, were causing funny feelings in her tummy, but she was determined to see this through. It was time she played hostess, and Hunter Maguire would admire the way she carried out the task. Why she craved his admiration she did not question.

Maggie had longed for years to take her mother's place as hostess of Treemont, and she had long thought she was ready. Tonight she would prove it to her father, and to that handsome devil Hunter Maguire.

And he *was* handsome—beautiful, as Florence would have said. And Maggie liked his manner, for while he appeared to be a gentleman, she felt he was also quite daring. After all, how many men would have sat quietly in a tub and talked to a woman? Her behavior had not been at all proper, and the memory of her afternoon visit stirred Maggie's sense of adventure. She should never have entered his room, but being naughty was a bit breathtaking, like sneaking out of the house in the middle of the night to gaze at the stars. The fact that it was forbidden only made the experience more exciting.

Leaning her head against the doorframe, Maggie closed her eyes, listening for any sound that might indicate the men were finished with their drinks. She was famished! Only the thought of seeing Hunter Maguire's brilliant, devastating smile seemed to be keeping her upright. And then she heard the near murmur of male voices as they moved into the dining room. Maggie straightened, smoothing her gown in unaccustomed concern for her appearance. Normally Maggie was more concerned about running and riding free and unhindered, but tonight it suddenly seemed very important that her best blue dress be crisp and clean and that every strand of hair be in place. She had brushed out her hair and left it to flow down her back in a very bold move toward adulthood. She prayed her father would not scold her for her daring and wished she were old enough to possess a sophisticated ankle-length dress.

Taking a deep breath and forming her pink lips into a brave smile, Maggie quietly pushed the double doors aside, pausing in the opening only briefly as two sets of startled male eyes turned in her direction.

Gratified when the two men rose to greet her, Maggie swished into the room and stepped to the place to the right of her father.

"Daughter?" he asked.

Maggie chose to ignore his confusion as she frowned at the table as if in surprise. "Father," she said softly, "you really must speak to Anna. She has forgotten to set my place.''

Hunter stifled a laugh behind a subtle cough while Alastair drew himself up in shock.

''Now see here, Margaret,'' her father said as Maggie smiled up at him brightly.

''Don't worry, Papa. I shall get my own place setting.'' And she raced into the pantry while Alastair could only bluster.

''Perhaps it's not my place,'' Hunter offered quietly as both men continued to stand and await her return, ''but would it be unforgivable of me to suggest that we enjoy her company? You did say that in a few months . . .''

Stymied, Alastair could only shake his head in dismay while he plopped down onto his chair. A moment later Maggie happily raced back into the room, plate and utensils in hand, and he found he could not deny her.

''Very well,'' he muttered to no one in particular, and Maggie's heart lurched as she set down her burden and graced their guest with a beautiful smile.

Playing her game, Hunter moved around the table and held the back of her chair while Maggie sat in a motion so well practiced he was amazed by its grace. And when he returned to his own chair and sat smiling across the table at her, Maggie knew she had truly found her first love.

''Now we shall engage in some engrossing conversation,'' she said.

Alastair stared at her, perplexed, before shaking his head. Hunter coughed suspiciously.

In fact, Maggie proved herself to be an engaging conversationalist. Although she was still somewhere between childhood and young womanhood, she was nevertheless an interesting table companion.

For her own part, Maggie found the strain of maintaining an adult mien quite draining and was feeling wilted by the time dessert was served. In truth, she would have preferred being in her bed to struggling through more conversation. She had already slipped a time or two and said something outrageous. The last time her father had scowled in her direction, and so she had fallen silent until the men had been served coffee.

That was her cue!

"Well, it has been delightful," she said, rising to her feet and feeling gratified as both men rose in unison. "I shall leave you to your brandy and cigars." Seeing a strange and unreadable expression in her father's eyes, Maggie felt a moment of doubt. "Am I not correct, Papa?" she asked and knew instantly that she had spoiled her exit.

Her eyes darted to their guest. Maggie's heart seemed to stop, but it missed only a single beat before it began to thunder as Hunter Maguire bowed slightly to her.

"Good evening, Miss Downing," he said in his deep, resonant voice. "And I thank you for the pleasure of your charming company."

Maggie was not certain how to respond to that and felt it better not to respond at all. And so, blushing madly, she curtsied and fled the room.

CHAPTER

❧ 3 ❧

Maggie Downing slept little that night and what sleep she did manage to get was fitful at best. In the morning she had no desire for food and fussed over her appearance during the time she would normally have spent eating breakfast.

Deciding she had best not push her luck, Maggie plaited her hair into a single braid. The style was practical and more adult than the twin braids she normally wore, yet not adult enough to earn her a scolding. Satisfied that her hair would do, she donned an emerald-blue day dress that she had been told flattered the light blue of her eyes, wishing once again that she could wear full-length skirts. Still, she felt she passed muster when she exited her room and made her way quietly down the corridor toward the guest room.

And only just in time!

Anna was ascending the back stairs, tray in hand, and walking toward her. Ducking back into her own room, Maggie closed the door all but a crack and watched as the housekeeper knocked once on the door to Hunter's room, then left the breakfast tray on the floor in the corridor. Maggie thought it rude that their guest would not be served properly in his room, but the priggish Anna would never enter a room occupied by a male guest. Later she would straighten the bed, but not until Hunter Maguire was well away.

Maggie eased her head around the doorframe and watched until the top of Anna's head disappeared from sight.

When the corridor was deserted, Maggie darted the few paces to Hunter's room, knocked on the door vigorously, and stooped to pick up the tray of coffee and warm cinnamon rolls.

Hunter groaned softly, his face half buried in his pillow, as he became aware of a knocking at the door. Normally he was up and cheerfully greeting the dawn, the best time of day. But this morning he was reluctant. He cautiously opened one eye to stare out the French doors. The sun was already high and bright. He must have been more tired from his journeys than he realized.

The sound came again.

No help for it; he could not lie abed all day. Reluctantly, he turned over, propping a pillow behind his back even as he called, "Come!"

The door opened partway, and a round, smiling face, framed by wisps of white-blond hair, appeared. "Are you decent?" she asked and he laughed shortly as he ran his long, lean fingers through his hair.

"I never seem to be when you come skulking about."

"I am not skulking," Maggie retorted indignantly as she stepped into the room and closed the door behind her. "Anna left your tray, and you took so long waking up that the coffee was growing cold." She stopped short a few steps from the bed. "Oh! You don't wear a nightshirt!"

"No, I don't wear a nightshirt," he returned wryly as he made certain the blankets covered his torso to the waist. "You really are shameless."

"I know," she agreed, then placed the tray across his lap. "Are you going to look at the horses today?" she asked as she plopped herself down on the bed beside his right hip.

Pouring coffee from the small silver pot, he smiled, shaking his head as he steadied the tray with his free hand. "I am."

"I could help you choose," she offered and reached out to take the small piece of roll he offered.

"You fancy yourself a good judge of horseflesh, do you?" he asked.

She nodded, chewing on the roll. "There is a prime little mare that is in foal, and I don't believe Papa knows." She reached for another piece of roll. "You could have two for the price of one!"

Hunter stared at her in amazement. "Now, that's disloyal of you, Miss Downing," he said. "And how is it you know that the mare is in foal and your father does not?"

"I was there when Salamander mounted her, that is how," she said with absolutely no hint of embarrassment. "I just happened to be in the loft."

While Hunter believed that young people should be aware of the act of procreation, he somehow did not believe Alastair would share his views. "Is your father aware that you've witnessed such things?" he asked quietly.

Maggie's brows arched upward. "Good heavens, no! Papa would be scandalized."

"And you are not?"

Shaking her head, Maggie said, "The breeding was a mistake actually. The stable boys let Salamander get away from them, and of course once he smelled the mare, the boys could not keep him away. They would have been injured if they had interfered. Still, Papa wouldn't be happy to know about their blunder."

Hunter could visualize this sprite witnessing that particular event; it was a wonder she had not fallen headlong from the loft while she strained to see! "I don't think it would be fair of me to dupe your father that way, do you?" he asked.

Maggie shrugged her shoulders, licking a sticky finger. "You would be saving the stable boys from a scolding," she said. "Unless, of course, the breeding didn't take and the mare is not in foal. Then Papa would never know what happened."

Hunter chuckled, thoroughly enjoying her company; she was such a delightful minx. "You had best get out of here, Miss Downing," he said a moment later. "I do believe you're corrupting me."

Maggie merely shrugged.

"I'm serious, Maggie. I am about to get out of bed."

Maggie flew into action then, knowing she had over-stepped the bounds of propriety again. At the door, she turned her head back. "You won't tell Papa I was here?"

Hunter shot her a good impression of a frown. "I'll have to give the matter some thought," he said.

"You won't!" She laughed and raced from the room.

The day was bright and sunny and not overly humid, considering the time of year. Just mild with the smell of freshly cut grass and hay mingled with the headier odors of animals.

Hunter propped one booted foot on the lower fence rail while his forearms rested on the upper rail of the corral. Several mares were paraded by for his inspection. Treemont boasted some fine horseflesh. He was having a difficult time choosing.

Maggie had changed into her best forest green riding habit, hoping Hunter would select a mare and want to take her for a jaunt. If he wanted to ride, of course, he would need an escort. Someone who knew every inch of the plantation. Someone, namely her.

Coming up beside him, Maggie placed both feet on the

lower fence rail and boosted herself up, then turned her head to smile at him on a much more even level. "Hello," she said. "Have you decided?"

Hunter smiled and returned his attention to the center paddock. "The roan, I think. She appears to be healthy and strong but she has fine lines and intelligent eyes."

"She is not the one," Maggie whispered.

Her father was standing to Hunter's right. "Good choice," Alastair said. "One of my finest mares, and she has already given me an excellent colt. Tried and true," he added.

Maggie had heard her father repeat the same words a hundred times. "Would you like to take her out?" she asked Hunter. "You can better judge her temperament once you have ridden her."

He knew her game for what it was, but he played along. Besides, he enjoyed her company. "Will you join me?" he asked and drew an immediate response: Maggie raced for the stables.

Alastair watched her run through the open doors and shook his head. "That girl is something beyond me," he said. "Last night she was a perfect lady. Today she is racing around like a hoyden. I've never seen her like this."

Hunter smiled and turned his back to lean against the wooden rails. "You have four daughters, my friend. You had best prepare yourself, for they seem to be growing up."

Alastair straightened away from his post and stared at Hunter as if he had gone mad. "They're babies," he said firmly. "Each and every one."

"Not Maggie," he returned. Alastair looked alarmed. "Relax, man," Hunter said. "I recognize puppy love when I see it." But in his own mind, he wondered if the man's alarm stemmed not so much from the shock of realizing his daughter was growing up as from the knowledge that she appeared to be attracted to a man who was beneath her station and a Cherokee to boot. He hadn't seen Alastair

since Hunter was a boy, and had met him only a time or two
at that; it was difficult to know the bent of the other man's
mind. Still, remembering that his father and Alastair had
once been close friends, Hunter wanted to give the man the
benefit of the doubt.

In the stable, Maggie was rushing about, finding the best
and most suitable saddle for Hunter to use, even as she
urged the stable boys to set a faster pace.

When the two mounts were finally ready and led out,
Maggie followed, her heart beating joyfully until she saw
the concerned expression on her father's face. Surely he
would not demand an escort for them! She stopped before
the two men, looking into her father's eyes and awaiting
some word from him.

It was Hunter who spoke first. "I'll take care, Alastair."
He smiled when the older man looked his way. Give the girl
her moment, his eyes seemed to say, and Alastair reluctantly
nodded in agreement.

Maggie knew she had missed something, but she also
understood that an agreement had been reached. Taking that
as confirmation that her father was permitting her to ride out
with Hunter, Maggie turned and prepared to mount. Taking
up the reins in one hand, she awaited a boost up from one
of the boys and was pleasantly surprised when Hunter bent
to the task. Taking her small booted foot in one hand and
placing his other hand at her waist, he lifted her high with
ease and steadied her until her right leg was settled securely.
Totally flustered, Maggie could only nod her thanks and
pray she did not blush.

Smiling secretly, Hunter turned away and mounted the
mare he had chosen.

One of the proudest moments of Maggie's young life
occurred when Hunter turned slightly in the saddle, keeping
his mount steady until she could draw up beside him. It was

the first time she had actually been allowed to ride out alone with a man—although she had secretly ridden all over the county with one local boy or another—and she knew she had just taken her first step to womanhood.

They rode in silence for a time; Maggie was suddenly tongue-tied. And while Hunter was clearly enjoying the silent ride, Maggie began to panic because she could not think of a suitable topic of conversation.

"It is a beautiful day!" she finally said in a rush.

Hunter turned his head briefly and smiled. "Yes," he said softly.

"Is that all you have to say? Yes?"

He laughed briefly. "Yes."

"Are there times when you don't like to talk?" she asked, narrowing her eyes.

He nodded.

"Is this one of them?" she ventured, and he laughed again, startling the mare and having to pull her back to a more sedate walk.

"Are there not times when *you* do not wish to talk?" he returned.

"Not many," she admitted.

"All right, little one," he said softly. "What would you like to talk about?"

"Well, I have wondered." She frowned in her hesitation. "You are not what I expected you to be."

Hunter's smile slipped momentarily, but looking into her soft, questioning blue eyes, he decided there was no malice in the comment. "And what did you expect, Maggie?"

"I'm not certain," she said truthfully. "I've never known an Indian before, and I thought you would be much different."

"You expected me to ride in half naked and threaten to take your scalp?"

Maggie didn't care for his tone and drew herself up,

shoulders back in indignation. "Well, if you cannot tolerate my natural curiosity . . ."

He laughed ruefully and shook his head; he had overreacted with a child. Curiosity was healthy as long as it was not malicious. "I apologize, little one." He reached across the short distance between them to pat her hand by way of indicating his sincerity. "You may ask whatever you wish."

"I simply did not know what to expect, and I suppose you . . . surprised me," she returned softly.

"Why is that?" he asked, turning sideways in the saddle to face her.

"I am not certain," she offered, puzzled by her inability to sort the matter out. "You . . . Well, you have gentle ways."

He smiled again, indulging her now. "And do you not know many men who have gentle ways?"

"Some," she said after a bit of thought.

"And do you not consider an Indian a man?"

Blushing furiously, she nodded, and Hunter laughed, not unkindly, this time reaching out to touch her cheek with his fingertips. "There, little one. You have addressed your own concern."

There was a moment of silence before Maggie offered quietly, "I feel silly."

"Don't," he said succinctly. "Not with me, Maggie."

Maggie stared at him, swallowing heavily as her mind raced around the possible meanings of his statement. But he had turned back and was facing straight ahead as he encouraged the mare into a gentle lope. She could not see his eyes, could not guess the true intent of his words, but she hoped he meant she held some special place within him . . . just as he held a special place within her.

She did not understand this attraction, this feeling of

being drawn toward him, for it was all very new to her. New and unique.

Urging her mare forward, Maggie caught up and turned her head to smile at him when she reached his side. "I have a new calf," she said breathlessly. "Would you like to see her when we go back?"

How could he refuse?

Maggie had difficulty maintaining her adult calm and reserve as she pictured her new friend's possible reactions to the clever little calf that was her pride. The Downing girls did not lack for much, but Alastair insisted they attend to their studies each day and be responsible for the things he placed in their care. And he considered pets an excellent means of teaching responsibility.

Most girls would have requested a kitten or a pup, but Maggie had insisted she could care for the calf from the moment the creature was old enough to leave its mother's side. And secretly she looked upon the animal as a way to demonstrate her cleverness.

"I've spent hours with her," she boasted now as she led Hunter down the long, dim stable corridor. "And she's clever," she added as he smiled indulgently.

Maggie stopped at the last box stall in the row and reached up to remove a lead rope from the nail in the wall beside the door. She peeked over the top of the closed lower half of the door before allowing it to swing open. "Hello, Boxcar," she said, entering the darkened stall. "I'll bring her out," she called.

Hunter stepped forward, resting his elbows on the gate-like door, knitting his fingers together as he grinned. "What do you call her?" he asked, certain he had not heard correctly.

Maggie wrapped her arms around the small light brown calf. "Boxcar," she said, kissing the calf gently above its left eye.

"Where on earth did you get such a name?" He laughed.

"From trains." She snapped the lead onto the calf's halter. "You'll see when I bring her out!"

Hunter could see them in the dim stall, but Maggie and her calf were not about to make an entrance into the brighter light of the corridor. The heifer had planted her forefeet wide and was bawling miserably as Maggie pulled on the rope, attempting to get the animal to move. "She does walk on lead," Maggie insisted. "I just have to get her started!"

He laughed softly, not wanting to dampen the girl's hopes; that calf was not about to budge.

Looking around, he spied a wide harness strap hanging from a peg on the wall. When he had it in hand, testing its length, he entered the stall and stepped to the animal's side as he studied the stubborn calf. "I believe she needs a little nudge," he said. "Leave the lead draped over her neck and go around her," he directed softly. He stared at the calf when she turned her head to examine him. "Boxcar," he said, "you are a stubborn girl." The calf turned her head away, facing the open door, chewing her cud.

Hunter passed one end of the section of harness across Boxcar's back. "Take this," he directed his accomplice. "We're going to put it around her rump and see if we can nudge her forward."

Maggie nodded and did as he directed. When the wide leather harness was in place, Hunter and Maggie stood on opposite sides of the animal's head. "Hold tight to the strap," he said, and Maggie smiled.

"It's like putting her in a sling!" she said gaily.

But Boxcar didn't care for this treatment at all. Almost as soon as she felt the pressure on her hind end, the calf bolted forward and out the open door.

Maggie stumbled, and Hunter laughed as he too had to regain his balance after the sudden release of resistance on the strap. But he simultaneously managed to reach for

Maggie's upper arm and save her from going down in the straw.

They were both laughing now, and Boxcar was free.

As soon as Maggie realized her pet had bolted far beyond the stall door, she was on the move. "I'll get her!" she called, and Hunter smiled as he gathered the harness and stepped into the corridor; Maggie was racing out of the stables.

A moment later he joined her in the noon sunshine, where she was proudly promenading with the calf on the lead!

She smiled as she walked toward him, leading her pet. "I told you she could do it," she said.

Hunter laughed, shaking his head at his own ineptitude. "I apologize for setting her free. I confess to being knowledgeable only about horses."

Maggie merely smiled up at him; nothing he could do would be wrong.

"So, tell me," he said, burying his hands in the pockets of his breeches. "Why do you call her Boxcar?"

The mischievous twinkle in her eyes made him wary, but Hunter complied when she said, "Walk around behind her."

He stood there feeling a bit foolish as he stared at the calf's rump and high, bony hips. He looked at Maggie, who was smiling, and then he looked at the high, protruding hipbones again, and suddenly he understood: The calf was square!

"See?" Maggie laughed.

CHAPTER

4

The days of Hunter's visit at Treemont flew by until they numbered seven.

On the eighth day he would leave.

At dawn of the seventh day, Maggie had stood at the foot of his bed, dressed only in her nightclothes, breathlessly asking that he ride with her.

Hunter had stared into her earnest blue eyes and wondered if he had miscalculated. Had he overstepped the bounds? The last thing he wanted was to hurt her, but she needed to understand that hers was merely an infatuation. And yet to tell her so would wound the tender heart that had tried so hard to beat like that of a woman.

Perhaps it was unwise, but he decided to ride with her one last time before he left. Within months she would no doubt forget him.

He found that thought caused him dismay. He had stared at the pretty young girl who promised to reflect her mother's beauty in the years ahead. It would be interesting to see how she turned out, how her youthful spirit matured. In fact, as his dark eyes roamed over the untamed fair hair that flowed over her thin shoulders, Hunter had begun to wonder if Alastair would allow him to visit again in two or three years.

He threw off the thought, more concerned during these early morning hours with the problem of leaving. Clearly Maggie was infatuated with him and he would leave her . . . but he just might return.

He had smiled at her, agreeing to her request, and Maggie had raced out of his room, obviously eager to prepare.

By the time he emerged from the house, she was waiting at the stables with the roan mare he had purchased from Alastair saddled and standing beside her own little mare.

At the moment Maggie was obsessively happy, blatantly ignoring the fact that he would be leaving in the morning and might never return. This was their last private time together, and she intended to enjoy each moment, for she felt the end of an important phase of her life fast approaching.

They had ridden some distance from the house before either spoke, but Maggie had become more comfortable with these periods of silence. It was a very adult thing.

It was Hunter who broke the spell. "Maggie," he said softly, "we must talk."

Shaking her head in a fashion that reminded him of her youth, she refused to look in his direction. "I do not wish to talk."

He smiled sadly, understanding. "I know," he said quietly. And then, spying a pretty pond, he led her in that direction and dismounted at the water's edge.

Maggie's mare stopped beside Hunter's mount without any signal from her rider, but Maggie kept her seat, refusing to join him.

"You cannot avoid the inevitable, Maggie my girl," he said firmly. He stepped up beside the mare and reached up to grasp her waist in both hands. "Come down now."

Bracing her hands instinctively on his shoulders, Maggie stared down into his dark eyes before he lowered her to the ground. "I know what you're about to say," she told him. "And I do not wish to hear it."

He laughed shortly and stepped back a pace. "And what am I about to say?"

"That I am just a silly girl and you are a *man*."

He smiled at the small pout formed by her mouth. "You are not a silly girl, little one. You are a delightful young woman."

"But too young," she offered forthrightly, squinting up at him, for the sun was at his back.

"Yes, too young for some things." He cupped her elbow in one hand and led her toward a fallen tree.

When they were seated side by side, Hunter leaned forward, bracing his elbows on his knees and lacing his fingers loosely together.

"I shall wait for you, you know," she said.

Hunter turned until he could see her profile. She was staring out over the pond, and he could feel her sudden sadness. "You will soon be meeting many, many young men, Maggie. You will go to parties and picnics and make many friends as you grow up. You'll soon forget me."

She turned her head abruptly, and he could see moisture gathering in those bright blue eyes. "I will never forget you," she said firmly. "You must promise to come back."

"I have enjoyed my time at Treemont, Maggie," he said evasively. "And I shall miss your company. But it is time for me to go."

"Why did you stay in England for so many years?" she asked, changing the subject.

He studied her expression in hopes of gleaning some purpose to the question. "I was getting an education."

"And after that?" she asked, refusing to look his way. "You stayed for many years after that."

Clearly perplexed, Hunter responded warily, "I visited farms to learn about planting and breeding horses."

"You have been away from your home for many years," she said quietly. "A few more days will not matter."

"Oh, Maggie." The tender way he spoke her name seemed to be more than she could bear.

Maggie jumped to her feet and moved quickly away to stand staring out over the small pond, as if seeing nothing. "This was one of my mother's favorite places." She flinched when his hands settled lightly on her shoulders.

"Maggie, look at me."

"I know it's hopeless," she said, her head falling forward, "and I'm sorry, Hunter. You think I'm just a girl, but I don't feel like a girl. This is all very confusing. I can't seem to help myself."

He knew she was crying. "Maggie," he said again, turning her around and holding her against his chest. "I am sorry, little one. I've been a fool."

"No, you have not!" she returned fiercely, struggling with her tears because she did not want to disappoint him. She wanted him to remember her as happy and pretty, and instead she would look ugly crying. She tore herself away from him then, stepping back a pace . . . a pace too far.

Teetering, Maggie grabbed for his hand and pulled Hunter off balance. They both plunged into the pond.

Maggie landed on her back, as did Hunter, who twisted away so as not to fall on top of her and drive her deeper under the water. Gaining enough control to sit up, Maggie watched him struggle to right himself. The astonished look on his face when he turned her way sent her into fits of laughter.

Finally seeing the humor of it all, Hunter gave in and joined her, even as Maggie threw herself at his chest, almost choking him when her arms went around his neck.

"Oh, Maggie," he said, laughing. "I will miss you!"

Maggie's cheek settled firmly against his as she responded. "I am going to grow up, Hunter Maguire," she breathed. "And you are going to miss all of that."

In that moment of closeness, Hunter Maguire made a decision he felt he would never regret: He would speak to Alastair Downing about the man's eldest daughter before he left.

CHAPTER
5

Treemont Farm, 1883

The tree-lined road to Treemont mansion had not changed a great deal. The oaks were older, of course, as was he. The crushed-stone path was as neat as he remembered, and the red brick edifice in the distance appeared the same. But the columns and dormers seemed more gray than white as the sun concentrated its beams there. Beyond the oaks the brush had sprouted up, adding to the deep shadows along the lengthy route.

Hunter Maguire pressed the soles of his booted feet firmly into the stirrups, stretching his long muscular legs by standing up in his saddle. The journey from his home near the James River had been tedious, although not overly long. He knew what really made him weary was making the decision to return to Treemont. But, being perfectly honest, he *was* in the market for a good stallion. So far his trip had been profitable, and he did not doubt that Alastair would have some good stock. A great stallion to match the two excellent mares already on their way to his home.

He relaxed once again in the saddle. Soon he would enjoy a thirst-quenching drink and, he hoped, a long hot bath.

Over the years Hunter had corresponded with Alastair Downing occasionally, and the man had extended to him an open invitation to visit Treemont. Curiosity, as much as the desire to find a champion stallion, had fostered Hunter's decision to return. He had often thought of the bright, delightful Maggie. He wanted to see how she had grown, wanted to know the woman she had become, even though he understood that she could well be married by now, though Alastair never mentioned her in his letters. She had shown great promise of becoming a beauty, and her spark for living had touched Hunter in some way. A way that no other woman ever had.

As he rode along the stone drive he removed his hat and raked his long, lean fingers through his straight black hair. Then, replacing the hat, he surreptitiously scanned the trees to his right. The house was near enough now, and he was certain there was no cause for concern, but still . . . he felt that he was being watched.

Margaret drew herself up as thin and tall as possible in order to remain unobserved, although she was certain the thunder of her rapidly beating heart would reveal her presence.

She'd heard the muted clip-clop of a horse's hooves, and though it was childish, she was hiding behind a tree. She frowned and considered why she was really hiding as Hunter Maguire rode by her secret place. He had taken her by surprise, of course. That was a major reason. She just had not expected to see him so suddenly, and she was not prepared for a meeting.

She peered around the tree at his retreating back. He sat his horse proudly and confidently, his fine-cut coat moving slightly as he swayed with the rhythm of the horse's movements. He was still a fine equestrian.

Maggie ducked back behind the tree, frowning as she quickly looked about for an escape route. But when she dared to peek up the road again, he had vanished.

Maggie sensed danger of exposure and moved deeper among the oaks where the shadows were darkest. The last thing she wanted was to meet Hunter Maguire here beside the lane, before she had prepared herself.

She darted to the safety of the next tree.

Hunter had ducked between two giant oaks and tied his horse at the edge of the high brush. He then backtracked under cover of the scrub until he could emerge near the spot where he had spotted the spy. He had caught only a glimpse of a hat brim as he rode by and had calculated the person to be short—either that or the man was squatting low as he watched.

Coming out from the thick underbrush, however, Hunter saw no one as he looked among the trees. It appeared his daylight stalker had moved on.

He cautiously stepped out onto the gravel surface of the road, his eyes darting warily from left to right. No one was in sight. Perhaps he was so tired he was imagining things. Perhaps what he had thought was a hat had been a tree limb or a clump of shadowed moss.

Shrugging his shoulders, he had started walking back to his mount when suddenly the horse charged out onto the road from between the trees. Hunter stopped in his tracks, his mouth falling open in amazement. His horse was being ridden away by a man in a black hat, black breeches, and a white shirt!

Horse and rider raced up the road toward the house, bits of cut stone flying upward in their wake. The man could be admired for his horsemanship, Hunter thought, as he watched his transportation fleeing. But then his thoughts turned far less charitable. He now had one hell of a long walk ahead of him!

As the figure grew smaller, Hunter once again halted in his tracks. The rider's hat had flown off in the wind, and long white-blond hair billowed out behind her.

Her!

He grinned slowly as he realized he had been duped. Duped by a small woman, at that. "Maggie," he said softly. Strangely, her trick amused him despite his weariness and the long walk ahead. She'd obviously lost none of her fire.

When he finally reached the house, he knocked on the door, prepared to wait a moment or two for someone to traverse the large foyer. He imagined Maggie was still at the stables, so he didn't expect anyone to answer promptly. He turned around, frowning at the bubbled and split paint on the columns that supported the roof over Treemont's wide porch. The place needed painting.

The scraping of wood on wood drew his attention then, and he whirled to smile down into the face of a slim young girl who blushed when his eyes met hers.

"Hello," he said softly.

"Mr. Maguire?" she inquired, and he nodded. "Papa is expecting you," she added shyly and stepped back, pulling the door wide in invitation.

She was a girl of about thirteen, he decided. "Let me see," he drawled. "You must be Florence."

She nodded eagerly, and dropped her eyes. "If you will be seated in the parlor, Mr. Maguire, I shall let Papa know you've arrived."

The entrance to the house was bright, airy, and elegant, its polished rosewood banister and wall panels reflected in the white tile stairs and floor. Hunter glanced briefly up at the curved staircase that led to the second floor, relieved that the interior of the house appeared to be in good condition.

The disrepair of the exterior of the house had concerned him.

Hunter entered the spacious front room, noticing that little had changed in the decor. But he looked only briefly around the room, for his eyes were drawn to the portrait above the mantel, just as they had been three years ago.

And he envisioned Maggie looking exactly like this now.

"If my Margaret were still alive I would have to keep my eye on her with you about," Alastair proclaimed from the doorway.

Hunter laughed and turned around, extending his hand in greeting as he walked toward the man. "You would, Alastair. For a certainty."

The older man raised his eyes briefly to the portrait as he always did when he entered this room, but then he gave his full attention to his guest. "Welcome, Hunter. I hope your journey has been a pleasant one?"

"Profitable so far," and then he teased, "We'll see what you can do to ravage the remainder of it."

Pretending to be affronted, Alastair Downing drew himself up to his full, elegant height, which left him half a head shorter than Hunter. "I understood you were seeking fine horses," he blustered.

"Yes. But not at the expense of your owning my last shirt!"

Alastair cuffed his guest on the shoulder. "Ungrateful pup!" But then he laughed. "Come to my study. Perhaps I can soften you up before we strike any bargains."

Once seated comfortably, brandy in hand, Hunter took a moment to study his host; Alastair was still a fine-looking man, but some of his former vibrancy was missing.

Alastair settled back in his chair, crossing his knees as his gaze traveled quickly over his guest in a like inspection. Hunter had changed little; he'd matured, perhaps, but the man was as strong and fit-looking as ever, and his features had become almost aristocratic. The one change Alastair did note was a certain sadness, and perhaps wisdom, in the dark eyes.

"And all is right with you?" he asked.

Hunter smiled. "Fine, Alastair. And you?"

The older man nodded, smiling ruefully, but Hunter had an odd sense that something was not at all right with his friend. "Times are good, and my daughters are driving me mad," Alastair said lightly, belying Hunter's concerns. "All appears right with the world."

Hunter laughed at the derisiveness in his friend's voice. "The girls cannot be as bad as that. They are practically grown by now."

Alastair leaned forward like a conspirator. "Trust me, my friend; if you ever have daughters you should know that they become more difficult with each passing year."

Hunter chuckled. "I'll remember that."

Settling back, Alastair eyed the younger man. "Perhaps you do have a daughter or two by now? I've failed to ask."

Hunter merely smiled and shook his head.

"No sons? No daughters? A wife, perhaps?"

"No."

"Well, your time will come, without doubt."

They were both skirting the issue of Maggie.

Suddenly Alastair's tone changed abruptly as another thought struck and he knew he had to speak on the matter. "I was sorry to learn of your mother's passing, Hunter. She was a fine woman."

Hunter's smile instantly disappeared, and he sat forward, studying the glass that rested loosely between his cupped hands. "She was a remarkable woman, and I am not the only one who misses her." He straightened then, determined to lighten the mood. "I believe her only regret was that I had not married and given her grandchildren." He smiled at the thought, for he and his mother had engaged in some heated discussions on the matter. But all of Rebecca's attempts at matchmaking had failed, for Hunter had been too intent on his work and improving their lot in life.

"And who is minding your affairs while you gallivant around the country?" Alastair asked.

Hunter relaxed in his chair again. "A good and very old friend of my parents. You may have heard them mention Jason Longstreet. He managed the farm for Mother for years while I was in England. He stayed on after I returned home."

"And you've waited too long to visit us again," Alastair said sincerely.

"It's been three years, Alastair. I recall our last discussion. We agreed . . ." Hunter stopped in mid-sentence, suddenly aware that Alastair had paled and seemed to be having difficulty breathing. Alarmed, Hunter set his glass aside and sat forward in his chair. "Are you all right, man?" he asked abruptly.

But Alastair was shaking his head, holding up one hand to signal that his friend should remain seated. "Fine," he said, forcing himself to remain calm. "It's just that . . . Perhaps I should have written to you, but . . ." Looking directly into the younger man's eyes, he blurted guiltily, "You will find Margaret greatly changed, Hunter."

Frowning, Hunter reached for his snifter of brandy and sat back. "I expected her to change, Alastair. She was fifteen years old when I last visited."

Alastair was now looking decidedly uncomfortable.

When he did not immediately respond, Hunter prodded, "I expect Maggie has become a very beautiful young woman by now," he said, but his smile disappeared when Alastair looked at him sadly.

"Indeed she has," he said softly. "Almost as beautiful as her dear mother. But . . ." He took a hearty pull of brandy before staring directly at Hunter again. "I believe I should warn you, Hunter: Margaret was involved in an . . . accident, of sorts, about a year ago.''

Hunter was growing concerned about the direction this conversation was taking, and his frustration level was not particularly stable, either. Sitting forward in his chair again, he said, ''Alastair, I do not understand what you are trying to tell me. What sort of accident?''

Visibly uncomfortable, Alastair appeared to be choosing his words carefully. ''I would prefer that Margaret explain the details. Perhaps once the two of you have had some time to renew your acquaintance . . .'' He held up a hand to silence his friend when he saw that Hunter was about to interrupt. ''I admit to being deliberately evasive, my young friend, but I have my reasons, and I hope you will come to understand. I do want to warn you, however, that Margaret is scarred.''

Hunter stared silently, feeling as if his gut had just turned to stone. ''She was badly injured?'' he asked softly and felt a slight lessening of the pressure in his chest when Alastair shook his head.

''The scar is relatively small,'' he said softly. ''But there are greater wounds.''

CHAPTER
❧ 6 ❧

Dressed only in a soft, sheer shift that accented her young woman's curves, Margaret Downing stood before the open doors of her clothespress and rummaged through the multitude of gowns there before selecting a garment suitable for the occasion.

Holding the gown aloft she frowned, first over her decision and then over the few wrinkles in the skirt. Dropping the gown to the floor, she paced to the open window and stared out over the neatly clipped lawns of her beloved Treemont.

Hunter Maguire had come to her home. She wasn't sure how she felt. Certainly strangely unsettled. But she would be in control of her faculties by the time evening arrived and she descended to the parlor to meet him for the first time in three years. Margaret had become a master at controlling her thoughts and emotions over the past year, and tonight would be no different. Many men came to visit her father to negotiate the sale of crops or horses, and Margaret dealt with them all; Hunter Maguire would be no different.

Then why did her insides feel as if she had eaten too many green apples?

Striding back across the thick Oriental carpet, Margaret took her thoughts firmly in hand, scooped up the gown she'd left lying in an ice-blue puddle on the floor, and opened the door of her room intending to call for Anna. To her surprise, she was met by the grinning, freckled face of her youngest sister.

"He's here!" Nine-year-old Jennifer grinned up at her. "I came to tell you."

"I know he's here." Margaret frowned and looked right and left down the wide corridor. "Where is Anna?"

Jennifer's eyes lost some of their happy shine, but her smile remained as she boldly entered her sister's room and plopped down on the edge of the bed. "Somebody stole his horse!" Jennifer piped up and then laughed lustily. "He had a really long walk." Jennifer eyed her older sister with curiosity. These days Margaret seldom smiled, but Jennifer had heard that she used to be fun and that she had often played tricks on strangers. "Have you seen Mr. Maguire's horse?" she asked.

Margaret frowned at the girl. "Now, what would I want with another horse? We have a barn full of horses." The twinkle in her eye told Jennifer all she wanted to know, and she grinned up at her idol, until Margaret's manner changed. "Perhaps he should take better care," she said unkindly.

Jennifer frowned, getting to her feet. "What's wrong?" she asked softly.

Margaret held the blue gown up, more agitated than Jennifer had seen her in years. "What's wrong?" the older girl parroted. "Look at this gown. It was put away wrinkled, and there's a smudge near the hem. I can't wear *this*. Anna should be here," she continued impatiently. "She knows I have to see to the running of the house and the farm. I can't be expected to do everything. I asked her to prepare this gown, and now look at it,'' she said again, waving the dress around. ''I have to get ready for this evening, and I can't even trust her to see to a simple task.''

Jennifer was often puzzled by Margaret's shrewish behavior, but she tried to soothe her sister. ''She has extra chores today, Margaret. You know she has to do all of the cooking now.''

''Father should never have let the cook go,'' Margaret muttered, pacing the room.

Jennifer had wondered about that, but she shrugged her bony shoulders as her sister paced away from her again.

''Anna is not attending her duties,'' Margaret said. ''Father should have let *her* go and kept the cook!''

Jennifer giggled at the thought. ''And then we would have even more chores to do. At least Anna helps with the cleaning.''

''Well, we need more help in this house!''

Jennifer tried to puzzle out the possible reasons for her sister's bad temper. When Margaret was this irritated it was best to leave her alone. She felt it was time to go about her own business. ''*I* didn't fire the servants, Maggie,'' she said quietly and hurried across the room, closing the door behind her as she left.

With Jennifer's departure, Margaret turned to her dressing table and perched on the delicate bench, trying to tamp down her agitation. This was just another business meeting, she told herself as she reached for her brush and attacked her waist-length blond hair.

But she knew it wasn't.

Through the years she had often visualized her reunion with Hunter Maguire—at first with pleasure, later with trepidation, but now with icy fear. Margaret had carefully noted the reactions of men when they were introduced to her, and she was well aware of all the signs of distress. Hunter Maguire would be no different, although he might be more deeply shocked than the others. After all, he had known her before, and would expect her to be beautiful. . . . Yes, Margaret expected his reaction to her ugliness to be quite something.

And that was just as well. She suspected Hunter had come for more than a peek at the grown-up Downing girl. Perhaps he was still thinking of a match. It would be better if he was put off immediately, for there was no sense in prolonging the agony. Margaret could not marry him. Not ever. With shaking hands, she threw the hairbrush back on the table.

She was losing control, and she didn't understand why. She had learned to control her emotions months ago.

But Hunter Maguire was not just another guest. He was the only man she'd known as a friend. She had even thought for a brief time about marrying him.

The time she'd longed for had come, but all of her dreams had been shattered.

Whirling suddenly, clutching her middle, Margaret raced for the chamber pot beneath the bed and dragged it forward just as her stomach reacted to the turmoil within her.

The faithful Florence found her on her knees beside her bed. "Margaret?" Concerned, she rushed to her sister's side.

But even as Florence knelt and lightly touched her back, Margaret struggled to regain control. "Please go away," Margaret whispered with difficulty as she got to her feet. "I'm fine now."

The usually reserved Florence was too worried to be put off. "You don't seem fine, Margaret. You haven't been *fine* for weeks now."

Margaret, who normally dealt gently with this shy, delicate sister, struggled with her impatience to be alone. "I'm sorry, Florence. Don't be worried. I am really quite all right."

"What's wrong, Margaret? Why were you ill?" And then

with sudden insight, she added, "You haven't been well since father told us Mr. Maguire was coming to visit."

Maggie tried to laugh that off as ridiculous as she turned toward the dressing table again. "Don't be a ninny, Flo," she said.

"I thought you liked Mr. Maguire," Florence whispered, truly confused and concerned for her sister.

Maggie turned back, a smile pasted on her pretty lips. "Florence, darling, shouldn't you be dressing for supper?"

After a moment's indecision, the younger girl turned toward the door. "You will be nice tonight, won't you, Maggie?" she asked apprehensively as she stood on the threshold.

But Margaret took the comment in stride. "Of course, Florence," she returned patiently. "Mr. Maguire is an old friend."

Alone again, Margaret poured water into the floral-patterned ceramic bowl on the washstand and, dampening a soft cloth, let the cooling effect of the water on her face ease some of the tension within her.

It was time to collect her thoughts, and past experience had taught her that she always gained control and felt better after the illness had passed. She would be prepared to meet Hunter Maguire, just as she had been prepared to meet every other man who had set foot inside her home in the past year.

Yes, she would be prepared, and she would deal with him quite nicely.

After all, she possessed more than one attribute that would keep him at bay.

Freshly bathed and dressed in a crisp, high-collared white shirt, beige trousers, and a royal blue coat, Hunter Maguire stepped into the entrance to the parlor. He was not surprised that he was actually looking forward to this meeting now that he was here. He had been greatly concerned when he learned that Maggie had been injured, but he was as eager to see her as he had been through all the years of waiting. He had been slightly annoyed at Alastair's reluctance to explain the circumstances of her accident, but upon reflection, Hunter knew it would take much more than a scar to change his opinion.

Stepping into the room he was immediately, if distantly, aware of the presence of several people, but his attention was immediately drawn to a young woman standing in front of the fireplace. Hunter raised his eyes briefly to the portrait above her and then allowed his gaze to fall again. If he had not known that Downing's wife had died . . .

She was standing almost in profile to him as she spoke with another young woman who was seated before her. When she became aware of his presence, she raised her eyes and turned slightly to offer him a subtle, almost shy smile.

Hunter was entranced. It was as if the woman in the portrait had stepped down off the wall, intending to join them for supper. Here was a living, breathing replica of that exquisite beauty he knew to be his friend's wife. This was the charming child grown up, Margaret Downing's daughter, and such a legacy to leave the world!

The cascading silvery hair waved softly back from her face and over her bare shoulders, a perfect foil for the ice blue satin gown she wore. He had only a glimpse of her eyes before delicate ivory lids fluttered over them, but that glimpse was enough to identify the large pale blue eyes that had reminded him of the winter ice that could be found around the edge of a clear pond.

With some disappointment Hunter saw his host approaching.

''Hunter, come and meet my daughters after all these years.'' Alastair clamped a warm hand briefly on his guest's shoulder while leading him to one of the sofas in the center of the room. The two girls seated there came to their feet as the men approached.

"You are already reacquainted with Florence, I understand."

Hunter smiled as he stood in front of her and when she straightened from a shallow curtsy he bowed, taking her hand and bringing it briefly to his lips. "I had the distinct pleasure of meeting and conversing with Florence upon my arrival." And then he smiled in sympathy as the shy girl blushed dramatically.

"And this is Jennifer. You may remember her as the baby of the family . . . although she's nine now, so I suppose I should stop introducing her that way."

"I'm almost ten, Papa!" Jennifer informed him in a stage whisper that made Hunter chuckle.

Taking her hand and holding it for a moment, Hunter gazed down at her fondly. "You *were* a baby when last I saw you," he said warmly. "But you are quite the young lady now, Jennifer." He bowed over her hand while the girl smiled up at her father with something close to triumph in her laughing eyes.

Turning to join his host as Alastair led the way around the low table between the two sofas, Hunter said softly, "Beauty seems to run in this family, my friend."

The older man waved the comment away with a casual yet decidedly nervous gesture. "Obviously inherited from their mother," he muttered.

But that was not necessarily true. Alastair was still a fine figure of a man. He had thickened around the middle a little since their last meeting, but he had not developed a paunch, as did so many men who lived in the lap of luxury. Then, too, Hunter recalled that the senior Downings, Alastair's parents, had been a strikingly handsome couple.

As the men approached the other sofa, Hunter noticed that his vision in blue had moved to stand behind her sister and, although she was not presented totally in profile, he could see she was frowning.

Surely she could not resent the attention he was lavishing on her sisters? She couldn't have become so petty. With her beauty, she had no need to resent anyone. Still, some of the most beautiful women he had met could be insanely jealous on some occasions. God, he hoped she hadn't turned out to be one of those. What a disappointment that would be.

"And this is Denise, my second daughter, if you will recall," Alastair announced with a note of pride. "She is to be married before the year is out," he added.

Denise stood and dipped into a graceful curtsy. Hunter smiled before bending over her hand. "A pleasure to meet you once again."

Denise smiled. She obviously accepted herself for what she was, a reasonably attractive young woman approaching seventeen who had inherited her father's auburn hair and gray-green eyes. Her most notable feature was her mother's ivory complexion, which glowed with a natural blush.

As Denise resumed her seat Hunter felt heightened anticipation as he stepped to his right to follow Alastair around the end of the sofa. As he came to stand behind her, his vision in blue turned slowly, and with great effect, to face him.

He knew, even though he had been warned, that he had not been able to repress a fleeting look of shock, and in those first few seconds of seeing her he realized *that* was exactly what she'd wanted. She had set the stage in such a fashion that anyone would be forced to display surprise. Was this a game she played often, he wondered, or had she acted simply for his benefit? Did the awkwardness of the moment give her a perverse satisfaction? No awkwardness on her part, however, he noticed. She stood regally before him, a cool, disdainful smile on her beautiful lips, and Hunter felt his anger overcoming his initial shock and sadness.

"My eldest daughter, Margaret," Alastair announced, not so much with pride this time as with wariness, Hunter decided.

Margaret did not curtsy as her sisters had but held up her hand to him, an almost triumphant smile on her face.

Hunter dutifully kissed her hand briefly before she snatched it away. He did not smile when he straightened but crossed his powerful arms over his chest as he stared at her. Waiting.

"I believe you made some comment about our beauty, Mr. Maguire?" she challenged stiffly.

"Margaret!" Alastair cried, aghast.

The combatants ignored him.

"Indeed, you are exceptionally beautiful, Miss Downing," Hunter returned. "But would you have believed me if I'd told you that?"

Margaret's eyes flashed as she stated evenly, "I do not believe you now!"

"As you wish," he returned, gazing into her ice-blue eyes. "I am considering withdrawing the comment at any rate," he said after a moment's reflection. "True beauty is not found only on the surface." With that he turned to his host. "I believe you mentioned a drink earlier, my friend," he said in a voice that sounded more steady than he felt.

Alastair cleared his throat, obviously unsettled by the confrontation, and glanced briefly at his eldest daughter before responding. "Yes! Yes, of course."

As Hunter followed his host across the room he wondered briefly if he had reacted too harshly, but immediately decided he had not. His only regret was the dead silence that now hung over the room; the younger girls were obviously uncomfortable with what had taken place.

The scar was a damned shame, he admitted to himself, an unsightly interference with perfection, but it was made ugly only by the way she drew attention to it.

The mark ran jaggedly along her right jawline for a length of approximately two inches. It was pink in comparison to her complexion, but not livid, and it did little to mar her exquisite beauty.

But he knew that she'd plotted to put him off guard.

"I must apologize for Margaret's behavior," Alastair murmured as he prepared their drinks.

"Margaret is no longer a child, Alastair. She should apologize for her own behavior." Cocking his head slightly to one side, Hunter smiled ruefully at his friend. "But somehow I don't believe that happens often," he said softly.

Alastair looked up briefly, then across the room to his eldest daughter as he shook his head. "No," he said. "But it is not a minor blemish in her eyes, you see."

"I am sure it is not."

"In the beginning I was relieved that Margaret was not going to hide herself away in embarrassment and shrink from others. Still, I have never seen her act quite so hostile. I *do* apologize."

The man's voice was tinged with regret and almost unbearable sadness. Hunter had the distinct impression his host was afraid to challenge his own child and wondered at this attitude. But that was really no business of his, he decided. If Alastair could not discipline his children that was his own problem, but he need not expect Hunter to stand meekly by and allow Margaret Downing to make him a fool. She had caught him unaware once; she would not have a second chance to do so.

And still he wondered about the old Maggie. Surely she existed somewhere. . . .

Across the room, Margaret Downing was collecting herself. He was arrogant, she decided. Why had she not seen it all those years ago? He was obviously not a gentleman, and she wondered how she could ever have thought of him as one. Then she scoffed at herself. Most men were not gentlemen. They only presented a display of manners when they were guests in someone else's home. Although Hunter was no gentleman, at least he was brave. Most men shriveled in embarrassment and revulsion upon seeing her for the first time, and it gave her some satisfaction to see them squirm. After all, they were the reason she was disfigured.

Margaret closed her eyes briefly as she took a small sip of sherry, trying to blot out the next thought. Thoughts about the true nature of man and what she had learned: She made certain the same statements were echoed in her thoughts every day in the hope that she would be totally convinced of them. But the exercise was always ruined by a remembered childhood dream and a hollow, empty feeling she could only describe as an ache somewhere in the vicinity of her heart.

But Margaret knew she must keep trying to convince her stubborn mind that a liaison with a member of the opposite sex was not possible, that such relationships were not at all like the dreams she'd had as a girl.

She glared across the room at the tall, dark stranger quietly talking with her father. She wondered what her father had told him. Margaret had never discussed the "accident" with anyone, and Papa would not allow anyone at Treemont to mention it. She did not even think about it anymore. She hadn't for a long time now. But she remembered the lesson.

She walked around the settee to sit beside Denise.

Denise was already a lost cause, proclaiming herself madly in love with that young doctor from Williamsburg. She was still a child, and yet she was to be wed within two months. Margaret was saddened by thoughts of the harsh lessons that Denise would have to learn. It was so senseless, when they could all be perfectly happy living out their lives at Treemont. As the girls matured, they would come to understand that a life without men could be gratifying and peaceful.

Denise leaned close to her sister and spoke softly. "I believe he has become even *more* handsome, if that's possible," she said.

Margaret groaned and turned her head to frown at her sister. "Really! Watching Florence gush and coo is bad enough. I thought you had more sense."

Margaret did not frighten Denise. She ignored her sister's old-ladyish behavior. She even boldly teased her on occasion, hoping that Margaret would one day come to her senses.

Now she merely shrugged away Margaret's attitude. "I state only obvious fact, sister." She paused and took a delicate sip of sherry. "I believe he must be very brave also." Another pause, another sip from her glass. "You did misjudge this one, Margaret."

Margaret narrowed her eyes and primly straightened her spine, turning her head forward. "I don't know what you're talking about."

"He did not become all flustered and tongue-tied, did he?"

"You're being ridiculous," Margaret hissed.

"Not at all," Denise responded calmly. "You present yourself as if you were some ugly beast and treat every man who comes near you as if being a man were a sin."

"You have no idea what—"

"Oh, do I not? Well, you are not ugly, Margaret, and all men are not responsible for that silly scar. When are you going to realize that?"

"This is neither the time nor the place for this discussion," she said in her most condescending voice. But she saw that Denise was not to be stopped. What had gotten into the girl tonight? Was she losing all authority over the younger girls?

"When is the time?" Denise looked quickly around the room before her eyes returned once again to her sister. "We are all family here, with the exception of Mr. Maguire, of course, and somehow I feel he would enjoy a heated discussion of your attitude toward men."

"My attitude toward men is the only sensible one, as I have tried to tell you." Maggie now stared pointedly away from her.

Margaret was stubborn and vexing when it came to this subject. "Oh, yes, you've tried," Denise said sadly. "Margaret, do you really want to wither away here at Treemont?" Her voice had risen angrily.

Suddenly Alastair was before them. "What is going on between you two?"

Margaret realized that their conversation had grown intense and they were nearly shouting. She looked up at her father and then across the room at Hunter Maguire. He was looking in their direction, of course, and the man was smiling. Oh, God! How much had he heard? She was mortified.

Turning to her father, Denise said softly, "Papa, I'm sorry."

"We have a guest," he reminded them evenly.

"I apologize also, Papa," Margaret said quietly as she stood and placed one hand lightly on his forearm. "Shall I discuss the showing of the horses with Mr. Maguire?" she asked softly. Although she was suspicious of men, she still loved her father. And she had ways of calming him during moments like these.

"That would be nice," Alastair said derisively.

Margaret squared her shoulders and turned away from her family. As she walked stiffly across the room it occurred to her that she should not have taken such pains with her appearance tonight. It appeared that her plan had not affected Hunter Maguire the way it had previous callers. But then, Hunter was not like the other callers. She suspected he had come here to bargain for more than a stallion.

He was to remain with them for one week. At the end of that time, Margaret would see that he had completed his business and was on his way home.

Alone.

She approached him now and spoke in a cool, stilted tone as she stopped before him. "Mr. Maguire," she said as she raised her head to look directly into his eyes. "You must forgive my brief lapse in manners. My sister and I became engrossed in conversation, and I have neglected to welcome you to our home."

Hunter's face betrayed nothing, but he was surprised. She acted as though they had never met before. "I understand, Miss Downing," he responded warily.

"Papa informs me you are in the market for a good stallion, Mr. Maguire," she said before lifting a delicate glass to her lips.

"There was a time when you called me Hunter," he said quietly.

A slight frown creased her forehead. "We have some excellent stock to show you," she hedged. "I think you'll be pleasantly surprised."

"Will I, indeed?" A *pleasant* surprise would be a nice change, he thought. But as he looked at her, he realized her indomitable spirit was still present. It had merely been warped since her accident. It might be interesting—as well as worthwhile—to see if he could bring back the old Maggie.

"We have a particularly fine mare as well," she said, continuing her businesslike manner. "Would you like to see her?" she asked reasonably, feeling the discussion was going quite well.

A twinkle developed in Hunter's eyes. "I bought a fine mare a few years ago. Do you remember?"

Maggie raised her glass, the action neatly breaking their eye contact.

"But at the time you wanted me to choose another," he teased.

She remembered, but she didn't want to. Remembering was painful. Margaret's shoulders stiffened visibly as she lowered her glass and looked up at him. "You should have taken my advice," she said coolly. "That little mare gave us a good foal. Perhaps you'd like to buy the stallion. He's an excellent two-year-old."

Hunter felt stung again. She was being deliberately distant, but this time he could see a spark of the young girl he had known. She was reacting toward him with an air of authority, and *still* he could see her intensity when she spoke of the horses. She was too rigid to appear exuberant, but there was something there that he remembered.

Tipping his head to one side he asked curiously, "And should I take your advice about the stallions?"

Margaret smiled confidently. "Definitely."

Hunter nodded and sipped his brandy thoughtfully before asking, "You consider yourself a good judge of horse-flesh?"

"Definitely."

"And of men?" he asked, frowning as her body stiffened in reaction.

"I don't know what you mean," she said, turning away to place her glass on a nearby table.

"Do you also consider yourself a good judge of men?" he pressed.

Margaret's eyes frantically darted toward the dining room. "If you'll excuse me," she said, "I must see about supper."

Hunter reached out to touch her forearm, wanting her to stay. But Margaret snatched her arm away. The icy stare she sent him momentarily distracted Hunter from his course of questioning. He quickly regained the track, however. "You're running away," he said quietly.

Margaret reacted with a semblance of a laugh. "Don't be silly. I'm going to see if our meal is ready."

"You haven't answered me."

"Mr. Maguire," she said with the air of one striving for patience, "a silly question hardly deserves an answer."

"Was it silly?" he asked reasonably.

"*I* thought so." She started to turn away again.

Hunter shook his head and set his own glass aside before crossing his arms over his chest. "I am interested in hearing more about your 'sensible' attitude toward men."

Margaret's complexion turned a glorious flaming pink. "It's very bad manners to eavesdrop on private conversations," she returned evenly.

"I'm sorry, Margaret," he offered sincerely, "but your conversation was hardly private, and I must admit to being curious."

"I once heard of a boy who was *curious* about a rabbit trap, Mr. Maguire," she said evenly. "He could have lost more than his finger."

Hunter grinned with obvious admiration. "Well done, Miss Downing."

"I thought so."

So she could still give as good as she got, he thought with something akin to pride. "Perhaps I should return to the subject of horses," he offered.

Margaret nodded. "Perhaps you should."

"Very well, then," he drawled. "You wouldn't have an inkling of what happened to mine this afternoon, would you?"

"You really must excuse me," she said, and this time, with a hearty laugh, he let her go.

Margaret hurried through the dining room, her eyes scanning the table to make sure nothing had been forgotten.

Only four places had been set. Florence and Jennifer would take their evening meal in the kitchen. She made a mental note to see that both girls went to bed after their supper; the hour would be late.

Entering the kitchen, Margaret silently prayed that Anna was ready to serve the meal. The end of their supper would signal the end of the evening, and Margaret had already grown weary of being in the company of their guest.

Seeing Anna spoon small peas into a bowl, Margaret asked, "Is the meal ready, then? Shall I take the platters through?"

Anna did not care to be rushed and frowned as she nodded toward the thinly sliced lamb. "Take that and the potatoes. I'll bring the rest."

"Will you call everyone to the table, please?" Margaret asked and earned a glare from the older woman. "We have to do this properly, Anna," she said firmly. "We don't want to embarrass Papa."

"Always trying to please *Papa*," the woman muttered as she placed a shoulder against the swinging door and disappeared.

Margaret sighed wearily and lifted two large platters of food before following. Why did Anna always have to be difficult? she wondered. And the woman always seemed to choose those moments when there was a lot to be done.

Sometimes Margaret thought that she alone was responsible for seeing to all that needed attention at Treemont.

Arranging the platters carefully on the table, just as Anna was returning from the parlor, Margaret heard the soft voices of Florence and Jennifer as they bade Hunter good night. Her eyes scanned the table once again, noticing that the meat fork was missing. Whispering a soft expletive, she turned and raced through the kitchen door.

When she returned to the dining room, Denise was seated

and her father and Hunter were patiently standing beside their chairs.

Maggie placed the fork where it belonged, but before she could touch her own chair, Hunter was there beside her, pulling it back from the table and waiting politely for her to sit. Somewhat flustered by this attention, Margaret smoothed the back of her skirt with both hands as she gracefully sank into her place. "Thank you," she murmured softly, her eyes darting to her sister even as she reached for the linen napkin beside her place setting.

Denise smiled brightly, and Margaret frowned.

From his place at the head of the table, Alastair looked at his eldest daughter and then at his friend. They were seated to his right and left, facing each other, and he wondered if the tension he could feel in the room would be a breeding ground for indigestion.

"Margaret has been telling me you have some very good stock for sale, Alastair," Hunter said as he speared a slice of lamb and placed it on his own plate.

"Indeed. We have several young stallions and one older fellow for you to inspect," Alastair said, accepting the platter of meat from the younger man. "The older horse is the only one of the lot we know to be true, you understand."

Margaret's eyes snapped up to her father's. "You're not speaking of Pride, Papa?"

Alastair looked at her briefly before attending to the matter of filling his plate. "He's the only young stallion we have at the moment who has been put to a mare."

Margaret lowered her fork to her plate and braced both forearms on the table edge. "You can't mean to sell Pride?" she asked anxiously.

"He's to be offered for sale along with the others," her father returned firmly.

Maggie bit her lip, fretting. She loved all the horses, but Pride was special. He was worth a dozen of the others, and

Treemont needed the foals he would produce. Surely her father understood that? Still, Margaret knew she could not argue the matter here in front of others. She would discuss the future of Pride when she and her father were alone.

Hunter had watched the interaction between father and daughter very closely. Clearly Margaret was shaken by her father's announcement about this particular horse. Hunter wondered if her reaction was due to an attachment to the animal or to the fact that a decision had been made without her knowledge. Since Margaret gave the impression that she was in control of a great many things, it would surely hurt her pride to have a decision made without her concurrence. On the other hand, Hunter could understand strong emotional ties to certain animals, and as he stared across the table, the look he gave Margaret was one of compassion.

Raising her eyes from her plate, Margaret encountered the dark eyes of their guest and immediately decided she had given too much away. He seemed to be offering pity because she did not want to lose a good horse. She did not want pity from him. For any reason.

Wanting to discharge the uncomfortable moment, Margaret straightened her spine and smiled at her father. "In any event, I believe we should reconsider selling *any* horses to Mr. Maguire, Papa," she said tightly. "He seems to misplace them."

Alastair lowered his fork and frowned.

Hunter threw back his head and laughed.

CHAPTER
7

Hunter now understood Alastair's worry over Maggie. Obviously the woman was riding roughshod over the household and no one was stopping her. Someone should have taken her in hand years ago, but then, years ago Maggie had been a sweet, laughing, fun-loving girl. She hadn't yet become Margaret the ice princess.

What had happened to Maggie? She certainly hadn't come to bring him breakfast in bed.

Swinging his legs over the side of the bed, Hunter stretched, twisted his torso, and got to his feet all in one fluid motion.

It was still dark outside as he padded across the room to retrieve his breeches and a plain white shirt. He wondered if any of the household would be about. Actually, he hoped to have a quiet moment to sip some coffee before he was forced to face a whole herd of Downings.

Quietly leaving his room he walked soundlessly along the wide corridor toward the curved staircase. The girls, with the exception of Margaret, appeared to have retained their good nature. Yet how could one small scar have made such

65

a dramatic difference in her disposition? There had to be more.

Last night he had seen much about her that he did not remember and only snatches of the young woman he had known. She was now stiffly in control, while he remembered her as carefree. She now smiled coldly, while he remembered laughing warmth. She now tried to avoid him, while he remembered her seeking him out. But the wit was still there and the intensity, as witnessed by her fervor when talking about horses. Her passions appeared to have been channeled in a different direction. She could obviously run the household as if she were born to order troops about, but he sensed no happiness. Something had destroyed the sunny side of her nature, and he intended to find out what that something was. He wanted her laughing and smiling again.

The housekeeper was in the process of laying out a multi-course breakfast when Hunter entered the massive dining room. He smiled apologetically at the woman who was busy setting platters on the sideboard.

"My apologies. I hope I am not disrupting your plans? I'm an early riser."

Anna Crosleigh was a thick-waisted woman of perhaps sixty who possessed an unpleasant manner. Hunter had sensed that she disliked him during his previous visit, and he sensed it again now. She was unfriendly and unsmiling, and he recalled Alastair saying that he kept the woman only because she worked like a horse and seemed to like it that way. Well, as far as Hunter was concerned, a good day's work did not compensate for having to suffer her rudeness. Perhaps Maggie had been associating too much with Anna, he thought, and smiled.

"Things is ready," Anna said before hastily leaving the room.

Hunter was pouring his first cup of coffee when he heard

running feet. He was not to have a few moments alone with his coffee and his thoughts.

In the next moment Jennifer charged headlong into the room, executing a well-controlled maneuver and managing to stop without bouncing into him or the sideboard.

"Good morning!" she chirped, grinning up at him while she reached for a plate. "Are you up to facing the wicked Downing girls today?" She helped herself to bread and ham.

Hunter smiled as he took his coffee to the table and sat at the place he had occupied the previous evening. "I can tolerate some better than others," he responded lightly.

Jennifer carried her plate to the table and sat opposite Hunter. "I'm glad you get up early," she said, slicing into a thick piece of ham. "Now we can chat."

Hunter suppressed an urge to laugh and raised the cup to his lips. "And what would you like to chat about?"

"Well," she said, "I should tell you that Denise feels very bad about last night. She told me so when I went to wake her this morning."

"Denise need not feel bad," he returned.

She attacked another piece of ham. "She said we were not very polite. She meant when she and Margaret were arguing. But then, they always argue."

"Indeed?" He raised a dark brow in question.

Jennifer looked around the room before leaning toward him. "She's the only one who stands up to Margaret."

Hunter leaned back in his chair and drew a small cheroot from his pocket. "Why is that, do you think?"

"Because no one else would dare to defy Margaret. We always do as she asks and let her go her own way."

"Is that what you do, Jennifer? Do you let Margaret go her own way?"

Jennifer studied her fork as a frown crossed her pretty face. "Sometimes Margaret is nice to me, but not much anymore, so I just leave her alone. She used to be fun, but not since the accident."

Hunter got to his feet and moved to the sideboard. As he returned with the silver coffee pot in hand, he asked, "What sort of accident was it?"

Jennifer shrugged as he took his seat. "I don't know. Anna told me I was not to talk about it." She chewed thoughtfully on a slice of toast. "I don't think Denise and Florence know either. Some man hit her, but I don't know why he would do such a thing. He must have been a beast, don't you think?"

"An ogre," Hunter said quietly.

She smiled at him. "I'll bet you never hit a woman."

He smiled in return. "Never."

"I knew that!" she declared with confidence and then took up serious study of her now empty plate. "I don't remember when you were here before, but Margaret used to talk about you." She raised her eyes shyly to his. "She was quite gushy about you, really."

Hunter laughed. "Gushy?"

A smile lit her eyes at his reaction. "You know . . . silly. Like older girls are sometimes?"

"Yes, I believe I know what you mean," he said quite seriously.

"Time to get ready for school, Jennifer," a quiet voice announced from the doorway.

Two pairs of eyes turned in that direction, and Hunter's darker ones widened in disbelief.

The vision of loveliness of the evening before had vanished, only to be replaced by a severe and unfeminine specter. Today Margaret had pulled her glorious hair back until it stretched the skin around her eyes, and her attire was that of a stable hand. He could not imagine anyone putting a rough plaid shirt and stiff dungarees next to a woman's delicate skin, but she had done just that. Clearly she was challenging him.

"I've had Pride turned out to the paddock so you can see him running free," she said as she picked up a cup and saucer.

"Coffee is here," he said dumbfounded.

"Thank you," Margaret returned with strained politeness.

"What have you done to your hair?" he asked stupidly.

Margaret frowned as she reached in front of him for the coffee pot. "You are a very rude man, do you know that?" She frowned at him briefly before pouring the black brew into her cup.

"I suppose I am," he returned. "But I've never seen a hairstyle quite so severe."

Margaret raised a hand in an unconscious gesture and patted the neat knot on the top of her head. "It keeps my hair out of my face when I'm working with the horses," she said matter-of-factly. Margaret stared at Jennifer as she pulled a chair away from the table. "Go and get ready for school now," she said.

Jennifer looked unhappy, but she obeyed.

Once her sister had departed, Margaret lifted her cup to her lips.

"You're not going to eat?" Hunter asked.

She shook her head. Her stomach had been behaving nervously, but she was not about to tell him that. While she might have to deal with him on a business level, Margaret had no intention of engaging him in personal conversations.

"The stallions are ready for you to view," she said simply.

"Your father won't be joining us?" Hunter asked with obvious confusion.

Margaret set down her cup. "The horses are my responsibility, Mr. Maguire. You may dicker with Papa over price, but I am in charge of training and conditioning the animals." She got to her feet.

"Along with the training and conditioning of your family!" he muttered.

"I have to see that the girls are preparing for school," she said, frowning because he had spoken so softly she had not heard his comment. She was certain it hadn't been flattering. "I'll meet you at the barn in a few moments."

She turned toward the door as Hunter looked out the window. The sun was barely up!

"Surely it's too early for school?" he asked quietly.

Margaret spoke over her shoulder. "And girls will dawdle away the hours if they are not reminded of their responsibilities."

He watched her go, frowning as he wondered if *she* ever dawdled away an hour or two.

"That is Passion's Pride," Margaret announced as she joined Hunter at the corral gate. "The beast," she said fondly.

Hunter noticed she continued to frown. "He's a magnificent animal, Margaret." He turned his attention back to the center paddock. Passion's Pride pawed the ground and snorted before throwing his head back and racing to the far fence. A magnificent specimen of muscle, sinew, and spirit all drawn up tight as a drum in a sleek black package. "He needs to run," Hunter murmured, keeping his eyes on the horse. "He might treat his ladies a little more gently if he had the freedom to run often enough." He turned to her. "Was he bred here?"

Margaret nodded, her manner businesslike. "Sired by my stallion, Eclipse, out of a mare called Desert Passion. Two of my finest animals."

"Truly outstanding," Hunter murmured, as they returned their attention to the paddock. "He is fine to breed for saddle stock and that is where the best money lies for me. And he has me intrigued."

"If you're feeling up to a challenge," she said, nodding toward the prancing beast, "be my guest," she added with a false smile.

Hunter cast his eyes briefly toward the clear blue summer sky. "And I thought the sun would shine all day," he said softly.

Margaret did not miss his message. She had thought twice about facing Hunter this morning, but the horses were her responsibility and her pride. She had dressed plainly for the second part of her plan, and for the third she'd decided to ignore Hunter Maguire for the better part. By now he must be thoroughly disillusioned, so she would survive the few remaining days of his visit. Then life would return to normal.

She was glad her father had promised to join them at the stables. Alastair had long claimed that Hunter was a master horseman, and Margaret saw this as an opportunity to put the man to the test.

And so she ignored Hunter's comment, smiling a greeting as her father walked up to the paddock fence. She hoped he was about to see his friend land on his rump in the dust.

Pride was a valuable animal and one they could not afford to lose. And since her father would not listen to reason on the matter, Margaret knew it was up to her to dissuade Hunter from purchasing the stallion.

Smiling sweetly at her father, she said, "I shall have the boys get Pride saddled, Papa."

Alastair nodded absently as she left, but he was more concerned when she returned, smiling softly.

"This should only take a moment," Margaret said in an odd tone, and Alastair frowned in confusion.

She did not give her father an opportunity to question her as she watched two lanky youths enter the paddock. One hefted a saddle onto the fence railing, then followed the other boy who clutched a bridle. It took some time and quick maneuvering to corner the proud black animal, but they eventually managed to catch hold of the horse's halter and deftly got bit and bridle into place, carefully avoiding the hind legs. The horse prancing between them, they started toward the gate, but Hunter had already entered the large enclosure and was upon them.

"Leave the saddle," he said, reaching for the reins. "If this fellow is truly not a gentleman, I want to feel him moving beneath me. Perhaps then I can detect any tricks he has in mind before he unseats me."

"Yes, sir," one of the boys managed to say as they both moved away, wide-eyed. "There's goin' to be hell to pay when that man breaks his neck," he muttered to his companion.

Hunter stood and talked quietly to the animal, rubbing the soft muzzle and velvety ears.

"My God," Alastair whispered, "he's going to ride without a saddle."

"I'm certain he knows what he is doing, Papa," Margaret said as her heart began to beat a wild tattoo. Her plan had to work, she thought, as she maintained total concentration on horse and rider. She couldn't lose Pride. But part of her admired Hunter's nerve.

Hunter continued to talk soothingly as he caressed the animal's neck, then ran his hand along his back. Still talking, he grabbed a handful of mane at the withers and easily swung up onto Pride's back.

The great stallion stood still, awaiting a command. Not

until Hunter gathered the reins more firmly in his hands did the horse appear distressed.

Hunter knew he had trouble.

Pride tossed his head fretfully and began to worry at the bit. As Hunter tried to turn the animal's head, Pride burst into action. Hunter kept the reins firm and short; if Pride managed to get his head down he would buck. Instead, the horse twisted and ran toward the far fence. Hunter immediately understood the trick. Pride would turn at the last minute, raking his rider along the wooden rails.

Hunter was stunned that he had absolutely no control over this horse. The animal was not unschooled after all. The damned beast must have the bit between his teeth!

After that there was no more time for thought, other than to seek the best means of escape. If he did not bail out now, he could lose his right leg. So . . . over the side he went, rolling several times as he hit the ground before lying flat on his back.

Margaret flinched visibly at the sound of man hitting solid earth.

"Damn!" Hunter muttered and beat a fist into the dirt.

"Get that animal back in his stall!" Alastair blustered.

"No! Wait!" Hunter was on his feet and calling to the stable boys. "Wait! Let me see him!"

Margaret turned her head long enough to see the worried expression on her father's face. "Mr. Maguire is an experienced horseman, Papa," she said, trying to alleviate his fears. "I'm sure he has taken many falls."

Alastair cast her a baleful look. "And that makes *this* fall acceptable?"

Margaret shook her head, frowning as she returned her attention to the paddock. "Not acceptable, Papa," she said softly. "Necessary."

Alastair's frown intensified. "Margaret . . ." But he grew quiet as his attention was drawn again to the stallion.

The stable boys had captured the horse once again, and Hunter stood staring at the beast. Pride continued to worry at the bit, and the froth from his mouth was speckled with blood.

Hunter stepped forward and, keeping the reins around Pride's neck, dropped the bit free. His lips tightened and his eyes darkened as he saw the severe curb. "What bit does this horse usually wear?" he asked the older boy.

"A snaffle, sir," the boy answered quietly.

"Then why did you put such a harsh bit on him today?" But he did not need to ask as the two boys looked fearfully at each other and then, pleadingly, back at Hunter. In an attempt to quash his anger, Hunter ran his fingers through his black hair and took a deep breath. "Miss Downing's instructions?" he asked softly, and the older boy managed a slight nod of affirmation. Sighing heavily, Hunter asked, "Is there a hackamore in the tack room?"

The boy smiled. "Yes, sir!"

"Get it for me. This animal's mouth is sore enough." He turned to the younger boy. "Can you hold him here on your own?" The lad nodded, reaching for the reins. "I'll be back. And make certain you hold him well. There is about to be a ruckus, and I don't want him frightened into running."

Hunter moved with a strong, assured gait as he crossed the paddock and left the gate wide open when he rounded the fence toward the two who stood watching. His gaze remained determinedly fixed on the blue eyes that were growing larger with each step he took in her direction. When he had only a step or two to take, Margaret sensed his purpose and bolted. But not quickly enough. Hunter seized her upper arm and spun her around to face him. "Come with me," he said evenly.

"Let me go!" she snapped. "Papa?"

Alastair stood by, his arms crossed over his chest as he watched the proceedings. Hunter Maguire would not harm his daughter and he was at a loss as to what to do with her.

Hunter started to move back toward the paddock but with that first step, Margaret dug in her heels. "I said let me go!" she shouted, pulling back against his hand.

Knowing he would bruise her if she insisted on being dragged, Hunter changed his tactics, and Maggie quickly found his arm around her waist as he hauled her against his hip. "I want to show you something!" he said firmly and grunted when one of Margaret's flailing feet caught him soundly on the shin. "Stop that!"

"Put me down!" she cried in panic and continued to kick and struggle, hoping for any chance to escape him.

"I said stop that!" He was breathing heavily from the exertion of trying to control her; the woman was twisting and bucking like a harnessed mustang. Thinking of Passion's Pride, standing a few feet away and already snorting at this wild creature, he snapped, "You'll get us all killed!" When she continued to kick and strike out with her hands, Hunter set her roughly on her feet. "Now stop!" Glaring into eyes that expressed her shock at what he had done, he tightened his grip on her arms, for he could see the explosion coming just as sure as the sun would set.

"How dare you!" She tried to raise her hands to scratch his face.

Hunter captured both wrists with one hand and wrapped his arm around her waist again, drawing her against his side where she could do less damage. "How dare I?" he muttered. "I dare because, by God, you are going to see what you have done!"

Margaret was beginning to weaken, and she knew she would lose in a battle against him. She was no match for this man's strength, but the fear of being held so close against him made her struggle until her last ounce of strength gave out.

When finally she sagged against him, Hunter set her on her feet once again, taking a deep breath as his arms loosened their hold even while he continued to offer support at her waist. He stared down at her, her head bowed in defeat, wondering why she'd continued to struggle against him when he had posed no real threat. "Why did you fight me?" he asked softly. "Do you fear me so much?"

Maggie's head snapped up, and her beautiful pale blue eyes narrowed with loathing. "You act like a madman," she said, "and you have the nerve to ask?"

"I was angry, yes," he said reasonably. "But surely you cannot fear me so much that you would fight like that? We were once great friends, Margaret." He studied her face as she looked away. "You did not fear me then. In fact, I recall you were fond of me. What happened, Margaret? What has changed?" he urged.

Margaret tugged feebly against his hold, her eyes downcast as she studied the buttons on his shirt. "I simply want you to leave me alone."

"Why?"

"Because it is my wish." She raised narrowed eyes to reinforce her words. "Just go away and leave me alone."

He studied her expression for a moment, deciding her words masked some greater meaning. He could understand that her feelings for him could have diminished over the years, but there was much more about her reaction to him that he failed to understand. "I cannot do that," he said and dropped his arms from her waist, taking firm hold of one wrist. "Will you walk or must I carry you again?"

"I'm not going anywhere with you," she said and tugged again at the hand clamped firmly onto her wrist. Why was he being so damned pigheaded? Surely he must see that there was no longer anything between them; she was not the raving beauty everyone had expected her to become. So why had he not taken to his heels and run at first sight of her? Because of some pretense of buying a horse? She did not believe that was his only reason for coming, after the way her father had been talking about the man's visit. Well, she no longer had anything to offer, so he might as well return to his home and leave her alone!

Hunter listened to her words and shook his head in frustration. No matter her reasons for not wanting him near, she would walk into the paddock or be carried. "You are a foolish woman," he said softly. "Will you be embarrassed when I pick you up with witnesses present?" And as Margaret's eyes roamed the fence line, staring at the people she had known most of her life, he added, "Take heed, dear one, for carrying you in my arms is not a task I would loathe."

Her eyes snapped back to his and grew wide. "Why are you doing this?" she muttered, and he knew she did not relish a scene in front of family and stable hands.

"Someone has to take you in hand. You are entirely too thoughtless."

"And you are going to save me from myself?"

Hunter grinned ruefully. "Something like that," he said and turned, pulling her along in his wake.

Maggie could barely contain her anger at his high-handed manner, but there'd been enough commotion already. Whatever his purpose in dragging her toward that damned horse, she would endure his treatment and hope she could then escape the attention of all the eyes that were following their every move. And her father stood there watching! She had the distinct impression that Alastair was joining ranks with this heathen. That did not bode well for her. Her father's failure to come to her aid only fueled her suspicions that her dear parent had plans that she would not like.

When Hunter reached Passion's Pride, he spoke softly in order to calm the nervous animal. He pushed Margaret closer to the black head, placing both hands on her shoulders to keep her there. "Look at his mouth," he said softly.

Margaret flinched as Pride continued to toss his head in agitation, spraying the air with foam. She could see blood mixed with the white foam that had formed around his mouth. She felt sick at the sight. "His mouth is bleeding," she whispered shakily. She hadn't stopped to consider that she could actually harm Pride in her effort to keep him with her.

Hunter's lips were very close to her ear as he stood behind her and said softly. "Dammit, Margaret, you have been raised around these animals. You must have seen this before. Why did you allow it to happen?"

Margaret lowered her eyes. Remorse made her voice quake. "I didn't think," she whispered and turned away when Hunter dropped his hands from her shoulders.

Knowing Pride was too nervous to be ridden now, Hunter ordered the young stable boy to take the horse inside and tend his sores. But his eyes had not left the profile of Margaret Downing for one moment. "Does it bother you, Maggie, seeing the horse in that condition?"

"Of course it bothers me."

"Then why would you do such a thing?" he asked again, trying to understand. "Could you possibly hate me so much that you would endanger that animal?"

Margaret raised her head and stared at him, although she

did not face him fully. "Why are you here?" she asked, throwing Hunter off balance.

And the fact that she had asked the question in such a way made him wary. "There was a time when you did not want me to leave," he returned evasively.

Margaret shook her head. "But that time is lost. Can't you understand that?" Not giving him time to respond, Maggie raised her head proudly and walked slowly away.

CHAPTER

8

The following morning Margaret took herself off for some quiet time to think and was comfortably ensconced in the hayloft when she heard the chatter of her youngest sister. Opening the small door used for dropping hay to the animals in the paddock below, Margaret had a perfect view of Hunter Maguire preparing to ride Passion's Pride for the second time.

Jennifer had climbed up to sit on the uppermost fence rail and was offering encouragement. "The hackamore should be good!" she called.

Hunter turned his head, smiling in her direction. "We can hope," he said ruefully, remembering his tumble the previous day.

Alastair stood beside his youngest, as if hoping he could keep her from falling. Margaret could see her father was carefully watching the proceedings, although she was relatively certain Hunter knew what he was doing. It irked her that Alastair was taking such inordinate interest in their guest's every movement.

Margaret stretched out on her stomach to watch Hunter

gentling the big black stallion with soothing words and soft caresses. Clearly the man was good with the animal, and she became fascinated by the quiet, confident manner that, despite herself, she remembered well. Hunter exuded power, yet his gentleness was clearly visible. And within her, a pang of disappointment caused her heart to twist painfully. She fought against it, just as she had fought for the past year, because nothing could change what had happened and nothing could change what she had become. While his presence had revived her childhood dreams, Margaret knew that if she could just get through the next four days she would be able to take control of her life again and find some contentment in the security of Treemont.

Hunter continued to talk to Passion's Pride as he adjusted the hackamore, which was now in place. Gently he tested the tension of the lamb's-wool pad across the horse's nose, then dropped his hand to caress the black muzzle, even as his peripheral vision took note of his audience high above the paddock. He could see only the top of her fair hair but he was grateful that she cared to watch what he was doing. It gave him hope.

Turning his attention back to the horse, he whispered, "I know your mouth hurts, old boy, but there will be no more pain with this." There was no bit in Pride's mouth to cause further irritation. The animal would be controlled by gentle pressure on his nose from the bridle and against his neck from the reins . . . in theory at least, Hunter thought ruefully. After all, this was an English-trained mount who was used to having his head pulled around rather than responding to pressure from his rider and the equipment. Hunter smiled as he gazed into the animal's eyes. Either Pride would respond or the rider would end up in the dust once again.

Passion's Pride initially responded with confusion to the new headgear and the unfamiliar signals from his rider, but it was clear that the beast was not mean. He was high-spirited and lacking in exercise, but he was intelligent. The stallion needed only strong and knowledgeable handling.

Hunter spent some time putting the horse through several paces in and around the area of the barn and paddocks before deciding they had both had enough for one day. Tomorrow he would take the stallion out again and just let him run.

Margaret had been able to see most of the stallion's exercises and was impressed by what she'd witnessed; Hunter possessed a knowledge and expertise far above that of any handler she had seen. She sighed and dropped her forehead onto her folded hands. Her attempts to scare him off had failed, and her feelings were in chaos. . . . There was too much to admire about the man. She would be hurt again when he left, and this time it would be for entirely different reasons. And she'd be doubly hurt, since it appeared her beloved Pride would leave as well.

Time passed as she sorted through her jumbled feelings until suddenly the fine hair on the back of her neck stood up and Margaret turned onto her back in reaction to the soft shuffle of the hay near her feet.

"Jennifer and I are going out for a ride," Hunter said quietly. "Join us."

"You frightened me to death!" she gasped.

He smiled apologetically and dropped down to his haunches at her feet as she sat up. "Sorry, Maggie."

"And don't call me Maggie."

He raised black eyebrows mockingly. "I don't know you well enough to call you Maggie?"

"My name is Margaret," she snapped.

"I'm aware of that."

"Then why don't you use it?" she asked, looking for a way to get around him and escape; she was boxed in up here.

"I was once very fond of a young girl named Maggie," he said conversationally and grinned at the glare he earned. "Don't suppose you could bring her back? I miss her."

"You are being ridiculous!"

He laughed at her disgruntled tone. "Oh, no. Not me. I'm dead serious!" And with that he stood, holding out a hand to help her up. "Come on. Ride with us."

"I'm not in the mood for a ride," she mumbled, ignoring his hand.

"Very well," he said reasonably. "What will your mood allow?" He stepped back a pace to allow her to struggle to her feet under her own steam, which he knew she manufactured in abundance.

"Work," she said simply, brushing hay from her britches.

But when she took a step toward the ladder that led below, Hunter placed a hand gently on her forearm to stop her. "Afraid?" he challenged, his black eyes homing in on hers.

Maggie stiffened her spine and her resolve. "Perhaps I simply do not care for your company. Have you considered that?"

"Frankly, no."

She was so taken aback by his calm arrogance that she had to choke back an astonished laugh.

"Jennifer is waiting," he said when she continued to stare at him.

"My mare is lame," she said with inspiration.

"Then we shall find you another," he returned, equally inspired. "We could stay up here and verbally fence the day away, so why not give in while the sun is still shining?"

"Why are you so determined?" she asked.

"Why are you?"

"Oh, for heaven's sake! Let's go for the damned ride!" she said as she flounced down the ladder in frustration.

"Gotcha!" he whispered after a moment and followed her down.

Jennifer eyed her sister warily as Margaret flounced out of the stables with Hunter Maguire following on her heels. "I had Maribelle saddled for you, Margaret," she said, smiling and hoping it would encourage her sister to do the same.

"Maribelle is lame," Margaret said.

"No, she's not," Jennifer returned. "I saw you ride her earlier."

Margaret glared at her sister and then raised her hands in resignation, letting them fall to slap her thighs.

Hunter chuckled softly and came around to the side of the little roan. "Leg up?" he asked.

Maggie glared, shaking her head. Without a word to him she led Maribelle over to the mounting block, climbed the three steps, and settled herself astride the mare.

Hunter had become accustomed to her garb and had decided the fitted shirt and britches held some merit. His Maggie might act like an aged aunt at the ripe old age of eighteen, but that outfit accented beautifully the maturing curves of a woman.

Jennifer was dressed in breeches and a coat and was not so reluctant to accept Hunter's offer of a leg up. He easily raised her high while she swung her right leg over the saddle, then smiled her thanks at him while she gathered her pony's reins loosely in her hands.

"Could we please not trot?" she asked. "My pony jiggles my insides when we trot."

Hunter laughed as he moved off and mounted the horse he had chosen.

"Jennifer!" Margaret admonished.

The younger girl turned to frown at her sister. "Well, he does!"

"Do not say things like that."

''Why not?'' Jennifer asked, perplexed. ''That's what happens.''

''She has a point there,'' Hunter teased and led them off down the nearest lane.

Margaret did not appreciate his interference and decided the best way to survive this outing was probably to remain silent. Still, the man was vexing, to say the least.

They rode past row upon row of drying sheds, which would not be filled with tobacco leaves for several weeks yet. At least Hunter hoped that was the case in the southern part of the state, for he wanted to be home by the start of harvest.

He noticed as they rode that Alastair had left several fields to fallow. He pulled back, slowing his mount until Margaret was beside him. ''Are these fields played out?'' he asked.

Margaret looked around her. ''I wouldn't have thought so,'' she said and then shrugged casually. ''Perhaps Papa decided to leave them for another year.''

Hunter was surprised that, except for the horses, Maggie knew so little about the running of the farm. Surely she and her father discussed such things, at least casually? It also surprised him that Alastair had not chosen an alternative crop that would be easier on depleted soil. Few planters could afford to leave fields lying fallow for many years. But then his thoughts were directed elsewhere as Jennifer drew up beside him. He slowed his horse to match the pace of the pony while the girl chattered on about several topics.

But still his thoughts remained a few paces behind . . . with Margaret.

Soon they had left the fallow fields behind and were riding through a pretty forest that smelled of evergreen and sweet damp earth and wildflowers. When they emerged from the trees, Hunter suddenly recognized the location.

''I remember this pond!'' he said, smiling as he turned to

look at Margaret. "You must remember as well!" he said.

"Why?" Jennifer asked, looking from one to the other.

"It was one of Mother's favorite places," Margaret said demurely.

Hunter laughed. "Your sister and I took a little dip here," he said.

Jennifer's eyes widened. "You went swimming?" she asked, shocked. "Together?"

Margaret began fidgeting with her reins, not wanting to remember that afternoon when she had cried as only a foolish child could cry. She knotted the end of the reins, picking at the leather to avoid looking at the man who had managed to bring back more memories in two days than she'd thought she could dredge up in a lifetime.

"We didn't swim intentionally," Hunter explained as he lifted Jennifer to the ground.

"You fell in?" she asked, squinting up at him with a grin. "You fell in!" she crowed when he nodded his head. Then she turned to tease her sister. "Did he pull you in, Mag?" she asked, dropping the pony's reins and running toward the water; it didn't look very deep. She turned back to Margaret then, awaiting a full explanation, frowning in confusion when her sister refused a hand down. Hunter shrugged casually and turned and left her to her own devices.

"I pulled *him* in," Margaret said, setting the record straight.

"Ah, you did not!" Jennifer was incredulous. "He's too big!"

Hunter was smiling as he walked toward the water and sat on a fallen log at its edge. "It's true, monkey," he said. "She pulled me in."

"Jiminy! Maggie's stronger than I thought!"

Maggie stubbornly remained mounted, but she was watching her younger sister closely. "Don't get too close to the water, Jennifer!" she called and then was startled when

Maribelle began prancing. Maggie frantically grabbed the saddlebow to avoid being unseated. It took her a moment to realize what had happened; the mare had dropped her head to nibble the grass and the knotted reins had slipped forward on the animal's neck with enough slack so that the mare's forefoot had stepped through. When Maggie called out, Maribelle had abruptly lifted her head with the rein now trapping her foreleg.

The mare whirled and began to panic when she could not lower her leg to the ground.

"Hunter!" Jennifer screamed as she turned from the water and saw her sister's desperate attempts to stay in the saddle while the frightened horse whirled and pranced with increasing hysteria.

Hunter needed no more than a quick glance to understand what had to be done. He was on his feet and running before Maribelle's first squeal rent the air.

He had no time to think of the consequences. He circled the mare at a run, leaping up to drape himself over her neck. Maribelle was forced to bow her head, but she continued to whirl frantically. The mare was almost rigid with fright, but Hunter's weight was enough to force her head down and he was able to push the knotted reins over the animals ears. As soon as the tension of the leather was relieved, Maribelle stood on all fours, blowing and snorting while he attempted to calm her as he gathered the reins safely out of harm's way.

Hunter then freed the knot as he stepped around the mare's head and looked up at Margaret. Her normally glowing complexion had gone pale, and her hands continued to grip her saddle as she stared down at him, stunned by the thought of the near tragedy that had been avoided by his quick thinking.

"Come down," he said softly and reached up to grasp her around her waist. Margaret did not refuse his aid this time.

When she stood before him, he ducked his head, examining her eyes closely. "You're all right?" he asked.

Maggie nodded her head. "Maribelle?"

"She seems all right. Can you stand on your own while I take a look at her?"

Once more Margaret nodded, and Hunter reluctantly removed his hands. He dropped to one knee and ran his hand down the length of the mare's finely boned leg.

Jennifer ran to her sister's side and put her arms around Margaret's waist, hugging her close. "You scared me, Maggie," she said. She tilted her head back, frowning, when there was no response.

"I'm sorry, darling," Margaret managed to say, but tears had come to her eyes and her voice was strained. Margaret touched the back of her sister's head and pulled her close as the shock gripped her.

"Don't cry, Maggie," Jennifer pleaded.

Then Hunter was there, placing one hand reassuringly on Jennifer's shoulder while, with his free arm, he gathered Maggie close against his chest.

"All right," he said quietly. "You're all right." And when he felt her stiffen against him, he added, "Come now, you can lean on me this once."

Somewhere within her a dam seemed to burst as two days of pent-up emotions chose this moment to be released. Margaret gripped his shirtfront as she buried her face against his chest and wept.

Jennifer was looking decidedly worried, and Hunter was afraid she, too, would cry in another moment. "Take Maribelle over to that small tree and tie her, monkey," he said, smiling at the girl. "Can you do that?"

Jennifer nodded and stepped around him, looking back over her shoulder to keep a watchful eye on her sister as she did as he requested.

"Put your arms around my neck," he whispered. He bent

his knees and scooped Margaret up in his arms before she had complied. For safety's sake she was forced to wrap one arm around him, but she would not raise her head, and her face remained hidden against his chest, her hand covering her eyes. "My brave girl wasn't this frightened," he said with conviction as he sat on the log and settled Margaret on his lap. "Would you care to tell me about it?"

Her initial response was to shake her head and scramble off his lap. But once she'd moved out of his arms, she did sit beside him.

Margaret's head was bowed, and she had turned her face slightly away so that he would not see her tears. "I was afraid Maribelle would be hurt," she said softly, wiping the palm of one hand across her cheeks as she fought to regain control.

"The mare is fine," he said. He let the silence stretch out between them.

"Why did you come?" she choked out suddenly. "Can't you see it's hurting me?"

"Yes, I can see it's hurting you, Margaret," he breathed. "And I want to know why."

Margaret sputtered something that was very close to a wry laugh. "As I recall," she said, raising her head to stare out over the pond, "I cried the last time we came to this place."

Hunter stared at her profile. "You cried then for a very different reason," he said quietly and held out his handkerchief to her.

"Yes. I remember," she said, pressing the linen square to her cheeks. "I was a foolish child back then," she added in a whisper.

"Why foolish?" he asked, frowning as he leaned toward her. "Love is never foolish, little one. It's something everyone desires."

Margaret had collected herself, and the tears were gone

when she turned to look at him. "Not everyone, Hunter," she murmured. "Not everyone needs love."

Margaret assumed she had made her desires fairly clear, but she had not anticipated one small but revealing detail—the subtle catch in her voice.

CHAPTER

9

When they arrived back at the house, Jennifer jumped down from her pony unassisted, leaving him to be cared for by others as she raced to the house to tell her father and sisters the news of Maggie's near calamity.

Hunter helped Margaret down from Maribelle's back, and once the two horses had been led into the stable, he turned her, with his hand on her elbow, toward the house. "Your father will want to see that you are not injured," he said. "But I want us to talk privately."

Startled, Margaret stopped in her tracks. "Talk privately? About what?" She raised cocky eyebrows, but Hunter was not fooled. Something was seriously wrong; something had hurt her severely, and he was going to find out what that something was.

"I want to continue the discussion we were having before Jennifer interrupted us."

"Oh, you do!" Margaret exclaimed. "And if I choose not to participate in this discussion . . . ?"

"I believe you do want to discuss something with me, Margaret," he said sadly. "And you are afraid."

Margaret clearly resented this and tried to be remote again, turning away.

She was not to escape that easily, however.

Hunter stepped in front of her, folding his arms across his chest and setting his feet apart. "You have asked me more than once my reason for coming here," he said reasonably. "Why do you think I have come?"

Margaret very quickly decided she had sparred enough with this man. Besides, she was tired and hungry and wanted a hot bath. "I suspect you have bargained with my father!" she said. "For me!"

When she tried to step around him, Hunter gently gripped her arm. "Bargained?" he asked, arching his brows. "You are hardly a side of beef, Margaret."

"I am not even the stallion you are buying!" she spit.

"All right," he said, deciding to be forthright. "I came here to see you. There was once something very special between us, and I want to know if it's still there."

"Trust me, Hunter, there is nothing there," she returned evenly.

"You have not given us an opportunity to find out," he said reasonably. "You've either tried to avoid me or talked about business since my arrival."

Exasperated, Maggie raised her palms to the heavens. "I discuss business when it is required of me, Mr. Maguire. And I like to be alone on occasion. Is that so unusual?" She wrenched her arm free of his grip.

He let her go, but not without a parting comment. "It's easy to hide one's fears beneath business matters or in solitude, isn't it, Margaret?"

With only three days remaining before he had to leave Treemont, Hunter Maguire was firmly convinced that he wanted to marry Margaret Downing. She was not only beautiful, but possessed a sharp wit and superior intelligence. And he loved her spirit, or he would once it was rechanneled again. There was only one difficulty. Margaret seemed to have convinced herself that she did not want him—or anyone, for that matter. But Hunter now firmly believed that to be a lie.

Today Margaret had exposed her true feelings. He was now certain that her aloofness and her prim ways were merely a means of concealing her fear.

So now he had two tasks. First he needed to understand her anxieties. Then he had to convince her that there was nothing they could not overcome together.

The opportunity presented itself the following afternoon when Margaret was entering her bedroom, having returned from a solitary ride, and Hunter was about to return to the lower level of the house to join Alastair for a before-dinner drink.

Since she had not fully closed the door to her room, Hunter strode in behind her, pushed her forward, and leaned back against the polished door, sealing them inside and, finally, alone.

"Here we are," he said cheerfully.

Margaret glared. "You cannot come into my room."

"In the past you often violated my privacy." He looked around, folding his arms across his chest. "If you want me to leave, you'll have to talk first."

"I have nothing to say." She strode away toward the tall windows on the opposite side of the room.

"Very well. I'm in no hurry."

"Oh, for heaven's sake," she snapped, turning to look at him.

"How about for *your* sake, Maggie?" he asked softly. "You know, I am not certain whether I want to talk with you, spank you, or kiss you," he said, moving farther into the room.

Maggie's eyes grew wide as she backed up against the

window seat, then teetered and plopped down onto the cushioned bench.

"Which do you think I should do?" he asked, halting before her with his arms folded over his massive chest.

"None," she said firmly.

He smiled, shaking his head slowly. "I think you are a very beautiful woman," he said sincerely. "But you don't seem to want to hear that. That makes me curious." He drew a dainty boudoir chair close to her.

"Easy words to say," she muttered as he made himself comfortable. The pulse in her temples started pounding painfully as her eyes darted around him, looking for a means of escape.

"I mean them or I would not have said them. You must know that much about me."

But could she believe him? And if she did . . . what then? She carried deeper scars than the one on her face, and she harbored dark secrets. Surely he would not be so tolerant of those. He would be repulsed by them, and she would have to say good-bye to him again, just as she had three years ago . . . and this time the parting would be forever.

"What is it, Maggie?" he asked, his dark eyes searching a young face that seemed to be growing older as he pressed her. "Why do you hate me so?"

She looked up and saw the vulnerability in his eyes; this man was sincere, but Maggie did not want to get close to him. She was feeling trapped and wary, and the sickness was threatening to return to her stomach. She was close to revealing her secret. And the thought of his reaction was almost more than she could bear.

Hunter leaned forward, resting his elbows on his spread knees as he loosely knitted his long fingers together. He was so close to her he had only to reach out to touch the layers of dark skirts she wore. His eyes searched her face. He knew she was frightened, but he couldn't back away now. He had to know. "Why have you been trying to drive me away since the moment of my arrival?" he asked reasonably. "Why did you try to injure me that day when I rode the stallion?" There was a long moment of silence when she refused to look at him. "Why, Maggie?" he prompted.

She raised her pale blue eyes to his much darker ones. "It was not my intention to harm you," she said softly. "I just wanted you to leave."

"Why?" He looked more perplexed than ever.

"Because you're here on account of some bargain you made with my father," she said. "And because I make my own arrangements now."

Hunter shook his head. "There is no formal arrangement."

"All to the good," she said brightly. "Then you are free to go, are you not?"

Hunter sighed, watching her as he sat back in the chair, his hands falling between his parted thighs. "Margaret," he said painfully, "don't you realize that I've come back for you?"

"No!"

"I've merely been waiting for you to grow up."

"You don't even *know* me!"

"That is precisely why I've come, so we can—"

Margaret shook her head, tears threatening to spill over the tips of her lashes as she gripped the cushioned edge of the window seat. "I don't want you here!" She leaned forward and added harshly, "I want you to leave!"

Hunter felt the sting of her words, but he remained calm and firm. "Tell me why you want me to leave. If I knew your reasons . . ."

She stood up hastily, skirting around his knees as if touching him would inflict some dread disease upon her. She whirled away from him when he quickly rose and put himself between her and the door. Moving to the fireplace, she gripped the edge of the white wooden mantel and stared down into the cold, empty cavity blackened by years of flame and soot and smoke.

Margaret stiffened her spine, then regally raised her head as she turned to stare at him defiantly. "Very well, Mr. Maguire," she said woodenly, but he noticed her hands clenching and unclenching at her sides. "I'll tell you why I don't want you here. I recall that you once seemed to care for me, you see, and I had hoped to avoid any unpleasantness between us, but the fact is . . . I am not beautiful, inside or out, as you said yourself. I am not what you think me to be, and you have—"

"Margaret, for the love of God!" he breathed, taking a step toward her as he stared at the silent tears streaming down her face.

"And you have wasted your time by coming here," she said, taking a deep, cleansing breath. "Go find yourself a virgin wife if that is what you are seeking, Hunter Maguire," she whispered.

Hunter stopped in his tracks only a few feet in front of her. "What are you saying?" he asked in a hushed tone.

That poor, sad smile was on her face again, even as tears washed past the corners of her delicate lips. "I am saying I was raped. I am saying—" She breathed deeply and turned away from the naked pain dawning slowly in his eyes. "I am saying . . . you are free to go."

Stunned, he stood staring at her back as his heart froze in mid-beat.

Her stance was totally unapproachable, and yet he felt a need to reach out to her, whether for his own consolation or hers he was not certain. He turned away from her then, away from the bent head and the stiff back, wanting with every ounce of his being to step up behind her and wrap his arms securely around her. He wanted her not to hurt, and *he* wanted not to hurt, but the pain was there and he had to find some way to get past this moment.

Maggie was clutching the mantel with both hands by the time Hunter walked over to the small chair by the window, turned it toward her, and seated himself before his legs gave out beneath him. Crossing his legs at the knee and folding his arms over his chest, he asked quietly, ''When did this happen?''

His voice sounded so cool, so detached, that Maggie's pain intensified. She dropped her hands and wrapped her arms firmly around her waist. She had known it would be like this. He was repulsed and no doubt disappointed. But that was what she'd wanted, wasn't it? She shook her head, her confusion warring with her emotions as the thought occurred that it would be wonderful to have him console her, to have him soothe away this heavy wretchedness that lay so heavily on her mind. If only he could understand and not look at her as if she were some tainted creature. She could not look at him for that very reason. She quickly whisked these thoughts away, for they were the wishes that a different girl would have had in a previous time.

Knowing he would not leave until she had answered all of his questions, Maggie dropped her arms, turning her back completely to him, and leaned against one end of the sculptured fireplace before responding. ''It happened a year ago,'' she said softly.

Hunter closed his eyes, his head dropping back briefly, before taking a deep breath and looking at her again. ''And you thought my knowing this would force me to leave?''

''Yes.''

''You were wrong, my dear,'' he said flatly. ''And you give me little credit.''

She faced him, the shock his words had caused clearly evident. ''I want you to leave,'' she said firmly, her tears beginning to dry on her cheeks.

"I'm sure you do," he returned quietly, staring across the room at her.

"We cannot possibly be more than . . ."

Hunter's dark brows drew together. "More than what?" he asked, getting to his feet and walking slowly toward her. "More than what?" he prompted again as she began to back away from him.

"Stay away from me," she ordered, but still he advanced.

"I wish I could have spared you that, Maggie," he said, still advancing slowly. "I could kill the man who hurt you. Now tell me . . . we cannot possibly be more than what?"

He was upon her now, the stuff of his shirt brushing her high-necked, pleated blouse. "Friends!" she cried, leaning toward him angrily. "Only that!"

"Sweet Lord," he breathed, reaching out with one hand and gently pulling her against him. "My innocent girl," he muttered under his breath as his arms went cautiously around her. "I am so sorry for what happened." He bent his head close to her ear as she began to cry in earnest.

Margaret Downing suddenly had the sensation that she could melt into this man's very soul and stay there, forever protected. But this gentle side of him was tearing out her very being as the tears kept coming and her fingers clawed at his shirtfront as if to escape the nightmare of what she had just told him.

As her knees began to sag along with her ebbing energy, Hunter scooped her up and carried her to the high bed. He placed her gently on the mattress, then sat and held her close to his chest for a time. He warred internally with anger and frustration at what had been done to her and his inability to resolve the situation or even punish the bastard who had committed this vicious crime. If only he could undo what had been done . . .

Margaret dared to cling to him for just a short time; it was like a purging of her dreads and deepest fears just to be held against that strong, warm place. Her mind totally cleared of thoughts for just a few moments, she acutally sagged against him for succor.

Her eyes were red and swollen by the time her mind began to take control of her runaway emotions and, with reality forcing itself upon her, Maggie began to pull away, knowing even Hunter could not make everything right.

Forcing his arms to drop as she pulled back, Margaret lay on her back only for a moment before rolling to her side away from him. "I am sorry for that," she whispered. "Please leave me to collect myself."

"Maggie," he said softly, placing a gentle hand on her shoulder, "I would kill him if I could, little one. Please know that. But this does not change my reasons for coming here."

"It does, however, change my past reasons for wanting you to come. Please leave, Hunter," she whispered.

And he understood that her words were not focused only upon his leaving her room.

CHAPTER

❧ 10 ❧

"Dammit, man! Why didn't you tell me?" Hunter raved as he paced the worn carpet in Alastair's study.

Alastair's expression showed surprise. Clearly he hadn't expected Margaret to tell him, and now Hunter wondered if the old man was hiding even more surprises. This feeling that he had been manipulated did not sit well with Hunter. He was angry that both daughter and father had obviously felt he would turn and run at the first indication of difficulty. He supposed Margaret was *hoping* he would run. But could Alastair have thought his feelings toward Margaret were so shallow?

Hunter crossed the room, dropped down into the chair opposite the older man, and rested one booted ankle on his bent knee as he sat back. "What were your thoughts, Alastair?" he asked with tight control. "Why didn't you warn me?"

"I felt that Margaret should be the one to tell you," he said quietly, retrieving his pipe and tobacco pouch from the small table near his chair.

Hunter leaned forward in his chair, his dark eyes piercing

103

those of his companion. "But your silence didn't help. Can you understand? I didn't handle the situation well, Alastair," he said. "I was so damned shocked I couldn't tell her half the things that were going through my mind. Not once, in all the times I had heard others refer to Maggie's 'accident,' had my dull wit imagined this." He smiled sadly at his own ineptitude. "Not very clever of me," he added.

"You had no way of knowing," Alastair said, then added apologetically, "I did what I thought was right." He sighed. "It's so difficult to know what to do with her."

Hunter sat back in his chair, thoughtfully scrubbing a forefinger across his chin. "Is there anything else I should know?" he asked suspiciously.

Alastair shook his head, contrite.

A long silence grew between them. "What will you do?" Alastair asked after a time.

Hunter raised dark thoughtful eyes from the study of his boot top. He had not yet forgiven, but he thought he understood Alastair's motives, and Hunter could not say he would have handled the situation any differently had *he* been Maggie's father. "It's true that Maggie is not the same girl she was. How could she have remained unchanged by this?" He sat forward in his chair again, resting his elbows on his spread knees and knitting his fingers together in his favorite thoughtful pose. What he would do needed no discussion. Little had changed for him. He was angry, for Maggie's sake, and deeply concerned about all that had happened to her, and he was honest enough with himself to understand the possible ramifications to both of them. But his feelings and desires had not changed. And in answer to Alastair's question, he said quietly. "It makes no difference to me, Alastair. My plans have not changed."

The older man sighed audibly before nodding his head in agreement. "I have been hoping you would say that," he said earnestly. "But"—he hesitated—"Margaret is openly hostile toward any man who comes into this house—"

Smiling ruefully, Hunter broke in. "I know."

Shifting uncomfortably, Alastair continued. "Yes, well, her hostility is understandable, wouldn't you say?"

Hunter nodded his agreement.

"She seems to have blamed all men for what happened," Alastair added, "and she has banished any would-be suitors. I know you wanted her to meet other men . . . younger men," he said, "so that she could explore her own feelings before you returned. But Margaret would have none of them and the young men were of a like mind."

"But none of them knew what I know, isn't that so, Alastair? None could understand what motivated her behavior?"

"That is so, but Margaret has firmly declared her intention to live out her life here, unmarried. In control of her own life." Alastair rose slowly from his chair, leaving that thought suspended between them as he moved to a corner table and poured brandy into snifters.

Hunter posed a question of his own. "Is that because she's afraid or because she feels that no one will have her?"

Alastair turned and stared thoughtfully at his friend for a moment before walking back to his chair, and Hunter noticed once again that the man moved with painful lack of agility. "I suspect both," he said.

"I agree." Hunter took the glass of brandy. "It should be easy enough for her to understand that I will have her for my wife. Her fears will take time and understanding," he added perceptively.

"And are you prepared to take on that task?"

Settling back in his chair, Hunter ran a forefinger around the rim of the delicate crystal glass. "I could wish the situation different, of course, for Maggie's sake and my own." His dark eyes held a tenderness that accompanied his next thought. "But I believe Maggie is well worth any difficulties."

And he had held her while she cried. Maggie had not only allowed him to hold her, she had seemed to take comfort in his embrace. Hunter felt that she had reached out to him in that moment, and that gave him hope. She had sought comfort from *him*. Once her fears were alleviated, she would seek more.

His next task was to convince Maggie of that.

Margaret had remained lying on her bed in misery after Hunter left her. She simultaneously applauded her own stupidity and cursed it; now surely he would leave . . . but he would leave knowing her secret. And it took considerable time to convince herself that that fact did not matter. The fact was that she *had* told him. Hunter Maguire would not return to Treemont, and she would never have to face him again once he rode away from this house. This had been her intention all along, and finally she had succeeded.

Having no desire for food, Maggie had made up her mind to go to bed rather than join the family for supper. She had only started to wash, however, when Anna gruffly summoned her to join her father in his study.

It was with some trepidation that Margaret discarded her wrinkled dress and replaced it with a fresh blue high-necked gown with long slender sleeves and layered straight skirt. She quickly ran a brush through her tousled hair, knowing it best not to keep her father waiting when he was angry. And there was no doubt in her mind that Alastair Downing would be furious this night! She had foiled his plans. By now he must be aware that Hunter would be leaving, probably with dawn's first light. No, Alastair would not be happy.

Hesitating at the closed door to the study, Margaret braced herself, willing to face her father's wrath for the sake of her own serenity, but a little concerned what form his anger would take. Alastair seldom lost his temper with his daughters, but on those rare occasions when he did, he could be formidable.

Screwing up her courage, Margaret knocked once briefly before opening the door and entering the dimly lit room, only to falter when her eyes took in the sight of Hunter Maguire standing off to one side, his elbow propped on a shelf of the floor-to-ceiling bookcases. He casually swept back his coat, his hand disappearing into the deep pocket of his trousers while he swirled brandy slowly around the bottom of the snifter in his other hand.

Margaret stared, frankly stunned by his presence, until he smiled at her. If that smile was intended to make her feel welcome, it had the exact opposite effect. Fighting the urge to run, Margaret turned away, her eyes searching the room.

"I was told my father wished to speak with me," she said, her eyes expressing her displeasure at not finding him present.

"*I* wanted to talk with you," Hunter said, his expression carefully blank.

"And you had to use a *ploy*?"

"Would you have come otherwise?"

"Of course not." She reached for the doorknob. "I think we've said all there is to say."

"You're wrong, Margaret. I have many things to say." A thousand things. "Will you sit?"

Maggie merely shook her head.

"You needn't fear me."

Maggie managed a semblance of a scornful smile. "I don't fear you, Mr. Maguire. But I have already spent considerable time talking with you, and I have other things to do."

"And what requires your attention now?" he asked, turning to face her squarely. "The horses? The supper?

Your sisters? What chore is so urgent that you cannot spare me a minute or two of your time?''

Margaret sighed heavily. He could be the most exasperatingly determined man. ''I should go and see to your supper,'' she muttered, knowing any meal she cooked would drive the man away for certain.

Her tone puzzled him, but he chose to ignore her statement. ''A moment or two, Margaret,'' he insisted.

Margaret's hand dropped to her side, and she frowned as he took a step in her direction . ''Hunter, there's little use in rehashing the past,'' she said.

''I don't want to talk about the past,'' he said quietly. ''I want to talk about the future.''

''We've already decided to be friends,'' she said, her pale blue eyes dropping away from the intensity of his dark ones boring into her.

''*You* made that decision, my dear, not I,'' he said, shaking his head in disagreement.

Margaret's head snapped up, and her eyes returned to his. ''Friendship is all I have to offer, Hunter,'' she said firmly.

''Oh, no,'' he said softly, standing a few feet away from her now. ''I disagree.''

Margaret tried to laugh at his earnestness. ''What does that mean?'' she asked, growing wary.

Hunter turned away from her, bending slightly to place his glass on a nearby table. ''I think you have a great deal to offer the right man,'' he said before turning back to her.

She did laugh at that. ''And you, I suppose, are the right man?''

''That's right.''

Maggie folded her arms across her chest, trying for patience. ''Hunter, as your friend it is not my intent to hurt you, but I'm not interested in whatever you're proposing.''

''Marriage, Maggie,'' he said quietly. ''I'm proposing marriage.''

Maggie's eyes grew round, and her lips parted in shock before she could find her voice. "After all you've learned about me?"

"Will you come and sit down?" he asked, reaching out to touch her arm.

Maggie backed away. "I think you've failed to grasp a simple concept, Hunter," she said harshly. "I don't want a husband. I have a good life here. I simply wish to be left alone."

"It is natural for you to be reluctant to leave your home and family for the first time. And—"

"I am *not* leaving."

"And your reluctance may be greater than most, but we can deal with it."

Maggie paced away in frustration and then faced him angrily. "Hunter, what will it take for you to understand? I simply wish to be left alone."

"Oh, I understand." He retrieved his drink and sat in the chair that afforded the best view of the room.

Maggie turned in his direction but remained well out of reach. "But you aren't about to leave me alone, are you?" she questioned flatly.

"No."

"I didn't want to say this bluntly, Mr. Maguire, but you have forced me to be direct." She paced away, her fingertips pulling thoughtfully at her lower lip. When she turned back, Margaret straightened her shoulders stiffly. "I reject your offer of marriage, Mr. Maguire. You are free to go."

Hunter laughed shortly, lifting his glass to his lips before responding. "You haven't enough years left, as young as you are, to see that happen, my dear."

"Why?"

"Because I want you," he said simply. "I always have."

"You are deranged!" she said scornfully. "I'm not pretty—"

"No," he said. "You are beautiful." He frowned as she nervously paced around the room.

Margaret laughed that off. "I'm not a virgin—"

"It was not your virtue that brought me here," he interrupted once again.

"Then what did bring you here?" she cried.

"I will have to teach you that," he said simply and crossed his legs.

Maggie stared at him, spun away, and whirled back again, all in the space of a brief second.

"You are making me dizzy, Maggie," he said lightly. "Please sit down."

"No."

He sighed. "This could be a very long evening," he told her, "unless you talk reasonably with me. You might just as well sit."

Margaret stubbornly took refuge behind a chair, her fingers digging into its soft back. "You cannot marry me, Hunter," she said.

"Why not?"

"I told you why!"

"You told me a distressing tale that makes me angry for your sake, little one," he said kindly. "But my mind is set."

Maggie's next remark died in her throat as the meaning of his words registered.

"Now please sit down and stop acting like a child."

She paced around the chair and sat on the edge of the seat, gripping its rolled border. "You cannot take me away from my home and my family," she said firmly.

"Can't I?" he questioned softly, reaching into an inner coat pocket and producing one of the small cheroots he liked to smoke.

Maggie flopped back in her chair. "You are hopelessly stubborn."

Hunter grinned. "That's how I get what I want."

"Wanting does not mean loving, Hunter," she said, trying a new tactic.

"Really?" he asked in feigned surprise. "And you are an expert on the two?"

"I know enough to understand what men want when they say 'want'!" she said haughtily. "I know enough to desire no part of it."

"Maggie, I strongly suspect you know very little," he said.

Growing frustrated with the conversation, Maggie turned to logic. "If you are determined to marry, Hunter, wouldn't you rather have a woman you could love as well as want?"

"Absolutely," he said, grinning again—the grin that set tiny lights sparkling in those dark eyes.

Margaret sighed with relief and dared a small smile of her own. "There, you see! That is resolved." Getting to her feet, she looked down at him and said earnestly, "I wish you well, Hunter."

He laughed shortly. "Sit down, Maggie."

The small smile slipped, and she frowned in confusion. "I wish to go to bed now, Hunter."

"Soon," he said, staring up at her. "When we have finished our conversation."

"But I—"

"Sit," he ordered quietly and, perplexed, Maggie sat. "I have suggested to your father—"

Maggie jumped on that comment. "You talked to my father?"

"Of course," he said simply. "He has agreed."

"But I have *not*!" she snapped.

"As I was saying, I suggested to your father that we hold the ceremony here in two days' time." He held up a hand when she started to protest. "I must get back to my own farm very soon, and therefore there is little time to plan an elaborate wedding, but you may wish to invite a close friend or two."

"Hunter, I cannot marry you!"

"We will spend our wedding night here," he continued, ignoring her remark, "and leave the following morning."

"I cannot bear the thought of you touching me!" she cried. Then her eyes widened; she was aghast at what she had said. She had wanted to appeal to him on a purely logical basis.

Hunter was not at all surprised by her outburst; in fact, he had been expecting it. Uncrossing his legs, he spread his knees to support his elbows and leaned forward in his chair, saying quietly, "Don't you think I've guessed that, Maggie?"

"Then why would you continue with this farce?" she pleaded.

"It will not be a farce," he returned adamantly. "I believe we can have a good marriage."

"But you must want children?" she asked, daring to read her own meaning into his words.

"I do," he said, nodding resolutely. "There will be children."

"But if you understand how I feel . . ."

"I understand and I will be solicitous of your needs. You surely do not believe I would throw myself at you without a care for your fears?"

That is precisely what she'd thought . . . and expected. This turn of events, therefore, gave her pause. If her father was determined to see her wed, she had no real choice. No matter how her mind rebelled. And Hunter held some merit over other men she had met; at least she knew him to be honorable. Well, perhaps that was questionable, given what she knew of men who *wanted* women. But certainly the time would come when he would expect her to perform as his wife, and, in truth, Maggie did not know if she could endure that. The memories of a different man crawling and panting over her were all too nauseatingly clear.

There was the possibility that she could put Hunter off for a good long time, however. In that time she might grow accustomed to him, as he suggested, making the getting of a child at least endurable. A brief flash of anxiety warned her that she could become *too* accustomed to him, but a child of her own might eventually be a comfort. She was woman enough to desire a child that would be hers alone, and she would simply have to maintain the right degree of control in order to achieve the quiet, secluded way of life she needed. Once she had conceived, she could persuade Hunter to find a mistress; perhaps she could even help him find one. She would have the child, and Hunter would have his lover! Margaret knew of that happening in many marriages, and she would see to it that it happened in hers.

And Maggie knew her father's code of ethics well enough to realize that he would not tolerate such a situation. Once she made it known that Hunter was unfaithful, Alastair would welcome her home with her child, and he would shelter and protect them.

Perhaps the notion held some merit. . . .

"You would not . . . force me?" she asked hesitantly.

Hunter shook his head and lightly touched her skirt with his fingertips. "Maggie, no words will convince you the act of loving bears little resemblance to your experience. Until I can persuade you to see the differences, I swear . . ."

Maggie mulled over his words until finally, knowing she would not be easily persuaded, she agreed to his terms.

He wanted to embrace her and kiss her, but instead Hunter sat back in his chair, eyeing her, looking concerned.

CHAPTER

❦ 11 ❧

"Margaret says she does not wish to marry you," Jennifer whispered to Hunter the following morning at breakfast.

He smiled ruefully and sipped his coffee. "I am aware of that," he said, grateful they were alone and her comment had not been overheard by her older sisters.

"Is it true Papa is forcing her?" she asked, squinting across the table at him as a ray of sunshine found its way through the heavy draperies.

"I suppose you could say your father's opinion probably plays some role," Hunter responded patiently.

"Well, I think she's a ninny," Jennifer said without a qualm. "*I* would marry you."

Hunter laughed. "Don't tempt me, monkey. I can't wait for still another girl to grow up."

Jennifer tilted her head to one side. "What does that mean?"

"Nothing. Eat," he ordered lightly.

Jennifer chewed thoughtfully on a hot biscuit before saying, "She's up there pacing her room," rolling her eyes toward the ceiling.

Hunter frowned at that. "Is she indeed?"

"Margaret seems awfully nervous, Hunter."

He smiled. "I expect all brides are nervous, monkey."

"Then I'm not getting married," she said firmly. "Margaret is more nervous than Pride when he gets around a mare!"

Hunter almost choked on the ham he had been chewing.

"Well, it's true," she said, watching him raise a white linen napkin to his mouth.

"Yes, I believe I understand," he said, after collecting himself. And then it occurred to him that this child was perhaps serious in her observations of her sister, and he did not want a lasting impression to warp her future with some fine young man. "Jennifer, this might be difficult for you to understand, but Maggie is nervous for a number of reasons. Not all brides are so . . . reluctant. Most actually look forward to marriage."

Frowning and staring thoughtfully across the table for a moment, Jennifer eventually asked, "Is it because of the 'accident'?"

God, how he hated that word!

But to her he said only "Yes. Because of the accident."

"Because that man hit her?"

"Yes. And there is a more complicated reason that I can't explain."

Jennifer looked disgusted. "You think I'm too *young*," she accused.

"Perhaps a little," he said, smiling in the face of her disappointment. "Let it suffice to say that some men do not behave respectfully toward women."

"And that has made Margaret nervous?"

"Yes."

Jennifer thought about that for a moment. "That man must have been very nasty," she said softly. "Margaret has been nervous for a long time."

Hunter watched her work it through.

After a moment she raised worried eyes to him. "Hunter?"

"Hmm?"

"You will behave respectfully toward her, won't you?"

"I promise, monkey," he said fondly.

Margaret was harried by everyone but Jennifer from the time she opened her eyes that morning. Denise and Florence had learned of the forthcoming wedding the previous evening, but their father had told them not to mention it until Margaret had a chance to get over the excitement.

Denise sincerely doubted that "excitement" would describe Margaret's feelings on the matter, and she was the first to reach her sister's room with tea and biscuits.

"I'm happy for you, Margaret," Denise said, setting the tray on the small table near the window. "I think Hunter Maguire is a fine man."

"Or a fool," Margaret returned heatedly.

Turning slowly from the table, tea in hand, Denise raised her eyebrows, but not in surprise. "He is not the man who left his mark on you, Margaret," she said softly but firmly.

Margaret looked startled for a moment, wondering if her sister was referring to more than the scar she bore. Shrugging into a pink eyelet robe, Margaret crossed the room and sat in one of the small chairs Denise had pulled up to the table.

"I'm happy that you have someone to love, also," Denise said. "I think life would be painful without a special someone to love."

Margaret stared at her sister suspiciously. "Do you, now?"

The younger woman nodded, suddenly intent on the bottom of her cup. "We've never had anyone to talk with us about the kind of . . . loving that I think you're worried about, Mag. But you mustn't think that being with Hunter in . . . physical love will be . . . unpleasant.''

Margaret laughed caustically. "And you are an authority," she accused.

Denise blushed shyly, having had no conversations of this nature with any of her sisters. "Sometimes Tim becomes very bold," she said. "But frankly, Maggie, when he touches me, I like it."

"Denise!" Maggie was utterly astounded.

"We don't do anything wrong!" Denise replied defensively.

"You are not to be married for two months!"

"I am still a virgin, silly," Denise returned. "I did want to see if I liked him touching me, though. That only makes sense."

"You are not *supposed* to like it," her sister said informatively.

"Now, who told you that?"

Margaret made no response.

Denise leaned toward her sister. "Tim says women enjoy it, too."

"He's lying to you, sister," Margaret said heatedly. "He's telling you these things so he can get what he wants."

"I will not listen to you." Denise got to her feet.

Margaret followed her to the door. "There is so much more here for us at Treemont, Denise," she said wistfully. "Life can be good . . . quiet and organized and peaceful."

Whirling on her sister, Denise replied, "Is that really what you want, Maggie? A life in which you never have to take a chance on being hurt? A life without children? Is *that* what you want?" Heading toward the door, Denise almost collided with Florence in her haste to leave the room. Reaching out a steadying hand, she stared at her younger sister and offered some sage advice. "Do not listen to her, Flo," she said harshly. "Margaret has warped views, and she will cause you to think as she does." Without further ado she angrily fled the room, leaving thirteen-year-old Florence totally confounded.

"What is she talking about, Margaret?" she asked.

Maggie waved a dismissive hand. "Forget about her," she said quietly, turning back to fetch her tea. "Denise fancies herself in love."

"And you, too!" Florence said. "I'm so excited for you, Margaret. I think Hunter is wonderful!"

"Obviously," Margaret muttered and sipped her tea as Florence's gay smile turned to a brief frown.

But Florence was never unhappy for long. "I've come to help you decide on a dress," she announced happily. "And I'll help you pack for your trip. Oh, Maggie," she said wistfully. "I can't believe you'll be leaving us in just two short days."

Those days would be far too short for Maggie, also. Particularly the current one.

That day and the following morning sped by as Margaret and her sisters packed trunks and suitcases with all of the items she would need for her new life as Hunter's wife. There were the linens she had painstakingly embroidered as a young, wistful girl, and the silver tea set that had belonged to their mother. Denise contributed a few household goods that she had collected for her own home but insisted that Maggie take with her; Denise would be moving into a well-established home.

And finally came the hour that Maggie had dreaded. She was standing at the top of the stairs, knowing her family and a minister awaited her in the parlor. She was too proud not to take pains with her appearance and had dressed in a pale blue dress with a high collar and a lace bodice. The same lace graced the long tubular sleeves and the hem of her skirt. Denise had swept Maggie's long, heavy hair loosely back off her face and secured the curls in two sections, allowing the longer lengths to fall past her shoulders and adding tiny blue flowers to both sides. Denise had thought her sister would balk at the style, preferring instead of have her long hair partly cover the scar on her face, but Margaret was long past the point of trying to hide.

As she hesitated on the landing, Margaret looked down to see her father waiting at the bottom of the stairs, a nervous smile on his face and his hand extended upward. "Come along, my dear," he said. "We are waiting."

She took her time, gripping the banister as she went because her knees felt slightly weak. When she reached the last step, she placed her hand in her father's.

"Margaret," he said, almost sighing. "You are as lovely as your dear mother." He smiled wistfully. "Do you think she'll forgive me if I say you're even lovelier?"

Margaret wanted to be angry with him for his part in this, for not sending Hunter away so that she could live in peace with her family and her horses. But she could not. Not today, her last full day at Treemont. She simply loved him too much. "Thank you, Papa," she said. "You lie so sweetly."

Margaret had told herself time and time again over the past two days that her father had done as he felt best and she could not accuse him of meanness or of not caring about her welfare. That thought had served to dim her indignation— with Alastair at least; Hunter Maguire was another story. The moment Margaret entered the parlor on her father's arm and saw her future husband standing there looking confident, at ease, and devilishly handsome, her resentment grew. He'd coerced her father into agreeing to this.

Hunter turned, as did the rest of the family, when he heard the approaching footsteps of his host and his bride. He found himself drawing in a deep breath, which his lungs refused to release. What man could notice a small pink scar when there was such total beauty to behold? In truth, Margaret was breathtakingly lovely. Once he found a way around her fears and stubbornness, Hunter knew that he would be a very fortunate man. He remembered the love of life and living that she'd had as a child, and he would see it return.

Here was woman in all her glory. Here was the summation of all his hopes and dreams. Here was a woman so delicate and lovely that he could not get enough of staring at her. And here also was the vulnerable girl who did not yet understand what being a woman was all about. Here was a woman who would need his assurance and understanding and loving in order for them to achieve their full potential as partners. Every single fiber of her being radiated some special kind of sensual warmth into his being, as no other woman had ever done, and he would have it all. One day, Maggie, he thought.

As her father led her forward, Hunter smiled at her, then took the delicate gloved hand that trembled slightly at his touch. And then they were turning together to face the minister and hear his words.

"Dearly beloved, we are gathered here . . ."

CHAPTER

❧ **12** ❧

Anna, with the help of Denise and Florence, had grudgingly outdone herself in preparing the wedding feast.

Maggie noted that a fresh young turkey had been sacrificed for the occasion, and she felt that was fitting. It fell in line with her thoughts of being the sacrificial lamb!

"You look so beautiful, Maggie," Jennifer said, leaning closer to her sister.

Margaret smiled down at the grinning girl. "Thank you, darling."

"I agree," her husband said softly as he stepped to her side. "You're exceptionally beautiful today, Maggie."

Maggie raised her head slightly, frowning. "You know how I feel about you saying that." she said in a controlled voice.

"I know you have difficulty believing in your own loveliness," he returned. "But I will have years to convince you."

Totally embarrassed now, Maggie crossed her arms over her chest in exasperation. "I used to think of you as a man of few words."

His grin broadened, and he took her hand. "That is still true. But you should remember I'm a man who speaks up when I have something important to say." He shrugged. "I happen to consider your beauty a pleasant topic of conversation."

"Well, it annoys me," she snapped.

"Then we shall have to change the way you feel." Leaning close, he whispered, "I will have you believing in what I see when I look at you, my darling."

By now Jennifer was smiling broadly at Hunter's attentiveness to her sister and was truly annoyed when Denise took her arm and dragged her away.

Hunter noticed the girl's departure and appreciated the fact that they were alone for a moment or two. "The ability to believe in your own beauty is only one of the things I will teach you," he murmured.

Taken aback by his intimate tone, Margaret could only stare at him as flattering color spread across her ivory skin. His manner was far from threatening. In fact, she thought it belonged somewhere between a caress and a playful barb.

And it confused her.

"I believe supper is ready," she said, ignoring both his grin and the anxious little spasm in her chest.

Hunter's eyes followed her as she walked to her father's side. She was still too nervous to play, he knew. But he would teach her slowly, and she would begin to relax once she realized he posed no threat.

Jennifer was frowning as she appeared again at Maggie's side. "I only wish you didn't have to move away," she said.

"I will not be so far from here, Jennifer," Margaret said kindly. She felt a terrible sadness in leaving the girl she had raised since their mother's death. "And we shall return for Denise's wedding after the harvest."

That seemed to brighten the girl's mood. As everyone began to file into the dining room and take their seats,

Jennifer decided she, in turn, should help promote Margaret's happiness. She motioned with a tap on the arm and a wave of her hand, and when Maggie leaned close, Jennifer whispered, "Hunter will behave respectfully toward you, Margaret," she said. "He promised me."

Margaret straightened abruptly in her chair. "What?"

Jennifer continued to smile and nod happily, although some doubt of the wisdom of speaking up began to seep into her thoughts.

Margaret frowned across the table at her husband, then reached for her wine while wondering what on earth Hunter had been saying to Jennifer.

All too soon the meal was over and the men had been left alone to enjoy brandy and cigars. Margaret and her sisters adjourned to the parlor, where they partook of tea and a heavy dose of awkwardness. Not one among them knew what to say to Margaret. They had heard tales of the wedding night, of course, but they could not offer advice to their sister. What little Denise had tried to offer had not been met with appreciation.

Jennifer and Florence sniped at each other good-naturedly, but Maggie, like Denise, chose to sit quietly with her own thoughts and sip a little sherry, having abandoned her teacup in favor of a stronger brew.

Before they could blink, they were asked to join their father in saying thank you and farewell to the minister at the front door.

Hunter stepped up close to Maggie's side after the man had left. "Shall we, too, say good night, Mrs. Maguire?" he asked softly.

"It's early," Maggie announced, suddenly panic-stricken. "I wish to spend more time with my family."

Hunter smiled softly and did something he had never done before. He ran the back of one finger lightly along the narrow scar on her jaw. It was a touch so fleeting that

Maggie was not certain he had actually come in contact with her skin. But there was a tingling warmth there. "You'll see your sisters at breakfast, Maggie, and we have a long journey tomorrow. I think it best that we retire for the evening."

"I do not think it best," she returned with quiet conviction.

Hunter's eyes left her face and looked up the long staircase. "Shall I carry you?" he asked in a soft, teasing voice, but Maggie took his meaning.

"Is that a threat?" she asked.

He grinned down at her. "No, it's not a threat, my dear, but I would be pleased if you would oblige me."

"Oh, for heaven's sake!" She turned away, saying her good nights and hugging her father particularly close.

"Be easy, my darling," Alastair whispered against her cheek as he kissed her fondly. "He is a good man. Give it time."

Margaret pulled back, her arms remaining around his neck as she stood on tiptoe and stared into his eyes. "Father, I . . ." But Margaret could not bring herself to speak. Anything she had to say—however honest or heartfelt—would only bring him pain. He had done his best for her; it was simply hard for her to accept that he would marry her off so abruptly. And so, rather than blurt out her confusion, Margaret kissed his leathery cheek. "I love you, Father," she whispered and then turned toward the stairs.

Maggie suddenly found Hunter's hand supporting her elbow as they made their way upward.

"You could turn and give your father a smile, my dear," he said. "You are not going to your death, you know."

Maggie turned, smiled sweetly, and waved to her family before glaring aside at her husband. "Am I not?" she asked under her breath.

Hunter heard, but was determined not to let her words

affect him. "I thought the service was nice," he said conversationally.

Maggie stared at him as if he possessed the intelligence of a turnip.

Hunter laughed shortly. "Well, it was. And the supper was excellent."

Maggie nodded. "Now, that we can agree upon."

"First time today," Hunter whispered.

"Pardon?"

"I said, have it your way."

Maggie seemed to gain some small degree of satisfaction from that, and Hunter laughed ruefully.

With each step Margaret took en route to her bedroom she wondered at the stupidity of what she had done. It had all seemed so logical when she worked it out two days ago, but now . . . She failed to recall all the wise and brave things she'd thought about their forthcoming relationship.

Then Hunter was stopping outside her bedroom door.

He leaned forward, not quite touching her shoulder, and swung the door wide open.

Margaret stood staring at him uncertainly when he failed to enter and did not encourage her to precede him into the room. "Will you knock on my door when you are ready to leave in the morning?" she asked hesitantly.

He smiled. "If you wish."

She laced her fingers together nervously, wondering how a wife bade a husband good night and then closed the door. "Jennifer will no doubt wake me up early. She will want to say good-bye."

"No doubt."

"Well," she drawled, looking away and into her room. "Good night."

"Good night," he whispered and continued to smile when she entered and turned toward him with one last wary look before closing the door between them.

Maggie breathed a heavy sigh, leaning back against the door as her legs no longer seemed capable of bearing her weight. She had done it! She would spend her wedding night with no threat from her husband. She had to believe that Hunter would be true to his word.

Exhausted from the tensions of the day, Margaret moved slowly across the room, unfastening the collarbuttons at the back of her dress as she went. The bed looked so inviting, now that she could relax.

"May I assist you?" a masculine voice inquired.

Maggie whirled on him, her elbows pointing to the ceiling. "What are you doing here?" she demanded. "I thought you had gone to your own room."

"I thought I might be of assistance. How do you get in and out of that dress on your own?"

"I can manage quite nicely," she returned primly, although it was a lie. It was not easy to undo the row of buttons that ran down the length of her bodice.

Hunter smiled, taking a step in her direction. "It will save a lot of strain if I help, I am sure," he said. "Turn around."

"I would prefer you to leave," she said.

"And I would prefer to stay. Now, don't be a stubborn little chit. Turn around."

After piercing him with those ice-blue eyes, Margaret turned, bracing herself for the first touch of his hands on her back; still, she flinched.

Hunter did not miss her reaction as he reached for the buttons at her neck; he simply chose to ignore it. He brushed the heavy cascade of curls over her shoulder, taking the opportunity to feel the silkiness of her hair between his fingers before Maggie's hand came up and swept the curls forward out of his way. "This is one of those genteel services a husband can perform for a wife," he said easily. "You see, you can find some use for me even at this early stage of our marriage."

She could feel his fingers moving down her back, his knuckles lightly brushing her shoulder blades. Inexplicably, gooseflesh rose on her arms. It was like taking a chill, she thought, looking toward the windows. They were firmly closed against all errant breezes.

His hands had worked lower now, approaching her waist. "What is taking so long?"

Hunter chuckled lightly. "My fingers are large, and the buttons small, Maggie. You will have to be patient with me."

When she felt his fingers working the buttons below her waist, Maggie closed her eyes, begging for the strength to stand still. She could not. As quick as a flitting butterfly she darted away, turning on him as she did so. "I can manage the rest, thank you," she said with feigned politeness.

Hunter smiled and moved around her, crossing to the table near the windows while Margaret watched his every move. "Would you care for some sherry?" he asked.

Her eyes widened as she noted the small tray with decanters and glasses. "When did you bring those in here?" she asked suspiciously.

"Not I," he said, pouring sherry for her and then brandy for himself. "I asked Anna to leave them here." He turned, a glass in either hand. "You know, I don't think she likes me very much." He smiled, holding forth the small sherry glass. "A toast to us, my dear."

Margaret stared at him warily as she cautiously accepted the drink he offered. Her mind was tossing around the possible ramifications of this game he seemed to be playing. She was feeling vulnerable, having to hold her bodice in place with one hand. There was a fluttering in her stomach as her senses reacted to the presence of the man, even before her conscious mind could sort through the reasons for his being here like this.

Raising the glass to her lips, Margaret followed him with

her eyes as he sat on the same chair he had used only two nights before. The chair was far too small for so large a man, and the sight almost made her smile. He looked ludicrous in the setting. She did not smile, however, for it was dawning on her that Hunter was settling in and had no intention of leaving!

"I would like to say good night now, Hunter," she said reasonably. "I'm very tired."

His eyes strayed to the hand-painted screen in the corner. "If you are feeling shy . . ." he said and left the remainder of his sentence dangling between them.

"You are not staying?" she asked.

"It would look a bit odd, don't you think, for the groom to spend the wedding night in one room while the bride sleeps in another?"

"You are not staying." It was not a question but a statement of fact.

He took a small sip of brandy and watched as she set her glass on the table beside the bed. "You need not panic because I am here, Maggie," he said softly. "You'll never become more comfortable with me if I sleep in the next county, now, will you?"

"Sleep!" she gasped. "Hunter, you are *not* sleeping in this room! My sisters care little whether we share the same room, and I—"

"And your father?" he asked quietly.

"I don't care what he thinks about our arrangement. He has married me off."

"Don't speak of him in that fashion, Maggie," he said in a soft warning tone. "Your father didn't sell you into bondage, nor did he betray you. The man loves you. He did what he felt was right for you."

Margaret didn't take kindly to this dressing-down, although she knew his words were painfully true. "You are changing the subject," she said evenly. "We were discussing your sleeping accommodation."

He looked down at the small, feminine chair that, he suspected, barely held his weight. "I do not believe I will sleep here," he said lightly.

A black scowl crossed Margaret's face. "You will not sleep in *my* bed!" she sputtered.

Hunter sighed audibly. "Issuing all these orders to your husband is not a grand way to begin a relationship, my girl. Why not step behind the screen and get out of that dress before you lose your hold on it?" He grinned for her benefit. "Not that I would object if that should occur, Maggie. I am only thinking of your modesty."

Maggie had lowered her eyes to inspect her predicament as he spoke, but his final attempt at teasing her fell far short of its mark. "Oh!" She flounced toward the screen. "You are a buffoon!"

He smiled, once more raising the glass to his lips, waiting.

"Hunter Maguire!" she cried, appearing around the end of the screen, holding a man's silk robe and shaking it as if wishing it were his neck. "Tell me Anna left this behind my screen!" she taunted.

"I did ask—"

Suddenly Margaret appeared defeated, and the hand holding the robe fell wearily to her side. "Hunter, please stop playing with me. You planned it all," she said more reasonably, seeking his understanding. "I don't like this."

His smile disappeared, and he stared across the room, all pretense of teasing gone. "I know you don't, little one," he said patiently, setting his glass on the table before getting to his feet and walking toward her. "Maggie, I didn't marry you to cause you pain or distress. I have more . . . tender reasons," he said softly, standing before her and bending down to take the robe from her hand.

Margaret's eyes followed as he straightened, and the obvious distrust he saw there gave him pause. When she backed up a pace, her nervous reaction actually caused him pain. "Don't," he said, wondering again, as he had for many days now, if he was capable of the firm but gentle handling she would need from him. He was about to put himself to a supreme test, sleeping beside her and not touching her. Still, he knew of no other way to make her trust him.

"You are my wife," he said quietly. "And I expect you to share my bed."

Margaret saw no way out of the situation. She *was* his wife and, if she dealt with him too harshly he would naturally retaliate. If she was to obtain her ultimate goal, she had to trust him to some degree.

She turned away from him, knowing he was watching her, and ducked behind the screen. Moving to the far end of the private corner, she placed both hands on the small table that stood there, leaning on it for support. How was she ever to get through this night? She closed her eyes, searching for guidance, and when none came, she shook her head in anger at herself and at the hand of fate that had brought her to this moment! After a time she gathered her wits and stood tall, allowing the blue dress to fall past her hips and to the floor as she reached for the white nightdress Anna had left there for her. She would brave out this night as she had done almost every night for the past year. The ghosts that came to haunt her dreams would still be there, along with a husband she did not want. Now she would simply have to deal with all of them.

Covered from neck to ankle and wrist by a cotton nightgown and robe, Maggie cautiously peeked around the end of the screen, her eyes growing round at the sight of Hunter Maguire in her bed! He was reclining as if he belonged there, reading a book, naked from the waist up.

And under the sheet from the waist down? She'd forgotten he didn't wear a nightshirt. How could she ever have thought that amusing?

She ducked back behind the screen, but not before he'd seen her.

"We have to get an early start tomorrow, Maggie," he said easily. "Come to bed now."

The words were so easy to say—"come to bed"—but it was difficult for her to force her stiff legs to move around the screen and across the room to the other side of the bed. She noted that his clothes were neatly folded, his jacket hanging on the back of the small chair. It seemed odd to see another person's belongings in the room she had never shared with another living soul. And now this great hulk was taking up more than his fair share of her bed!

She sat gingerly on the very edge of the bed, her back stiff as Hunter watched and waited for her next move. When she did not rise to remove her robe, he extinguished the lamp on the table beside the bed. "Good night, Maggie," he said softly, settling down with his back to her.

Maggie dared to look over her shoulder, miffed that he could so easily make himself comfortable under the circumstances. She hesitated, considered leaving her robe on, then decided she would suffocate in the hot room. Hunter had opened both windows, but still the room was too warm. No help for it. She stood, untied her sash, and dropped the robe across the end of the bed, noting that hers lay neck to neck with his robe. Sitting down once again, she slipped her feet under the light covers and eased her head down on her pillow, clinging close to the edge of the mattress.

"Don't fall out of bed," he said lightly.

She whipped her head around, only to see his back was still presented to her.

"You don't want to start your wedding journey with bruises."

"You are *not* funny, Hunter," she whispered in the darkness and heard his disappointed sigh.

"No, I suppose I'm not," he said quietly.

Maggie lay with her back to him, warily awaiting any sound or movement that might pose a threat. But all she heard, after a time, was Hunter's soft, deep breathing as he slept.

CHAPTER

❧ 13 ❧

Margaret spent a fitful night, rousing several times with a start when she sensed another person in the bed. Then she would foggily remember that the body next to hers belonged to her husband, and she would doze off again. Still, she was confounded in the early morning when she rolled over and found herself alone in the room; she had not been aware of Hunter leaving the bed. Somehow that was most disconcerting.

Sitting up, she noticed Hunter's clothes had disappeared from the chair and a small tray with tea and biscuits stood on the table in place of last evening's brandy and sherry. Margaret was surprised and a bit concerned that someone had been able to come and go without waking her.

Shrugging and putting it all down to the strain of the past few days, she swung her feet over the edge of the bed and padded barefoot to the table, where she gratefully poured some tea and ate one of the warm buttered biscuits. She realized, as she picked up her cup and looked out the window at the dawn, that in the past Anna had brought trays to her room only when she was ill. Hunter must have asked—

Hearing the click of the latch, Maggie turned in time to see Hunter pop his head around the door. "Good morning!" he said cheerfully. "Need any help with buttons or such?"

Her mouth full of biscuit, Maggie could only shake her head in response.

"All right, then," he said. "I'll see to the horses and the wagon."

"I have to . . ."

"Take your time," he added reasonably. "Your father and the girls are helping me pack up." His head disappeared and then popped back again. "By the way, dear wife, you look lovely like that."

She heard him chuckle at her dismay as he closed the door, leaving her alone once again. Margaret looked down at her wrinkled nightgown, her hair falling forward in a mass of wild tangles. "Lovely," she muttered.

Suddenly the import of his words registered, and she flew into action; everyone else was up and dressed and preparing for her leave-taking!

When Margaret stepped out into the early morning light, she was dressed in a dove-gray traveling suit with a fitted jacket and a dark gray hat and shoes that matched the piping on the jacket. She looked elegant, refined.

"And as stiff as a bloody board!" Hunter muttered as he checked the lead to Pride's halter.

Margaret was determined to survive her farewells and to keep her emotions in check. Certainly Florence would be emotional enough for them all!

And she pulled it off rather well—until Jennifer stepped forward and presented Margaret with her favorite doll. "If you keep her you won't get lonely," the girl said. She gave her oldest sister a brave smile that didn't quite pass muster. "And I'll have a doll to play with when I come to visit,"

Jennifer added before falling forward and wrapping her arms around Maggie's waist.

"Oh, Jennie." Margaret closed her eyes as she ran a hand down the length of Jennifer's auburn braids; this was the most difficult farewell of all.

The younger girl turned around then, fixing Hunter with eyes flooded with tears. "You'll bring her back, won't you, Hunter?" she asked.

He nodded, stepping toward her. But before he could utter a single word of comfort, Jennifer had run toward the barn.

Only Anna remained aloof and unaffected. She stood apart from the others and offered not one word of farewell.

Although chaos threatened to overwhelm them for a time, Hunter eventually saw to the security of the trunks and boxes and the two stallions roped to either side of the wagon. Turning at last to Maggie, who stood in the arms of her father, he took one of her gloved hands, squeezing gently to reassure her. "We must go now, Maggie," he said softly and nodded once to Alastair. "We'll be back," he said, "when the harvest is over and we can celebrate still another wedding."

Alastair seemed unable to speak, but he bent and kissed Margaret lightly on the cheek, then shook Hunter's hand and stepped away from the wagon.

"Let me help," Hunter said as Maggie placed one foot on the hub of the front wheel. He handed her up and then joined her on the high wagon seat.

"We should have taken the train," she muttered.

He adjusted the reins and turned his head to grin at her. "And miss sleeping under the stars? Never!"

But all thoughts of his reasons for borrowing the team of bays and the wagon from her father fled her mind as Hunter clicked the horses into motion. Margaret turned on the narrow seat, lifting her hand in farewell as she clutched

Jennifer's ragged doll to her chest. During the past year her
thoughts had been directed totally to her life on this farm.
She had never thought to be looking back, seeing her father
and sisters standing on the steps of her beloved Treemont,
while her husband drove her away from them.

But the picture was real, and the reality was painful.

Turning to face forward, Margaret bowed her head and let
her unhappiness fall heavily between them.

"You can cry, Maggie," he said, but she shook her head.
He had seen her cry too often. She would not cry now and
have him think her weak.

"We'll come back," she said with conviction.

"We will," he said softly. "I promise you that."

Maggie felt she had been riding that cursed buckboard
seat for a week by the time Hunter decided to make camp in
the late afternoon. She was physically exhausted and
ravenous with hunger.

And Hunter seemed to have this penchant for quietness.
Although she *should* have preferred silence to his attempts
at being witty or his shrewd questioning, Margaret found the
long silences a strain. He seemed perfectly comfortable,
however, and that irritated her no end.

He had scouted out the small clearing where they would
camp for the night and had returned to her side of the
wagon. He held up his hand to guide her down. Seeing her
struggle awkwardly in the voluminous skirt, he offered,
"Perhaps you should wear your britches. That outfit looks
wonderful, my dear, but it is hardly practical."

"A woman should hardly wear britches on a public
thoroughfare," she returned primly, extricating her hand
from his.

"Really?" He grinned as he went to the back of the
wagon and opened a small suitcase. "Denise gave me these
for you."

Margaret stared in amazement at the boys' breeches and shirt he held up for her inspection. "I never thought she would dare," she said with conviction. "She always hated when I wore those."

Hunter's grin was suddenly complemented by a fair twinkle in his dark eyes. "I think there's a lot you don't know about your sisters."

He draped the garments over the side of the wagon bed, giving her the option to choose elegance over comfort, if she so desired. And then he was walking past her again, and Maggie turned to watch as he removed the harness from the bays.

"These two are gentle enough for you to handle," he said, holding out a pair of leads. "If you take them down to the stream, I'll follow with Pride and take the colt down later."

"What?" she asked, raising disbelieving eyes to his. She was not a stable boy!

Lesson one, he thought ruefully. "There is work to be done each evening if you wish to fill your belly and seek some rest. But the animals come first. Always," he added pointedly. "Now these good beasts have earned a drink, but I can't lead the stallion near these geldings. Please take them."

Maggie had managed the entire household at Treemont for years, and she had taken over the management of her father's stables almost a year ago; she was used to *giving* orders, not taking them! And she knew as well as he that the animals required care. She was hardly a novice. But he seemed to enjoy ordering her about, and he used vulgar language to boot. Fill her belly, indeed!

She arrived at the water's edge, holding her skirts high and teetering somewhat as she made her way downstream to where the embankment was not so steep. As the thirsty horses drank their fill, Maggie realized Hunter had moved farther downstream with Pride.

"Anna seems to prepare most of the meals at Treemont," he called in her direction. "And I did not think to ask you before now . . . can you cook, Maggie?"

A slow grin curved her lips, and she turned his way. "I make a wonderful mash," she replied. "Hot water, oats, and molasses."

"I should be a horse," he grumbled to Pride, his hand stroking the muscular black neck. "But I guess *you're* all set, old man."

He tethered Pride on one side of the encampment, then took the bays from Margaret and led them well away from the big stallion.

"You could start gathering wood while I settle these two and take the colt for water," he instructed offhandedly.

Margaret looked at him blankly. Let him get his own wood!

After the bays were settled he led the colt to the stream. "No wood, no fire, Maggie," he called over his shoulder. "No fire, no food!"

When he returned she had perched on a flat boulder and sat glaring at him.

Hunter was not surprised.

She watched as he calmly, efficiently set up camp, gathered wood, and started the fire. After bringing water from the stream, he set a coffee pot on a rock near the flames and on the other side he placed a cast-iron frying pan. Soon the wonderful aroma of perking coffee, frying sweet Virginia ham, and Anna's molasses brown beans was filling the air.

Her empty stomach reacted to the sweet odors with a terrible rumbling that she was certain could be heard clear back to Treemont.

Hunter, however, had other thoughts in mind. He heaped

ham and beans onto a tin plate, poured steaming coffee into a tin mug, and sat down on a log. He had taken only a mouthful of the food when he looked across the fire at his dear sweet wife; her expression of utter disbelief almost broke down his barrier of firmness.

"Are you hungry?" he asked reasonably.

"Of course I'm hungry!"

"Marriage is a partnership, Maggie," he said quietly, as he scooped beans onto his fork. "When we share the responsibilities, we can share the results of our labors. But even though I prepared this meal all alone, I'm willing to share it." His eyes dropped briefly toward the fire where food remained in the pan. When he raised his eyes again, he was smiling.

Maggie felt slightly contrite at her own spitefulness in the face of his patience. Still, it was not easy for her to withdraw. "You are not a gentleman," she announced.

He grinned, then put a piece of ham in his mouth. God, he hoped not, he thought, watching as she scrambled down from the rock in her beautifully fitted suit. Oh, the outfit flattered her figure to perfection and he could not find fault with that, but it was impractical for this journey. Secretly Hunter was placing mental wagers as to the length of time it would take her to reach a maximum level of discomfort. His best educated guess was less than two hours.

Margaret totally demolished his theory, however. She had suffered through the heat of the day in a jacket that made her blouse cling to her skin, and the damned skirt made it almost impossible to find a comfortable position on the wagon seat. As for climbing up and down, she felt like an inept ballerina each time she tried to find her footing. Enough was enough! She would change as soon as she filled her belly. If her husband cared so little about her appearance, then why should she worry? If they chanced to encounter others along the way, he would have to suffer the consequences of introducing his wife—scarred and in boys' britches and shirt!

They finished their meal in silence, but Maggie could sense that he frequently raised his eyes to her across the fire while she ate, as if he were examining every inch of her. That made her uneasy, and when she dared to look at him, the tender look he sent her made her feel conspicuous. Instinctively she turned the right side of her face away, hiding the scar from his view.

Hunter frowned at the action, then placed his empty plate aside, got to his feet, and slowly circled the fire.

Maggie raised her head to watch him. She wasn't quite sure what he intended to do.

Stopping directly in front of her, Hunter placed his fingertips lightly on the jagged pink line along her right jaw. When Maggie flinched, his hand followed. "Never feel you have to hide this from me," he said softly.

"You were staring at it," she said. "It made me feel self-conscious."

"I wasn't staring at *it*, little one," he said, looking directly into her eyes. "I was admiring *you*."

Maggie looked away in confusion, her eyes darting everywhere except up at him.

Hunter smiled at her discomfort and stepped back a pace. "Proud husbands do that, Maggie," he said.

Her eyes did return to his with those softly spoken words. "I'm not used to that kind of attention," she said and followed his hand as he reached for her plate.

"Are you finished?" She handed him her plate, but he did not step farther away. "Would you like to change your clothes now?"

Maggie nodded and scrambled to her feet before he could assist her. She hastily snatched the clothing from the side of the wagon where Hunter had draped them and dashed off toward the brush in search of some degree of privacy. This marriage was a monstrous mistake. How was she to remain aloof when he was so insistent about wearing down her protective guard?

Lunging forward into the brush with the red plaid shirt waving in her hand, Margaret unknowingly ventured too close to Passion's Pride. No high-strung creature of any intelligence would stand still for a frantic woman's approach in a flash of skirts and frills, and Pride was an extremely intelligent animal. He sensed danger in this wild thing racing in his direction and acted accordingly. His head came up, eyes wide, and he dashed to the end of his tether. So trapped, he turned to fight, his front hooves flashing in the air once and then again before Hunter caught Margaret by the waist and pulled her away.

"Dammit, Maggie," he cursed fearfully. "One of these days a thoughtless action is going to get you killed!"

"I was doing just fine!" she responded heatedly. Although she knew she hadn't been.

He reached the fire, then angrily turned her to face him and placed both hands on her shoulders. "'Just fine'?" he roared close to her face. "You were practically under that horse's hooves."

"You're just trying to bolster up your silly male pride," she returned. "I know that stallion."

"Maggie, don't you realize that horse was trying to protect himself in any way he could? Don't you realize how much danger you were in?"

That was beside the point. Hunter was simply too overbearing for her liking. "I was raised around horses, if you will recall," she said tightly.

And she did not like to be challenged. He understood that. Sighing and running shaking fingers through his black hair, Hunter said softly, "But your thoughts were elsewhere," he said more reasonably. "I know you're facing a lot of changes in your life, but I'm asking you to have a care for your own safety.'' He also understood that he had reacted with anger because he was frightened. More frightened than he had ever been in his life. He could have lost her then and there, under the destructive hooves of a stallion who thought he was fighting for his life.

Once again Maggie found herself reacting to his tender concern. ''I didn't mean to frighten him,'' she muttered.

After a moment's thought Hunter shook his head, fighting the urge to smile. ''Maggie, you and that horse are like salt on an open wound. You sting him almost constantly.''

Margaret knew it was true. How many times had she and Pride caused him misery? But this time Hunter had forced her to act.

''You want to take over my life and order me around,'' she accused, ''so that I behave to suit your own needs. You want to use me for your own purposes. I have been used by a man for his own purposes before, and I will *not* permit that to happen to me again.''

Her words were like a direct kick to his midsection. ''Oh, Maggie,'' he breathed. ''You're confusing so many things. Sharing burdens does not constitute taking over one's life. Requesting help does not constitute ordering another about. Caring about your safety poses no threat to you. I don't want to take over your life, but to combine both our lives for mutual benefit. And I don't want to *use* you, but be happy with you, sad with you, rejoice with you, and cry with you. I want my purpose to become your purpose, and yours to become mine. I want us to start building a life together,'' he added, holding his palms aloft as he sought her understanding.

She looked away from him, pondering his words. He was too clever by half, she thought. But she wouldn't buckle so easily.

''I only want to make you happy,'' he said.

She stared at him warily for several moments, realizing that she needed to consider the things he'd said. He was right, of course. She reacted without thought most of the time; she'd always been impulsive. And they were not going to have much of a life together if they were constantly at odds; there had to be some way of finding harmony between them. The difficult part of all this was that Margaret's plans did not include a life with him, harmonious or otherwise. She'd had no time to adjust to her situation, and the fact that she was being forced to adapt her entire life to suit a man did not sit well. Still, memories of how she had once felt about him had been flashing back more frequently, and it seemed the farther from Treemont they traveled, the more introspective she became.

"Can you understand my position?" she asked quietly. "You are taking me from my home, although I did not wish to leave. You have married me, although I did not wish to marry." She raised her eyes, asking for his understanding. "And most of the time you make me confused."

"Be kind to yourself, love," he said, the endearment causing her to stiffen in surprise. "You're so wary you fail to see that you sometimes truly need protection. You make yourself vulnerable when you do that, Maggie. Just have a care," he added as the palm of his hand lightly stroked the right side of her face.

As he moved away, her eyes followed the long, confident strides that took him across the clearing to where she had dropped the boys' clothes. His movements were strong, and she realized as she watched that, for a large man, he was graceful, in a powerful way. He was tall and proud, and Margaret felt a surprising stirring of respect.

When he returned, Hunter stopped at her side, holding the shirt and britches out to her. "Will you put these on?" he asked reasonably. "I have something I want to show you, and your skirts will get in the way."

Staring up at him, she asked skeptically, "In the way of what?"

"I merely want you to walk with me," he said and handed her the clothes, continuing to hold out his hand.

Margaret stared at that hand for a good long moment; she had never willingly touched him. He had held her hand during the ceremony, and he had kissed her lightly on the cheek when the minister so directed, but she had yet to consciously touch *him*.

Hunter did not miss her hesitation. "Take my hand, Maggie," he prompted. Finally she placed her delicate hand in his work-roughened palm. He smiled at her warmly. "You can change on the other side of the wagon," and he smiled good-naturedly. "But stay away from Pride, will you?" His teasing tone actually won him a small smile, and Hunter was satisfied.

By the time Margaret returned to the fire, Hunter had cleared away the remainder of their supper. He was grinning as he held up a brown labeled bottle for her inspection. "Your father is a thoughtful man," he said happily. "This was tucked away with our food supplies." He rinsed a tin cup and poured a hearty draft of brandy.

Margaret frowned at the generous portion he'd poured. She didn't want a drunken man on her hands.

Hunter merely chuckled in the face of her concern. "We'll share this while we watch the show," he said and eyed her garb with approval. "Much more practical, don't you think?" he asked conversationally. In actual fact, he felt he might be a bit sorry he had given her the clothes; these britches seemed to fit more snugly than those he had previously seen her in, accentuating her rounded hips and narrow waist. And the shirt fit in a revealing fashion, as no allowance for female attributes had been planned in its design. His Maggie had a well-proportioned and very womanly figure, for all her youth, and Hunter was forced to turn away from the sight of all that femininity. It had been a long and trying day, and he wanted nothing more than to hold all of that womanliness close to his own body.

He moved off toward the river, and Margaret stared at his back for a moment before having the presence of mind to follow. "What show?" she asked, coming up beside him.

"You will see," he hedged.

Margaret stopped dead in her tracks. "If this is a trick, Hunter . . ."

"It's no trick," he assured her. "It's something worth watching."

Margaret narrowed her eyes as she watched him walk away, still carrying the brandy. What could he do here that he could not do elsewhere? she thought and shrugged in resignation before catching up with him once more. "Why are you being so mysterious?" she asked, reaching his side and attempting to keep up with his long strides.

He smiled at her. "It's a surprise."

"Out here?" She looked around at rocks and trees and the river rushing by and beyond their sight.

"Here," he said and led her along the river's edge to a high outcropping of rock. "I noticed this while I was watering the animals." He stopped at the base of the huge rocks. "Can you hear the rush of water? I suspect there might be some rapids beyond this point."

Margaret stared at the rushing blue-green water and then raised her eyes to his in puzzlement. "*That* is the surprise?" she asked as if he'd left a good portion of his wits behind.

Hunter continued to smile. "There's more," he said as he looked upward, studying the rocks. "Think you can make it?" he asked.

Margaret's eyes followed the path his had taken. "You expect me to climb up there?" she asked, not hiding her surprise.

"I'll help you," he returned, looking down at her again.

"Hunter, I don't care if you can fly me up there, I am not particularly fond of heights."

"How can you ride a horse if you feel that way?" he teased.

"That's hardly a height," she returned impatiently. "And riding is second nature to me."

"Then this will be third nature. You will feel the same way about sitting on top of the universe as you do about sitting atop a horse."

"You really are mad," she murmured and looked up with doubt.

"Quite," he agreed. He took her hand and guided her up the easiest face of the rocks, while he carefully protected the brandy.

Margaret climbed agilely in his wake, but when he felt her pull against his hand, he looked over his shoulder, guessing why she had stopped.

"Don't look down," he directed firmly and then grinned. "You'll spoil the surprise."

"The surprise being the fact that we are about to break our fool necks," she muttered.

"Faith, Maggie my girl," he said, imitating a good Irish lad. "A little faith, if you please."

"Oh, I have faith." She puffed as he pulled her up a long, steep section of rock. "But it doesn't extend in your direction."

Truer words were never spoken, he realized grimly, and tried to blank them out of his mind. The moment would soon be upon them, and he did not want to ruin it.

He had brought her here because he needed a little restorative peace, and he hoped she would benefit similarly from the experience. He could not force her, however, to reach within herself.

When they reached the top she was puffing with the exertion but not alarmingly so, and he smiled at her before looking around their perch. "This is it," he said proudly, but when he saw her eyes turn toward the river he lowered the brandy to the rocks and placed both hands on her shoulders, guiding her until she stood with her back to him. "Look out, not down," he directed, then tightened his hold. "No, don't look down." He reached around her shoulder and placed his hand under her chin to raise her head. "Always look outward first, Maggie, and then allow yourself to take in the lower views a bit at a time. That way you should become accustomed to the elevation."

She mumbled a protest, but did as he directed.

He let her stand there for a moment, then returned his hand to her shoulder, pressing gently. "Sit down, Maggie, and I am going to sit behind you. We have a few moments to wait."

Margaret complied, though wary of his nearness. Still, with such a steep drop before her, she was not prepared to argue too heatedly.

"Hunter, why are we sitting here?" she asked in exasperation.

"That will become apparent in due course."

She sighed, a great sigh that heaved her shoulders up and then down but did not ease the tension in her neck.

Behind her, Hunter smiled and reached back to where he had set the tin cup. Such impatience. Such suspicion. He took a sip of the brandy and bent his knees so that he could rest his forearms there, even as his eyes strayed to the silver-blond hair and tense shoulders so close to him. She had drawn her knees up also and wrapped her arms around her legs so that, from his view, she looked like a frightened little creature nestled between his legs. And the tension and anxiety that surrounded her came not from the height of her perch but from his presence. He knew that instinctively.

He raised the cup to his lips once again and then reached around her shoulder, extending it to her.

Surprisingly, Margaret took it, then watched his hand as he casually returned his forearm to rest on his bent knee.

"I don't know if you're familiar with brandy," he said quietly. "But you should sip it slowly."

She stared down at the cup, then cautiously raised it to her lips. Her eyelashes fluttered when the vapors of the drink rose up to assault her. She took a small sip and then another. She gasped when the liquid seared her throat. "Oh," she breathed.

He chuckled. "There are several things we should appreciate about this show, Maggie," he said conversationally. "We paid not a penny for admittance, the location of our seats is excellent, the size of the theater is restricted only by the distance we can see, and the number of players is limited only by our lack of imagination."

"Hunter, you're not making sense," she returned impatiently. "And I don't like this." He was entirely too close, and she was feeling trapped. To say nothing of feeling silly, waiting on top of a rock for something to happen.

"Have you ever tried clearing your mind of your anger and suspicion and fear?" he asked. "Just long enough to allow simple enjoyment of something beautiful and natural? Don't you believe you deserve some innocent pleasure?"

Her shoulders jerked upward. He leaned forward, just a little so as not to threaten her. "Clear your mind for a few moments, Maggie. Forget all beyond this place. Forget I'm here, if you wish. Think of the things your eyes bring into focus. Concentrate on those things and their beauty. Clear your mind and just look . . . and feel," he added on a hopeful breath.

As Margaret listened to his words an ache within her started to grow and fan out to encompass her entire being. She knew what he was doing, and she wanted to appreciate his efforts. But it saddened her that he needed to take these steps because she had somehow lost her way and could not even manage to enjoy an innocent pleasure, as he had said. All innocent pleasure had been snatched away from her, had become foreign to her existence, and Hunter, in trying to reintroduce such things into her life, was causing her to mourn the loss. And it occurred to her that perhaps, just perhaps, he would be the one with whom she would once again find simple diversions.

"Why did you bring me here?" she asked softly.

"I wanted to watch a sunset with you," he said in a hushed tone.

"I am never certain what to expect from you," she returned. The confusion caused fear within her, although she would never, never openly admit as much to him.

But he knew that she was afraid. He knew also that there was little he could do about it. His eyes searched the skies and the scene before them, as if nature held some simple answer. But there was no easy answer. He knew that, also. So he stopped thinking and opened his mind for a moment, as he had directed Margaret to do. "It's beginning," he said in a quiet, rich voice that brought gooseflesh out on Maggie's arms.

But her thoughts had turned away from him, away from the threat of him, as she silently concentrated on the scene before her. Margaret took another sip of brandy, enjoying the warmth of it as it descended to her stomach, then held the cup out to the hand dangling near her right shoulder. In a moment hand and cup disappeared from her peripheral vision, and it was several seconds before his hand returned, minus the cup.

She did as he suggested and looked straight ahead, noting that the sun was very low in the sky. Then her eyes traveled to the expanse of trees and rolling hills across the gully from where they sat. The shades of green darkened as the light diminished, and the sheer expanse of rock became a wall of gray and pink and black rearing up from the river's edge.

For the first time she noticed the violent roar of the river and realized he'd been right; to her left there were rapids, wonderful and frightening and exhilarating all at once, sounding like continuous thunder, as if the river were angry.

She raised her eyes as the sun dropped behind the farthest trees. The sky was streaked with a spectrum of reds, scarlet to palest pink, glowing colors that produced warmth within her and raised the fine hair on her arms. Why had she never noticed this beauty before? Why had she never felt this way before? As she leaned forward in concentration, Hunter's hands dropped to her waist as security against a fall. But Margaret did not object.

She stared out at the wilderness before her as it was slowly swamped by descending darkness. She felt it should have saddened her, this disappearing of something beautiful, but night was a peaceful intruder, and soon a strange serenity came over her and the harsh heat of day became a gentle, refreshing stirring against her skin and hair.

The darkness began to glow a warm gray as her eyes adjusted, and finally she let her head fall back and closed her eyes as she felt night surround her like a gentle, friendly shroud.

In time Margaret let her back rest against his chest, and Hunter returned his forearms to his knees. He would not stir, would not spoil this moment by frightening her, though he wanted desperately to put his arms around her and draw her back more tightly against him. But this was far too important to rush, this first tentative contact she had sought. He would savor it while he silently thanked nature for giving them this tranquil moment.

"It's strange," she whispered, "but I don't think I've ever felt quite this way."

"And how do you feel?" he asked softly.

She shook her head from side to side against his shoulder. "I don't think I can explain."

"Do you feel good?"

She nodded her head. She felt very serene. She could not remember experiencing this kind of peace any night for over a year now. And as her conscious mind realized that she was actually leaning against a muscled chest that warmed her back, Margaret's first reaction was that that, too, felt very good.

"I suppose we should go," she said with a sigh.

"We could stay here all night," he suggested lightly, and Margaret almost giggled.

"We can't stay up here!" She sat up, moving away from him with something akin to regret. "I refuse to sleep on anything higher than a bed."

"You won't be sleeping in a bed tonight," he murmured, getting to his feet and helping her up beside him.

"I'll sleep in the wagon," she stated as he bent to retrieve the cup.

"You'd best sleep next to the fire, beside me," he said, taking her hand and cautiously leading the way down the rock face. "Otherwise, you could catch cold."

Margaret didn't like the idea of sleeping on the ground, particularly beside him. "I'll sleep in the wagon," she insisted.

Hunter grinned in the darkness. "Fine," he drawled. "It may be a bit crowded for two, however." But that prospect held some merit.

"I didn't say I wished to have company," she complained as they climbed down the last of the rocks.

"Maggie," he said, turning to face her in the faint light of the half-moon. "Things sometimes go bump in the night, and you should sleep within sight and sound of me. I'm the one with the rifle," he added, turning to lead the way back to their camp.

"What kind of things might go bump in the night?" she asked with obvious concern.

He smiled when he realized she was sticking close to his heels. "Four-legged things. Things that prowl around looking for food."

"You're just trying to frighten me," she scoffed.

"Regardless," he said, "you'll sleep where I can make sure you're safe."

She thought about that for a moment and then grumbled under her breath. Why did he always, eventually, make sense?

CHAPTER

❧14❧

Margaret's first night of sleeping under the stars made a lasting impression. Her bones ached from lying on the hard ground on just a thin blanket. At some point during the long night she started to tremble with cold despite the fire.

She had laid out her bedroll across the fire from where Hunter had chosen to sleep, but each time she awoke, he was alerted by her shifting around in her attempts to find comfort. Eventually, noticing that she was huddled under her single blanket, he rose, taking his blankets with him and moved around behind her.

Maggie was fully awake, and her head swiveled as she followed his path. "What are you doing?" she asked at last as he spread one blanket beside hers.

"I am going to keep you warm," he muttered. "Perhaps then we will both get some sleep."

"If you would let me sleep in the—"

"Forget it, Maggie. You're not sleeping in the wagon." He spread the second blanket so that it partially covered her and left a little for himself. "Besides, it's even colder there."

But as he stretched out behind her, Margaret sat up and twisted around. "I don't want you here."

"That's too damn bad," he mumbled wearily and, placing a hand firmly on her shoulder, forced her to lie back. He lay on his side, waiting for her to accept the fact that he was not moving, nor would he allow her to move. "Face the fire," he said firmly.

"There you go!" she hissed. "Ordering me around!"

"I'll do more than order you around, foolish one," he said. "Now turn over and let me get some sleep."

She did so angrily, catching the baggy sleeve of her shirt under her and almost wrenching her arm as she tried to raise it. Rearing up, Margaret muttered an unintelligible curse.

He smiled at her back, watching her performance. "Are you settled now?" he asked as he moved closer to her.

"Back off," she commanded and started to roll toward the fire without thinking, intending only to get away from him.

Suddenly a firm hand landed squarely on her rump, and when she started to get up, a heavy arm fell over her shoulder, pinning her down. "Stop this nonsense!" he said, and Margaret immediately fell still. "I haven't made a threatening move toward you, and you needn't fear that I will, so don't try to be a human candle. Now settle down and go to sleep."

There was little she could do but lie there with his arm over her, weighing her down, but sleep she would not. And then, to further distract her, Hunter's hand covered one of hers and tucked it against her chest. His thumb lightly stroked her from wrist to fingers, and warm tingling sensations darted the entire length of her arm. It was unsettling, what he was doing. Yet it was comforting. And there was consolation, she had to admit; she was warm.

All through the following morning, as she rode beside Hunter in the wagon, she was mortified each time she thought of how she had turned to him in her sleep and awakened with his arms around her, holding her against his chest. It was the closest Margaret had been to any human being.

Thoughts of how his nearness had disturbed her brought back older, more ancient memories—of a mother tenderly hugging a daughter, of parents caressing each other, even in view of their children. It reminded her that a hug could give one a sense of security, of calmness, and of being loved. Oh, she could not extend this last to Hunter, for surely he did not love her. But her instincts and his behavior of the past few days allowed her to suspect that he harbored some affection for her. Certainly that was more than she had ever hoped to attain, and she was amazed to find that receiving affection mattered to her . . . mattered deeply. And she cautioned herself against becoming too comfortable with his small signs of attachment.

With these thoughts came a desire to end the long silence that had fallen between them. She remembered that Hunter enjoyed quiet moments, even when others were about, but Margaret was not yet comfortable enough in his presence to feel safe with those silences.

"What's your home like?" she asked.

Hunter smiled thoughtfully at her before returning his attention to the road ahead. "It's a farm like any other, I suppose. Not so old or so large as Treemont. But the house is warm in winter and the land supports us well."

"Us?" she questioned, surprised. "You have no family there."

"I have friends who live and work with me," he said warmly. "And now I have you."

The intensity of his gaze made Margaret uncomfortable, and she looked away, searching for another topic. "How many friends will live with us?" she asked.

Hunter wondered at the direction her questions were

taking. "Only Jason will live in the main house with us. Jeffrey and his wife have a cottage of their own."

"Jason?"

"An old friend of my mother's."

"Oh," she said softly, turning to look at him again.

Hunter frowned at her as he asked, "What does 'oh' mean?"

In fact it meant a great deal in her own mind, but Margaret didn't think he would appreciate the conclusions to which she had jumped. "Nothing," she said, shrugging casually. "Another woman lives there?"

Hunter grunted, "Marie-Louise and Jeffrey are newly wedded," he said. "Jason and I have been happy to have her around the place. She's a terrific cook."

"That's good," Margaret muttered. "At least we won't starve."

He laughed, returning his attention to the team.

"Anna hated having anyone in her kitchen," she explained, "except to do menial chores."

"Why doesn't that surprise me?" he said wryly.

"Will Marie-Louise and I get on, do you think?" she said.

"You're the same age," he said. "I think you'll be company for each other. She's certainly a good helpmate. She is a strong girl and a willing worker."

Having another woman around would be a comfort, Margaret decided; she would miss her sisters.

"I think we should stop for the day," he said after a time, examining the sky to determine the hour. "We should be home in decent time tomorrow, and this appears to be a good spot." He motioned beyond the brush at the edge of the clearing. "I suspect we'll find water over there, but let me check to be certain."

When he returned, he reached out a hand to help her, but Margaret had found new freedom in her boyish clothes and smiled as she took his hand and jumped down from the wagon seat. Proceeding to the back of the wagon, she began to unload some of the things they would need for the night as Hunter stared at her in surprised silence. But when she reached for the heavy sack containing the cooking and eating utensils, he stopped her. "I'll carry the heavy things, Maggie, in a moment."

She looked over her shoulder, nodded, and reached for the two bedrolls in lieu of the sack. Once she had dropped them in a place she considered suitable for a fire, she returned to the wagon and stood by patiently while Hunter unharnessed the bays.

He knew she was there, just behind him, and he was pleased . . . but he was also a little stunned by this change in her, and he could only wonder what had brought it about literally overnight.

He clipped a lead rope to each of the halters and handed both to her. Before she could turn away from him, he gently touched her cheek with the backs of his fingers. "Thank you," he said softly, and watched a look of confusion steal over her face.

She stood there for a brief moment, distracted by the thought that his touch had been warm and gentle and she had liked it. Then she whirled away. She had actually enjoyed his touch!

She turned back to face him, the lead ropes draped across her thighs as she dropped her hands to her sides. "How is it that you can confuse me so easily?" she said and then turned on her heel and clicked the bays into action.

"A little confusion is good," he said calmly.

Together they set up camp, and Hunter had begun to prepare a stew when he heard horses approaching from beyond the bend in the road. "Two riders are coming," he said as he casually reached for the rifle he kept near at hand. "Stay close behind me until we determine who these people are," he said lightly. She needed no second coaxing; she was on her feet and moving around the fire before he had finished speaking. Hunter stood with the rifle bore pointing to the ground while Maggie peered around his shoulder at the two men who came into view. From a distance they appeared to be gentlemen, but on closer inspection she saw they were men of meager means.

The younger of the two was Hunter's age, she guessed. He was a man of firm build, and although his clothes were relatively clean, his coat and trousers had seen better days. What disconcerted her most was the cruelty of his eyes— eyes that looked directly into hers.

The second man was somewhat older, of slovenly appearance with several broken teeth. He seemed primarily interested in expanding his paunch, and his attention was immediately directed to their supper simmering in the black iron pot. But his foolish gaping grin unsettled her.

And she was furious when Hunter invited them to join their camp that night. Her heart pounding with fear, her mind exploding with rage, she stomped off in Hunter's wake when he went to the stream to get water.

"What on earth possessed you to invite those . . . those men to stay?" she demanded as she ducked and skirted under and around the trees.

In a few short moments they emerged beside a slow-moving stream. Hunter knelt on the bank and lowered a wooden pail into the water. "I am only demonstrating polite hospitality, Maggie," he said. "Don't worry about them."

"But they're evil, Hunter! I can feel it. They'll rob us and . . . and—" She stammered to a halt.

"And worse," he murmured, knowing full well her thoughts. He set the bucket on the bank and straightened, staring back in the direction of the camp. "I agree."

"Then why?" she cried. "Please send them away."

He crossed his arms over his chest and looked down at

her, his dark brows drawn together in serious thought. "Maggie, if you knew there was a bobcat in the area would you prefer to have it skulking at your back in the night or within the light of your campfire?"

She stared up at him in confusion for a moment and then responded with a simple, quiet "Oh!"

He nodded when he saw that she had understood his meaning. "I want them where I can see them."

She nodded, deferring to his judgment as she turned and preceded him through the dense trees, retracing their path.

Suddenly Margaret stopped short, and Hunter found himself close to sending her sprawling before he could stop directly behind her. He opened his mouth to admonish her as water from the pail sloshed down the leg of his hide trousers. And then he noticed the reason for her action. Their friend with the paunch was grinning at Maggie, unconcerned that he was unfastening his trousers.

Margaret had already turned away, and Hunter put his free arm around her shoulders, drawing her close as he frowned at the man.

Hunter whispered, "Stay here while I have a word with him."

Margaret grasped the front of his white cotton shirt with both hands. "Don't leave me!" she pleaded.

"I'll be back for you in a moment," he said quietly, bending to leave the bucket beside her. "Just stand where you are." He removed her hands and stepped around her, placing a reassuring hand on her shoulder before he moved away.

Hunter approached as the man was refastening his trousers, longing to wipe the grin off the filthy face.

"A mite flighty, that girl of yours," said the man with the paunch, still grinning.

"That *girl* is a *lady*, and don't you forget it," Hunter ground out.

"Bit hard to tell, appears to me, bein' she wears pants 'n' all."

"Regardless of what she is wearing, she is a lady. If you upset her again, you and I will do more than discuss the matter."

Suddenly the grin disappeared. "Hey, friend," the stranger cajoled. "I was just answerin' the call of nature."

"Next time answer the *call* far away from the lady!" Hunter said angrily. "Do you understand?"

"Sure. Sure!"

"Good. And you might also warn your friend."

"Sure. Sure," he grumbled again and hastily ambled off toward the camp.

When Hunter returned to her, Margaret had not moved except to clasp her hands in front of her.

"He'll behave in a more gentlemanly fashion in the future," he said matter-of-factly as he bent down to pick up the bucket.

Margaret looked away, mortified. It seemed to make matters worse that such a thing had happened while she was in Hunter's presence. A perplexing thought, since she was also intensely grateful that she had not been alone.

Suddenly she felt gentle fingers under her chin, and Hunter was forcing her head around as he frowned his concern. "Don't worry," he said. "I won't have you subjected to such performances. He and his friend have been fairly warned," he added in a deadly voice that sent a shiver up her spine.

Margaret was grateful for this display of protectiveness, but she sensed a violence in him that frightened her. Instinctively she tried to lighten the moment. "I am being a child, Hunter. The man posed no real threat to me, after all."

"But this has raised another issue," he returned firmly, taking her arm and leading her back through the trees. "Something is sadly lacking in your education, my love, and I intend to correct that.''

Maggie frowned up at him, clearly puzzled.

Hunter was silent for a long moment as he mentally chastised himself for not having seen this before. Maggie had every right to fear men, and her fears could only be magnified by her sense of vulnerability. And she was vulnerable because she did not know how to defend herself in situations where she felt threatened. ''Tomorrow your lessons begin, little one,'' he said quietly. ''Tomorrow you will learn how to take control.''

She helped Hunter prepare supper and was rewarded with frequent understanding smiles from him. She stayed very close to his side, and he in turn kept a close eye on her as she moved about the camp.

As Margaret served the food, Hunter passed heaping plates to the two men, then sat close beside her while he ate. When she washed the plates he had collected, he sat directly behind her, his back supported by a boulder, one leg stretched out before him and the other drawn up, supporting his forearm. He casually held a cup of coffee in that hand, allowing it to cool while his eyes and ears took in everything around him.

She had almost completed the washing up, listening intently to the conversation of the men, when the younger of the two guests spoke.

''Good coffee,'' he drawled. ''Mind if I have another cup?'' His question might have been directed to Hunter but his eyes were fixed on Margaret.

Nevertheless, Hunter responded. ''Help yourself.''

The man smiled, and the action seemed to make his chin disappear and his eyes grow more fierce. ''The lady is right there.''

''The lady has had a long day,'' Hunter returned evenly.

"You are welcome to all the coffee you wish, but service is not included in the offer."

Glaring gray eyes remained transfixed by Hunter's dark ones. Then suddenly false smiles appeared on their faces.

"Of course," the stranger said carelessly. "You've been more than generous already."

As he moved toward the fire, Margaret backed away from the coffee pot.

"Come here, Maggie," she heard Hunter whisper, and she scurried toward him, dragging the seat of her britches in the dirt.

Hunter had spread his legs farther apart, and when she reached him he pulled her back gently to lean against his chest. His entire body seemed to envelop hers like a strong cocoon, and Margaret did not miss the message he was conveying: She was safe.

"You appear most protective of the lady, sir," the younger man said as he appeared intent upon pouring his coffee.

Hunter smiled with just the proper degree of menace. "*My* lady, sir," he said. "*My* wife. Does that explain the matter to you?" He waited for a protest from Margaret, but realized she was too frightened to disagree with anything he said. When he felt her shudder, his free hand went to her upper arm, even as he took a sip of his coffee, and gave her a small, reassuring squeeze.

The man placed the coffee pot back in its nesting spot at the edge of the fire and eyed her again.

"You do understand, sir?" Hunter asked in a controlled but meaningful voice.

"Of course!" came the hasty reply. "Of course, my friend. I have no desire to cause undue . . . strain upon you or your lady."

Tensions eased as a polite conversation followed, and

eventually those around the fire began to relax as the men discussed topics of general interest.

Margaret didn't speak a word the entire evening and moved only once, to refill Hunter's cup and pour some coffee for herself. Then she immediately returned to the shelter of Hunter.

Hunter was enjoying the nearness of her, her willingness to allow his touch. Although he did not delude himself as to her reasons for staying close, he was content to have her there.

Eventually he moved away, after telling her he would spread their bedrolls, but as Margaret's gaze moved from one stranger to the other across the flames, she lost what little courage she thought she possessed and jumped up to follow.

"I need some privacy," she said.

Hunter laughed softly as he dropped a blanket in a heap at his feet. "You won't find it with me, will you?" he teased, but he touched her cheek lightly with his strong, warm fingers. "Come along, then, love. I'll wait for you by the wagon."

When they returned to camp Margaret spread her blankets as close as possible to Hunter's, across the fire from the two men.

He laughed softly when he saw her ploy and whispered, "Better the devil you *do* know . . . ?"

She smiled. "I don't wish to disturb your sleep again when I feel cold in the night."

After removing her boots, she crawled fully clothed beneath her blanket.

Hunter placed the rifle on the edge of his blanket before removing his shirt and boots, all the time aware of the movements of their guests. He did not really believe they would attempt anything foolish, but one could never be certain what went through the minds of scavengers such as these.

He pulled his blanket to his waist as he lay on his side facing the fire, their guests, and Maggie's back.

"Maggie?" he whispered.

"Yes?"

"Turn to me."

"No."

He placed one hand on her shoulder and rolled her onto her back.

Looking up at him she said with quiet earnestness, "I want them where I can see them."

He laughed a rich, husky laugh. "You just leave them to me, my fractious filly. Turn over and face this way or you won't close your eyes all night. I know you at least that well."

She conceded his statement to be true and turned, settling herself once again.

She found it somewhat disconcerting to be staring at his naked chest, however.

Hunter awoke well before the dawn, with the first whisper of movement from their visitors. He lay perfectly still, holding Maggie against him with his right arm under her shoulder and curled around her back while he lowered his left arm between them until he could wrap his fingers around the butt of his rifle.

The two men gathered only their own belongings, however, knowing their host was not congenial toward them. Also, having seen the weapon he kept within his reach, neither wanted any truck with Hunter Maguire.

As the two strangers buzzed quietly on the far side of the embers of a dying fire, Maggie stirred, rubbing her cheek against Hunter's arm and raising one leg between them.

"Easy my pet," he breathed. "Sleep on." He did not want the distraction of her waking disoriented or alarmed.

But Maggie slept on, sleeping the sleep of the well protected, as Hunter eyed the two men until they had saddled their own horses and ridden away.

Hunter moved the rifle carefully out from between them and laid it along the backs of his legs, then used his left arm to enfold Maggie and draw her deeper into the possessive, protective shell he had made of his body.

If only he could hold her whenever he wished. Although lying with her like this did have its drawbacks. Certain parts of his anatomy had awakened long ago, and it was disconcerting to say the least, to find his britches painfully snug while knowing there was little he could do to relieve his discomfort.

He wanted her more than he had ever desired any woman, but he wanted her not for an evening, not for one brief moment of release, but for an eternity. And achieving such an end would require his forbearance now.

She awoke slowly, groaning softly against the aches the ground had caused in her body, stretching delicately like a soft, warm cat within the shelter of his arms. Her nose bumped his chin when she arched her head back, and he smiled with the pleasure of it while lying perfectly still for fear of ending the pure joy of this moment.

Margaret seemed alert suddenly, her body stiffening with some thought that plagued her as she whispered against his shoulder. "The two men . . . ?"

"They've gone, sweet," he murmured. "And good morning," he added lightly.

Margaret's lips tilted upward against his arm in response to the smile in his voice. "Good morning," she returned quietly and found, to her surprise, that she was loath to move away from his warmth. Daring to snuggle closer, elbows bent and arms folded between them, she asked sleepily, "Will we be home today, Hunter?"

Hunter's heart vaulted in his chest with the velvet texture of her voice, her use of the word "home," and the whispered sound of his name on her lips. Perhaps, just perhaps, she had begun to soften toward him. "Yes, we'll be home today," he said warmly.

"Must I get up now?" she murmured.

He chuckled deep within his chest. "Slugabed," he teased. "We won't be home in time for supper at this rate."

"You're not moving too quickly," she answered, her words muffled against his chest.

"I don't want to get up, either, pet," he said honestly.

Margaret stretched out fully then, her toes pointing north and her arms reaching above her head as she rolled away from him. And just as suddenly she was curling up against him again. "I seem to want to stay here," she murmured to his chest as his arms went around her again. "Is that bad of me?" she asked in a small voice.

Hunter shook his head against the rolled-up blanket he used as a pillow. "It's not bad of you, Maggie," he breathed. Then he spoke softly against her wonderful silky hair that so enthralled him. "Don't you know that this is a natural place for you to be?"

Margaret was silent for a time, breathing in the scent of him, as she woke more fully. She liked being close to him, she realized. It seemed as if all her childish dreams of him had suddenly grown up and come to life. But they had matured ahead of her, and Margaret did not think herself capable of seeing those old dreams through to their conclusion.

She felt his lips lightly brush her brow, and Margaret tugged back against his hold. "You kissed me," she accused, her eyes flashing.

"Guilty," he said softly, and when she tried to move

farther away, Hunter did not release his hold. "It was just a simple kiss, Maggie."

"There is nothing simple about a kiss," she returned, pushing against his chest with both palms.

"That one was simple, don't you think?" he asked conversationally.

The pressure she was exerting slackened for a moment as she stared at him. "Why did you do that?" she asked, wondering particularly why he had bothered if that was all he intended to do. And it had alerted her to watch carefully for his true intentions.

Hunter removed his right arm from beneath her and propped his head on his hand. "I kissed you because I wanted to," he said, and watched her frown deepen as her thoughts whirled around in her head. "You should try it sometime," he added. "It's a small, rather pleasant sign of affection."

Her ice-blue eyes turned wary. Margaret knew a trap when she saw one. "You feel affection for me?" she asked while wondering about his next move.

"Of course," he said. "Why else would I have married you?"

Her eyes roamed over his face as she tried to determine any truth to his words. Why indeed? She was no longer pretty and she had resisted him at every turn. So why had he married her? Failing to find answers to her questions, Margaret set up her protective walls again. "Well, I hold none for you," she said. That, she thought, should put an end to it.

"You don't?" he asked, obviously doubting the truth of her statement.

He was confusing her again, setting her own words against her and making her head spin with questions.

"You're afraid to try a simple kiss?" he prodded in feigned wonder.

Maggie's eyes met his again. "And you are playing some silly game I want no part of," she snapped, sliding out from beneath his arms.

But before she could get to her feet, he taunted, "Kissing is a simple pleasure, Maggie. Like the sunset."

She scoffed at that. "You think kissing *you* would be a pleasure?"

"You won't know until you try it."

She hated to be taunted, and she was in fact curious. She couldn't see that such a gesture held any real merit. "I've kissed my father's cheek because I have affection for him," she said.

He rolled onto his back as he gazed at her. "There's a difference between father and husband, Maggie," he said.

There was, certainly, but what could be the difference between kissing one man's cheek and kissing another's? Exasperated by her own growing curiosity, Margaret chose to attack. "This is a silly game and no doubt a trick."

"No trick," he said, and it was hardly a game when husband and wife could not share even a kiss.

She stared at him a moment, kneeling at his side and ready to escape if need be. "I don't want you to touch me," she said.

Hunter raised his arms and cradled the back of his head with his hands. He then turned his head in her direction, offering one side of his face as Maggie leaned forward and lightly pressed her lips to his cheek.

She did not linger, but sat back on her heels, frowning down at him. "No difference," she said. He grinned, lying there looking foolish until she found herself smiling. "You look ridiculously pleased."

"Actually I'm disappointed," he said. "You could have put some enthusiasm into it."

She actually laughed at that.

"It lacked substance," he said lightly. "I hoped for

something more than a friendly peck. Chickens peck, Maggie,'' he said.

''You're being foolish,'' she said as she started to turn away.

Hunter lightly grasped one of her hands. ''It's fun being foolish sometimes, don't you think? Just as it's fun to kiss with a little enthusiasm. But you have to have it in you, Maggie,'' he said with well-feigned doubt.

Her frown mocked him as she eased her hand out of his hold and rested both palms on her thighs. ''Now it's *it*? You know something, Hunter? You should speak to me in Cherokee. Then perhaps I would understand you better.''

''*It* is substance. A kiss must have substance.''

''Is this a challenge?'' she asked, arching her finely chiseled brows as she stared down at him.

''Absolutely,'' he said and again cradled his head with his hands.

She was timid, but she was also a little bit curious. Just being close enough to him to offer that light peck *had* felt different.

Maggie leaned toward him, and Hunter turned his head so that she pressed her lips against the corner of his mouth. That startled her, and she pulled back, but then she tilted her head to the side and her soft lips and warm breath caressed his cheek again.

Come, little one, he coaxed silently.

Maggie's senses heightened as she caught his pleasant scent and warmth. She experimented with the feel of his skin against her lips, and she moved upward, her lips lightly touching just below his eye. She felt strange, but pleasantly so as her lips trailed down one side of his face and toward his mouth, hesitating.

Hunter could feel the tension radiating from her, but knew it to be shyness and not fear. He turned his head toward her, even as he dared to raise one hand and cup her face, lightly holding her still. He took her beyond her hesitation by placing his lips against hers. When she started to pull away, he waited, hoping her curiosity would force her to return of her own accord.

Maggie stared down at the well-defined masculine lips so close to her own, then lowered her head, tentatively touching and withdrawing before returning to wonder at the pleasant sensation this kissing could promote. It was not at all threatening, touching him this way. And that was curious.

And the hand that touched her cheek was warm and gentle and a little bit possessive. That, too, was curious.

She backed off then, watching his hand fall to his side as she straightened, clearly perplexed. When her eyes moved higher on his face, Hunter was watching her with an expression she could not define and had never seen on his face before, but that look was entirely sensual.

Maggie swallowed hard and sought to ease the nervous tension that had sprouted instantaneously within her. "Should we cook breakfast now?" she asked.

Hunter laughed lightly. She had made him hungry, but not for food! "All right, little one," he said in a strained voice. "But I want you to know I thought that was a pleasant start to the day." He rolled lithely to his feet and used the act of pulling on his shirt and boots as an excuse for keeping his back to her. Clearly he needed a few minutes alone.

"I'll get some water," he muttered as he swept his hand down, easily tossed the wooden pail in the air, and then caught it and started off toward the river.

Maggie frowned at his strange behavior as she watched him disappear among the trees.

By the time Hunter returned, Maggie had the fire going and was struggling to shave thin slices off a side of bacon. Hunter left the water near the fire, then knelt beside her and took the knife from her hand, testing the blade with the pad of his thumb. "This needs honing," he said.

Maggie moved far enough away so that she would not be touching him as she began making the coffee. She was still getting over the kissing, but now she found she couldn't forget the feel of his hand on her cheek and the feel of his skin beneath her lips.

When the coffee had brewed, they sat on the ground facing each other and a few feet apart.

Maggie seemed to concentrate on her food for quite some time, and then suddenly her blue eyes snapped up to his. "Was that the lesson you said I'd learn this morning?" she asked suspiciously. "Was kissing you the lesson?"

Hunter smiled to himself. So she was thinking about that, was she? But to her he said only, "Well, I suppose it was a lesson of a sort, but there is another lesson, Maggie. After we eat."

"What?"

"I'm going to teach you how to defend yourself," he said.

"As in *fighting*?"

"Not fighting as men might fight. But a woman can learn to protect herself. Even a small woman can disable a man if she knows how."

Maggie's brows arched upward. "A man of *any* size?"

Hunter nodded, innocent of her intent behind that particular question. But then he frowned in turn as a glowing smile slowly spread across her face. The imp! "Not against *me*, woman!" he laughed.

Maggie chuckled and dipped her head while she scooped up a forkful of beans. She thought it an excellent idea to learn how to defend herself against him. In fact, she was beginning to think she needed lessons in more than physical defense.

Once they had eaten and tidied their campsite, Hunter

moved well away from the fire and motioned for Maggie to join him.

Feeling a distinct rush of anticipation, Maggie walked slowly and stopped several paces away.

"It occurred to me last night that this is something you should have been taught years ago, Maggie," he said, as he shortened the distance between them.

"I don't think my father has ever thought about self-defense," she said quietly. "And who else would teach me?"

That was true. Still . . . "There are bound to be times when you find yourself among people you don't know or can't trust, like those two visitors yesterday. You didn't trust them, and they frightened you because you felt vulnerable. Is that a fair statement?" he asked.

Maggie nodded, but she was disconcerted by how much he seemed to know about her. In fact, he seemed to know her better than she knew herself. She had never given a thought to her vulnerability.

"All right," he said, watching for any display of skittishness. "I'm going to walk behind you," he warned as he put words to action. "And then I'm going to put my arms around you."

Maggie nodded slowly, once.

Hunter stepped up behind her and folded his arms across her chest, locking one strong hand onto his forearm. "All right, little one?" he asked.

Maggie nodded again but swallowed hard. This feeling of entrapment was not at all comfortable for her.

"Now, how do you think you could force me to let you loose?"

Maggie thought about that as she raised her hands to test the strength of his hold around her.

"You can't pry my arms apart, Maggie," he said softly, his cheek against her ear. "But men do have some vulnerable points.'' He loosened his hold a bit, giving her room. ''Look down at our feet. If you were to suddenly grind your heel into my foot, the pain would cause me to at least loosen my hold. Once you feel that happen, and have enough leeway to turn, move your arm forward and bring your elbow sharply back into my ribs.''

Hunter put his hand around her forearm and demonstrated the movement.

''Is this the way the Cherokee fight?'' she asked.

Hunter laughed. ''Darling, when it comes to fighting, everyone will do whatever must be done.''

Darling?

Hunter hadn't been conscious of the endearment, but Maggie was fully aware . . . and surprised.

''Now we're going to try this,'' he was saying, as her mind began to drift in directions completely opposite of fighting. ''But remember,'' Hunter warned lightly, gaining her attention, ''I am your husband. You are not supposed to hurt me.''

Maggie chuckled at the thought. Hurting him would be the equivalent of a flea hurting a dog. Anything more severe than a pesty bite would be pure luck.

Hunter released her and took a step back. ''Are you ready?'' he asked.

''Ready.'' She choked, doubling in two as she turned hysterically giddy over her own self-doubt.

Hunter frowned as he watched her turn toward him, her hands covering her face as she straightened slowly.

Maggie's eyes roamed up from his boots to his wide shoulders, and the control she had been gaining was lost as she began to laugh again. ''I am really supposed to disable *you*?'' she asked. ''Hunter, that would be like a mouse trying to fell a tree. How is he even supposed to lift the ax?'' She howled and Hunter grinned. ''I'm sorry,'' she said, striving for control when she saw how patiently he waited. "It just struck me as funny."

But he liked to see her laugh. It was the first time he had seen her laugh since their first meeting many years ago. He crossed his arms over his chest and waited until she had sobered somewhat.

"I'm all right now," she said, choking briefly as she wiped laughter tears from beneath her eyes with her fingertips.

Hunter shook his head, doubtful that she would not fall apart again. "You're certain you're ready?"

"No!" she teased, but turned her back to him. "Yes."

Hunter stepped forward and threw his arms around his wife.

Maggie snapped her arm back, driving her elbow into his midsection with such sudden force that Hunter immediately released her.

At his grunt of pain, Maggie whirled to face him. "Oh, Hunter!" she cried, genuinely dismayed. "I didn't mean that to happen!"

"I know, Maggie," he said quietly as his hand massaged his ribs. And then a lopsided smile appeared on his face as he saw her distress. "Now you see how you can use the element of surprise as another weapon."

Maggie covered her mouth with her hand as she continued to frown in obvious concern.

Hunter was moved by her reaction and took her hand in his. Squeezing her fingers lightly he said, "It's all right, little one. I'm not hurt."

Maggie nodded but continued to frown.

"Now that you've mastered that maneuver," he teased, "I hesitate to go on to the next."

"Perhaps we shouldn't do this anymore."

"But you see now how easy it is?" he asked.

She did. And suddenly her concern for him was forgotten. This was serious business.

Rubbing his thumb slowly across her knuckles, Hunter said lightly, "Now that you're free of your attacker, you must run."

Maggie nodded and began to relax once again as he talked.

"If you aren't able to get away, there's something else that you can do." He dropped her hand and stepped very close to her. "Suppose you had been successful only in stunning him and he continued to hold you." He put his hands on her shoulders and smiled ruefully. "Little one, I ask you not to lose control of your actions this time. You could ruin our hopes of having children."

Maggie's frown deepened even as her cheeks turned pink with his words.

Hunter knew she was going to be uncomfortable with this and chose to speak casually, as if they'd had such discussions on numerous occasions. "The most certain way of disabling a man is to strike hard between his legs. If you are far enough back, you can kick him. If he has a hold on you, bring your knee up sharply. Once you strike there, Maggie, I guarantee you will be free."

Maggie groaned and turned her head away, mortified by this discussion. Her complexion had turned from subtle pink to blushing red as he spoke, and now she couldn't face him.

Seeing her embarrassment, Hunter decided to end the lesson. He silently pulled her against his chest and wrapped his arms around her, amazed that she would permit such an action. "Do you understand, Maggie?" he asked softly. And then he turned his head so that his cheek rested lightly on the top of her head. "Do you realize the power you have gained with that bit of knowledge?"

Maggie nodded her head against his chest.

"Remember, *you* have the skills to gain control of the

situation,'' he said, running his palm lightly up and down her upper arm before he let her go.

Maggie had collected herself by this time, although she felt foolish for having reacted that way. But then, talking about a man's anatomy was not something she did every day.

CHAPTER

❧ 15 ❧

During the few remaining hours before they reached Hunter's home, Maggie had ample opportunity to mull over his morning games. It was true she had noticed something she'd never before experienced in their kisses and his caresses. And it caused her considerable concern. She was concerned, quite simply, because she wanted to experience more. The kisses and the control that he had allowed her stimulated her imagination as to how much enjoyable play he would allow. But it was the touch of his hand that truly produced in her a yearning that stemmed from her imagination. She tried to envision what it would be like if he were to touch more than her face.

But what if he didn't like her kisses? After all, she wasn't even pretty.

She stared at his hands as they capably held the reins of the matched bays. She had watched those hands quiet a nervous animal and knew them to be gentle, but she had also watched those hands lift and work, and she knew them to be strong. Maggie also knew that the day would come when she would feel those hands on her, and she could not help shuddering at the thought.

Hunter's attention was drawn to her as the quiver that ran through her body brought their shoulders into brief contact. "What's wrong?" he asked.

Margaret turned her head away. "Nothing," she said quietly.

"*Nothing* would not set you to trembling, Maggie," he prodded. "Are you ill?"

"I am not ill," she said sharply.

"Don't be snappish, Maggie," he said in response to her tone. "I'm genuinely concerned."

Still feeling peevish, Maggie asked, "Why did you marry me, Hunter?"

He was startled by her bluntness and pulled back on the reins to halt the bays as he turned his full attention upon her. "Where did that come from?" he asked reasonably.

Maggie's right hand rose and fell in agitation as she stared straight ahead. "I've asked myself since morning why you married me, and I can't come up with an answer," she said.

Hunter softened in the face of her anxiety; he realized her mind must have been working frantically for the past hour or two. He placed both sets of reins in his right hand and turned her face toward him. "Look at me," he instructed when she stubbornly refused to turn. He dropped his hand to his lap then, not wanting to use physical pressure to make her turn. "What has brought this on, Maggie?" he asked quietly.

She exploded before his eyes. "I am going to a place I don't know! To live with people I don't know! With a man I don't know . . . and don't want to know! Does that explain it to you?" she cried.

He thought that was fairly clear.

He returned his gaze to the bays for a moment, sorting

through his thoughts and struggling for a means to diffuse her unease. Of course she was afraid. Everything would be new to her, and she would not even be able to turn to a husband she loved when she needed comfort. Most brides had *that* luxury, at least.

"I'm not a cruel man, Maggie. You must know that. It was not, nor will it ever be, my intention to hurt you in any way. The people you will be meeting are good people. They're looking forward to your coming."

Startled, she glared at him. "You told them about me?"

"Of course. I returned to your father's house for you, Maggie. I've told you that," he said reasonably, as his eyes returned to hers. "Why would I not tell my friends about the woman I was going to marry?"

"But you knew a *girl*!"

"That's correct," he said quietly. "I knew a girl who has grown to be a beautiful young woman."

"Don't flatter me!"

"Who happens to have a bad temper," he muttered and then turned to face her more fully. "Do you think I would tell you that just to hear myself talk?" he asked.

"I think you have other motives."

"Indeed," he murmured. "What might those be?"

"I think all you want is—" Unable to complete the sentence, she turned away from the heated look in his eyes.

"You do me an injustice," he said angrily, fully understanding the unfinished comment. "And I can find *that* anywhere." On that note he slapped the reins against the horses' rumps, and the wagon lurched forward.

Margaret turned her head away from his seething anger. *Fool*, she mentally berated herself. "I didn't mean to anger you, Hunter," she said softly.

He laughed caustically. "Really?"

"I'm trying to . . ." What? She didn't know anymore. He sighed. He was beginning to think he'd been wrong in giving her time to adjust to her new home and to him. Obviously she was building mental barriers against him. Perhaps it was time to discuss their relationship honestly and openly. "You are my wife, and I will take you, Maggie, but it will not be rape," he said quietly, studying the road ahead. His peripheral vision noted that she had turned her head to look at him, and he spoke before she could interrupt and further complicate the discussion. "What I said is true. I could satisfy my lust anywhere and with any woman, if that were my *motive*, as you so kindly put it."

"Hunter, I—"

"Please allow me to finish," he said firmly, and Margaret fell silent, studying her hands in her lap. "Therefore, we might deduce that my interest in you is not driven solely by passion. Would that be fair to say?" he asked, turning his head long enough to see her reluctantly agree by a nod of her head. "Don't take that to mean I don't want you in that way," he added bluntly. "I desperately want to make love to you, and there are other things I want, Maggie. I want us to build a relationship that will grow stronger with the years. I want us to raise a family and grow old watching the sunsets together." He turned and looked at her as she rubbed the palms of her hands up and down the legs of her britches. "Would you consider those reasonable hopes for the future?" he asked softly.

Her eyes darted to his and away again. "Yes, reasonable," she said.

"And could you desire such things for yourself?"

Maggie nodded, feeling very small for what she had been thinking about him.

"Then how do we go about attaining our dreams, my dear?"

When she did not speak, he prompted, "Would a little mutual trust be a good jumping-off point?"

"Yes," she returned quietly.

Hunter sighed. "If you only learn two things about me, little one," he breathed, "know this: I will always protect you, and I will never willingly hurt you."

And she knew the last statement to be a lie. He *would* hurt her.

Hunter stopped the team a few miles from his farm and allowed Margaret time to change into the traveling suit she'd worn the first day. When she returned to the wagon, she looked fresh and dignified, and she hid her nervousness well, he thought. It was obvious that she was nervous about meeting his friends, for she had brushed her hair and left it down so that it fell forward over her shoulders and acted as a shield for the scar on her face. This surprised him, since she had flaunted the scar at their first reunion. Then he remembered that her intent at that time had been to drive him away. It seemed she didn't have the same desire toward his friends. How was he ever going to make her understand that the scar did not detract from her beauty or her desirability?

Margaret's interest was piqued when they turned off the main road and entered a long narrow lane. The weathered two-story house was set on an incline somewhat higher than the road, and a huge oak tree seemed to bow over the place. To the left, and set back still farther, she saw a barn, a few outbuildings, and what looked like a small apple orchard. While the place could not be termed pretty, it did have a serenity about it.

"We're not far from Danville," Hunter explained as Margaret looked around at fields of tobacco and corn and, to her right, orchards of fruit-laden trees. "We take our tobacco to auction there and sell most of our fruit and produce. From Danville it's shipped north by rail. It won't be long before I'll have to round up picking crews," he added. "You can come with me if you like and see what the town is all about."

Margaret smiled, nodding her agreement.

"Well, here we are," he said, feeling slightly apprehensive; it was important to him that she like his home and his friends. He very much wanted Maggie, eventually, to be happy here, and even though his farm was not so large as Treemont, he could provide for her well with what he had.

He drove the wagon around the house and followed the lane that ambled off toward the large barn. Near a side door he pulled the team up, wrapped the reins securely around the brake handle, and jumped to the ground. But before he could walk around to Maggie's side of the wagon and help her down, the outer door flew open and a feminine voice demanded his attention.

"About time you got her here!" Marie-Louise called, running down the steps from the porch that circled the house on three sides. She was a plain young woman of eighteen years whose auburn hair had frizzed in the southern Virginia humidity, but her smile could light up anyone's day. "What took you so long?" she admonished, cuffing Hunter's shoulder, much to Margaret's amazement.

Marie-Louise took one look at the two stallions tied to the sides of the wagon and frowned, keeping her distance as she muttered, "More of those dang creatures."

"Watch your mouth," Hunter said firmly. Marie-Louise ignored him, turning a radiant smile up to Maggie.

"Hi!" She extended her hand upward. "I'm Marie-Louise Winter, in case his nibs forgot to tell you." She noticed Margaret's gloves and pulled her hand back, wiping it on her apron before extending it once more. "I'm glad you're here," she said as she shook Margaret's hand. "I'm sick of my own company, and these men don't talk about nothin' but crops." She whirled on Hunter who was leaning against the side of the wagon, grinning. "Mr. Maguire, you help her down here now." And she flashed another smile at Maggie. "I'll make you some cool lemonade, if he ever gets you down here."

Hunter laughed. "Slow down, for Maggie's sake," he teased, having given up trying to tame Marie-Louise months ago. "And come here and give me a proper greeting."

Marie-Louise flew at him then, her arms going around his neck with little hesitation, while Hunter squeezed her waist. "I missed you," she said and stepped back, dropping her arms to her sides as he grinned down at her.

"I won't tell Jeffrey you said that," he teased, and she laughed.

"Jeffrey won't care," she returned proudly. "I love him enough so he won't ever feel threatened."

Margaret was stunned and a little bit hurt that this girl could speak and act so casually with Hunter when she, Maggie, continuously tripped over her tongue or made him angry. And there seemed to be something naughty in her statement about loving Jeffrey!

"Besides, you have your own wife," Marie-Louise continued, turning back to Maggie. "You've got to have patience with him, Miss Maggie. He's like the other men around here . . . slow."

"Get in that house!" Hunter laughed and turned her by her shoulders.

"With any luck," she called over her shoulder, "he'll have you down about a week from Tuesday!"

Margaret chuckled lightly as she watched the girl disappear into the house.

"She's full of vim and vigor, that girl," Hunter said, reaching up and placing both hands around Maggie's waist.

"She's not usually like that, Hunter?" Maggie asked hopefully as she jumped to the ground.

"Not quite as . . . excited," he said. "She's been looking forward to having another woman to talk with."

Margaret smiled warily.

Hunter placed his hand on the back of her waist and guided her toward the house. "Come on, I'll take you in and then get some help to unload your trunks."

The kitchen was large and bright and clean. This appeared to be the room where they ate their meals; a large oval table and six chairs stood at one end. A row of windows ran the length of the outer wall, and a large cabinet and hutch took up most of the wall opposite. The cooking area contained a long L-shaped countertop, a cast-iron wood stove, and wooden storage bins set up off the floor. Cupboards had been suspended from the ceiling along the wall over the counter. In the center of the area stood a large cutting block.

Marie-Louise smiled up at them as she halved lemons with a long knife. "I was going to make new curtains for these windows," she said as she began to squeeze the lemons. "But I thought you might like to choose the material yourself. We can make them together."

Hunter laughed. "Could you give her time to unpack her knickers?" he teased and ducked out the door before either woman could reply.

Margaret blushed at his reference to her underthings and Marie-Louise huffed as she poured ample quantities of the fresh juice into two glasses. "What does *he* know?" she muttered. And then she was turning away. "Be back!" she called as she exited the room.

Margaret felt her head would spin if Marie-Louise did not slow down.

She took another step into the room as she looked around at her new home. Walking toward the large table, Margaret removed her gloves and unpinned her hat. Before she could be seated, however, Marie-Louise had returned, carrying a clear frosted pitcher of water.

"Sit," she said as she whisked by. "I keep water in the

root cellar so it stays cool." Having added water and sugar to the two glasses, she returned to the table and sat in the chair to Margaret's left. "There!" She took a drink from her own glass. "You'll like this, I hope. I don't make it so sweet that it's syrupy."

Margaret took a sip. "It's very good." She raised her glass for a longer drink. "I was thirsty."

Marie-Louise beamed with pride. "I'm very glad you're here," she said again. "I don't usually run on like this, but I haven't had another female to talk with for months."

"How long have you lived here?" Margaret asked, thinking of the easy relationship this girl had with Hunter.

"It's been six months and three weeks since Jeffrey married me and brought me here," she said, smiling happily. "And I love this place already!"

"You do seem happy." Margaret smiled and lifted her glass again; Marie-Louise made the best lemonade she had ever tasted.

"Oh, I've never been happier," she said with feeling. "The men are good to me, and I love my husband and this old house and the cottage out back where Jeffrey and I stay." Her eyes sparkled as she gazed quickly around the kitchen with glowing fondness. "All I need now is a baby."

Margaret almost choked on her lemonade. "So soon?"

"The sooner the better," the girl said lightly. "I'm not . . . yet, you understand. But I keep praying."

There was a commotion outside, and Marie-Louise pulled back the curtains. "Here's Jason and Jeffrey to help," she said, letting the white lace curtain fall back into place. "Come outside and I'll introduce you to my Jeff."

There were no two ways about it. Marie-Louise moved to the door, and she expected Margaret to follow. "Don't be shy," she said, seeing Margaret's hesitation. "Jason is a grand fellow."

Jason proved to be a mountain of a man who stood a half

head taller than Hunter. He was well muscled, without an ounce of fat, and sported flaming red hair and a bushy beard to match! And he greeted Maggie warmly.

The three men were standing at the rear of the wagon, having obviously already stabled the horses, when Hunter looked up and smiled as Margaret walked his way. *These are my friends*, his eyes told her.

Margaret smiled when she caught the meaning behind that look; she realized it was important to him that she like these people. Was it equally important to him that *they* like *her*?

As Hunter introduced her to Jason, Marie-Louise stepped closer to the younger man and folded her small hand in his. This kind of open display was new to Margaret, and she wondered at the intensity of emotions that would permit two people to so casually show their affection in front of others.

"So you married this lout!" Jason boomed, sandwiching her hand between both of his. "Well, I hope you'll be happy here, regardless."

"Thank you," Hunter returned ruefully, and Margaret chuckled. She suspected Jason was in the habit of putting Hunter in his place.

Hunter placed a gentle hand on her shoulder and indicated the young couple awaiting their attention. He smiled at Marie-Louise and asked, "Can you release Jeffrey long enough for him to greet my wife?"

The young man with sandy hair looked unhappily at his employer as he let go of his wife's hand. But, with the smile Hunter sent his way, Jeffrey realized the man had been teasing them. "Ma'am," he said.

"And that's all you'll be gettin' out of him!" Jason boomed. Then he clapped Hunter on the shoulder. "Let's get these trunks up those stairs."

Marie-Louise placed a slender hand on Margaret's forearm to get her attention. "I'll show you the house while the men are unloading the wagon," she said. Margaret nodded, following in the young woman's wake.

The tour was not totally complete as Marie-Louise pointed to the closed door off the kitchen that was apparently Jason's room. "I only go in there to collect the linens on washdays," she explained.

The front of the house was split into two rooms divided by a narrow hall and a flight of stairs leading to the second floor. One large room had been divided, she was told, to make a bedroom for Jason. The smaller room contained a desk, some bookshelves, and two comfortable-looking chairs situated before a small fireplace. This was Hunter's room. The second room, deeper than the first, was simply furnished with a settee under the window and four chairs grouped before the fireplace. The floors were clean and highly polished, and hooked rugs were scattered about. The room was bright and inviting, and Margaret could imagine a roaring fire on a winter's night.

The top floor of the house contained three rooms, one much larger than the others. It was to this room that the men were moving her trunks, she noted with interest.

"This will be your room," Marie-Louise told her and then the girl had the temerity to wink!

Margaret merely smiled politely.

"This is your room," the girl said again, "and Mr. Maguire's."

Maggie turned various shades of purple and retreated downstairs.

CHAPTER
❧ 16 ❧

Margaret returned to the second floor later in the afternoon when Marie-Louise told her firmly that she would not be helping with the supper on her first night in her new home.

Before she started to unpack her belongings, however, Maggie strolled through the upstairs rooms, stopping to examine the one directly across the hall from where her trunks had been taken.

The room contained a large bed with an iron bedstead, a small table, and a commode. Against one wall a wardrobe stood and, examining it closely, she determined it would hold most of her clothes. A braided rug lay on either side of the bed, and white lace curtains fluttered at the small window. It would do nicely, she decided.

"This was my room," a deep masculine voice informed her, and Margaret turned to face her husband. "My mother kept it this way for me all the years I was in England." He pushed off with a shoulder from the doorframe and stepped into the room. "I moved my things to the larger room before I left to get you."

Margaret frowned and clasped her hands together, considering her words carefully before she spoke. "I like this room," she said simply.

"I do, too. Perhaps one day we'll have a son who will sleep here," he said, glancing around the room before his eyes settled on her again.

Margaret hesitated before continuing but finally said frankly, "I thought I would take this room for myself."

Hunter's brows arched even as his eyes narrowed, and Margaret knew immediately that she had grossly miscalculated. "Did you, now?" he asked in a deceptively calm voice.

"It's a nice room," she added lamely.

"It is. It is not *our* room, however."

"Hunter," she pleaded, stepping back from him a pace. "You said you would give me time."

He nodded. "So I did, Maggie. But I did not agree to being estranged from you. We will share a room and a bed, my dear," he said firmly, and then he softened a little as he tried to understand and be tolerant of her concerns. He held out one hand. "Come with me," he said softly and led her into the room that was to be theirs.

He looked around the large rectangular room. It would be cool in summer; a large oak tree cast its shade over the roof and windows. And it would be warm in winter; the chimney that serviced the parlor provided also for a small fireplace on the end wall of the bedroom. Jason and Hunter's father had carved the bedstead, and Hunter had added two comfortable, well-padded chairs and a woven rug to a center spot before the fireplace, where he hoped to spend many a long winter's evening in Margaret's company.

He stood in the room he had planned for her before learning about her aversion to having a husband, and he felt the warmth of her small hand tucked neatly inside his much bigger one.

"Hunter, your friends will know . . ."

"Of course they'll know," he said quietly, leaning close to her as he pressed her hand against his chest. "Haven't you heard that husbands and wives sleep together, Maggie? Most people understand that."

"A *gentleman* would allow his wife to sleep in her own bed!" she insisted.

"Where did you learn that?" he teased.

"It is general knowledge!"

"Indeed? And did your mother and father sleep in separate beds?" he asked. "Is that where you learned this amazing news?"

Margaret tried to turn away from him but he wouldn't let her go.

"I suspect that they shared a room," he told her softly, his dark eyes staring intensely into her light blue ones. "I suspect they shared a bed. And I suspect they cared very deeply for each other. How else do you think they got four daughters, Maggie?"

In theory, Maggie knew the answer to that, of course. She had been raised on a farm and understood the continuance of a line. She simply did not choose to believe that such tawdry, disagreeable behavior had any place in her own life.

When she looked down at the floor, Hunter's other hand came up and held her hand against his shirtfront. "This is a simple place," he said softly to the top of her head. "And I'm a simple man. I have envisioned spending evenings here while you and I talk, or while I read and you sew. Quiet evenings, away from the work and the cares of the house and the farm." He smiled when she dared to look up at him, a small frown marring her loveliness. "A quiet place where we would escape the demands of our children." And when she would have turned her head away from him, Hunter gently forced her chin up again. "I have no mean or hurtful thoughts or plans for this room, my pet," he whispered.

"Everything I want to do with you here is about sharing. We will share the bed and our thoughts and our humor. We'll share our fears and our disappointments, and most important, Maggie, I want us to share our love."

Maggie's eyes turned stormy, and she tore herself away from him, speeding across the room to stare out the window. "Those are pretty words," she said. "But I think you've trapped yourself, Hunter."

He didn't move toward her; he simply turned until he was staring at her back. "How do you mean?"

"You returned to Treemont to get a pretty, laughing girl, and I am not that girl anymore. Once there, you were trapped by your bargain with my father, weren't you?"

"No!" he said firmly, taking a step toward her. "I was not trapped, and there was no bargain. Can't you see, Maggie? I had a choice. I always had a choice because there was no firm agreement. Your father and I agreed that I would come back when you were grown, and if there was an understanding between you and me—"

She whirled on him then. "But there was no understanding between us!" she cried. "I didn't want you!"

His dark eyes narrowed as he studied the torture in the eyes he had come to love during the years he had imagined her growing up. And in response to her statement he said only "Didn't you?"

"No!"

"I thought little girls dreamed of their first love."

"Little girls do!" she said. "But the realities are for big girls! And I don't want any part of them."

"You don't know what the realities are, Maggie."

"Really?" she laughed bitterly. "And what do you call my previous experience?" Her hands were clenched at her sides, and she was leaning toward him in anger and frustration.

Hunter thought he had never seen anyone so frightened

and trying so hard to hide it. "I call it rape," he said. "And it has nothing to do with two caring people expressing their desire and their need for each other."

"*Two* people?" she scoffed. "And what woman would ever confess to feeling desire and need?"

"My woman will," he said quietly. "As soon as I teach her that desires and needs are natural and permissible. As soon as I teach her that making love with me will not be frightening or painful or degrading. Does that about sum up how you think when you think about lying with me, Maggie?"

Suddenly Margaret seemed to crumble before his eyes, and her hands came up to hide her face as if she could not bear to have him see her any longer.

Hunter's reflexive reaction was to reach for her and try to comfort her by holding her close against him.

"I can't, Hunter," she mumbled against his shirtfront, her hands continuing to hide her face. "I don't think I'll ever be able to take a lover."

"You will, my pet," he breathed with a confidence he didn't feel. "You'll take *me*." He cupped her chin in the palm of his hand and raised her head until he could look into her troubled eyes. "You will take me," he said again, "and you will find our loving to your liking. I promise you."

"You're such a strange man," she whispered, staring up at him. "How can you dare to imagine such a thing?"

"I dare, Maggie, because we are going to make it happen." He lowered his head, his eyes intense and alert as he watched her until the precious second before his lips lightly touched hers. She started, but he shook his head, moving one hand higher on her back while he pressed the palm of her small hand to the center of his chest once again. "So soft," he murmured and tilted his head slightly this time as his lips moved across hers.

It was not a threatening kiss. In fact, to Maggie, it seemed

that he was paying homage to her. As if he cherished her
and wanted her to know that. Margaret didn't know how this
could be, but she felt it as certainly as if he had spoken the
words. Such a curious man. He coaxed her senses with
maddening ease with a combination of harsh demands and
soft words, determination and hesitancy, dream and reality.
He was indeed an unusual man, and he was cultivating some
spot within her, just as he cultivated the land surrounding
the house in which they stood.

The wide palm pressed against her back seemed to warm
her through the stuff of her blouse, and she thought he might
be charged with summer lightning as tiny shocks traveled
down her spine to the tips of her toes. It was a mysterious
thing, and she feared it because it was an unknown. But she
did not fear that he might go beyond the gentle, lingering
kiss. The kiss was all he wanted; she knew that instinctively.

She pulled her head back and stared at him with curiosity
and shock.

Hunter smiled down at her, realizing that he had moved
her in some small way; and any way that would make her
think of him in relation to herself was a major event in his
estimation. "Marie-Louise is in the kitchen preparing enough
food for a threshing," he said lightly. "Let's go down to
supper."

Supper! They had yet to resolve their dispute to her
satisfaction. But then Margaret realized the disagreement
would be resolved to *his* satisfaction one way or another,
and she might as well be kind to herself and give in
gracefully. It crossed her mind, however, as he led her from
the room, that if she put her mind and her meager brawn to
the matter, she could push him out of the bed a time or two!

Supper was ready when they returned to the kitchen; a
delicious smelling meat pie, thick with dark gravy by the
looks of it, was warming on the back of the stove. Carrots
sweetened with maple syrup steamed in a pot, and warm

popovers covered by a cloth had been set aside. Except for the food and the furnishings, however, the kitchen was empty.

"Where is everyone?" Margaret asked.

Hunter had no answer, but a clue jumped out at him when he turned toward the table. Marie-Louise had spread a neatly ironed white damask cloth across the table and set places for only two. A bouquet of freshly cut flowers stood in a tall pitcher, and propped up against it was a paper-wrapped parcel. Hunter smiled as he began to comprehend. "I believe they're giving us a gift, my love," he said and lightly tugged her toward the table. "Our first supper at home is to be for us alone, it seems." He reached for the parcel, turned it over in his hand, and held it out to Maggie. "I imagine this is for us."

Maggie stared at the thing for a moment before taking it in both hands. "A gift?" she murmured, staring down briefly before frowning up at him again. "Shall I open it?"

"Of course!" he said. "And quickly! I'm a starving man." He pulled back a wooden chair.

Margaret sat down, put the package on the table, and carefully opened the present. It was a small broom, as long as her forearm, gaily and artfully decorated with dried flowers, cones, and herbs and topped by a wide plaid bow. "How lovely," Margaret said. Although it caught the eye, she doubted its usefulness. And then she spied a square of paper folded under the woven handle and gave it to Hunter to open.

They read it together silently, struggling over the nearly illegible scrawl:

My grandmother often made these when I was a girl. She told me of the importance of a new broom to newlyweds or friends moving to a new home. The gift of a new broom brings good wishes for a new start, and the decorations are a symbol of abundance. This is our gift to the newlyweds and to the new friend who has moved to a new home.

We thought you might like to enjoy your first night in the house in peace.

Marie-Louise

Note: Jason will sleep in the cottage tonight.

Hunter laughed at the last line, and Margaret glanced up at him hesitantly. "Marie-Louise seems to be in charge of everything and *everyone*," she said and he nodded.

"I expect *Jason* thinks so about now."

Margaret held the broom up for his inspection. "Do you suppose she made this?"

"Oh, yes. Marie-Louise is quite talented." He stood beside her smiling as she examined the broom. "Do you like your gift?" he asked unnecessarily; he could see that she was pleased.

"It was very thoughtful of her," Maggie said quietly. Then, raising her head, she asked, "Could we hang it on the door, Hunter? It would be such a pretty thing to greet visitors to the house."

Visitors? They didn't get many of those, but if that was what she wanted . . . He nodded in agreement.

He returned the note to the table before moving across the room to fetch their supper. "I am truly a starving man," he said again. "Could we consider the gift of abundance to start with food?"

The gift had lightened Margaret's mood, and she followed in his wake. Hunter took the pie and a large spoon to the table while Maggie scooped the carrots into a bowl. And while she was pouring the syrup over the carrots, he returned for the popovers. He stepped close to her right shoulder and planted a light, quick kiss on her cheek.

Margaret started, unused to familiarity, but he only smiled and said, "Welcome home, Maggie."

And when she turned her head, intending to scold him for his presumptuous action, the happy look in his eyes made her smile. But the look and the kiss had completely confounded her. Maggie quickly moved around him and carried the bowl to the table.

Hunter turned to watch her, pleased with her reaction to the kiss. And this sudden shyness was a good sign, he decided as he took his place at the head of the table while Maggie sat to his left. He had expected shyness in his bride, but it could be overcome with time and patience. Her anger and suspicions seemed to have diminished greatly in just a few days; that told him that she had not entirely lost all feeling for him. Yes, as they sat down together for their first supper in the old house, Hunter Maguire was indeed a hopeful man.

He spooned a wedge of pastry and meat onto her plate, ladled gravy over the lot, and then served himself while Maggie waited patiently for him to start.

But he had taken only a forkful of food when he set his fork on his plate. "Good Lord, I forgot!" He reached for her hand. "Come with me."

"For heaven's sake." She hastily dropped her fork as he tugged her to her feet.

He led her out onto the porch, turning to her the instant she stepped outside under the overhang. "How could I forget?" He scooped her up in his arms and strode back over the threshold.

Margaret was so surprised she could only stare, mouth open, as she wrapped her arms around his neck.

"What kind of husband have you wed?" he asked, stepping farther into the kitchen. And then he was smiling at her. "Now I can welcome you home, Maggie." He planted a quick kiss on her lips before lowering her to her feet.

When Hunter returned to his place and picked up his fork, Maggie was still staring at him with astonishment.

"Should I expect to be hoisted up and dragged around with any frequency?" she asked lightly.

"Possibly," he murmured and turned his attention to his meal.

CHAPTER
❧ 17 ❧

That first evening of settling into a bedroom together was a night Margaret would never forget. Hunter was not gentlemanly enough to leave her any privacy, which raised her ire. Additionally he seemed to think nothing of shedding his clothing before her very eyes!

He removed his boots, then walked to the window and peered out into the darkness as he casually shed his shirt and dropped it on a chair. He turned to face her while he peeled off his trousers!

Maggie stared at the wall. She heard a slight creak from the bed and began rifling through her trunk. Somehow sharing a bed with him seemed much more frightening than sleeping next to him on the ground.

"Leave that," Hunter said as he propped himself up in the bed. "Marie-Louise will help you unpack your things in the morning."

Margaret stood with her back to him, holding a white cotton nightgown in her hands. "Could you put out the lamp please, Hunter?" she asked and waited nervously for the room to fall into darkness.

He lowered the wick, and the corners of the room fell into shadows.

Maggie whirled to face him, frowning.

"You need some light to find your way around." He had the audacity to look her straight in the eyes as he said that to her!

Margaret raced for the door and across the hall to the dark, empty room that had once been Hunter's. There she undressed without his watchful eyes on her. Once gowned from neck to toe, she hesitated . . . but she knew he would only come and get her.

When she returned to the room they would share, Hunter hadn't moved. He was sitting up in the bed, blanket pulled to his waist, watching her as she hung her skirt and blouse in the wardrobe, then sat on the bed with her back to him and began to brush her hair. Hunter watched as she tended the waist-length tresses that were so close to white they might have been touched and colored by a cloud. His eyes followed her long, slow strokes for a moment before taking the brush from her hand.

Maggie's head snapped around, and he smiled. "Sit back," he said quietly, and after a brief hesitation Maggie moved closer to him. Her entire body tensed when he raised his hand, but he ignored the reaction, running the brush slowly from her temple to the very ends of her hair on one side. He repeated the procedure over and over until Maggie, weary from the day's events, found herself quite peacefully lulled, her eyes closing as the continuous stroking of the brush soothed her.

When her head dropped back and her eyes closed, Hunter set the brush aside and lowered her onto her back. "It's time for bed," he said, pulling the light blanket over her.

Margaret's eyes opened, and she stared up at him.

Hunter had not been unaffected by the intimacy of what he had done and now he smoothed her nightdress with one hand, caressing her slowly from shoulder to wrist as he twisted his upper body and lowered his head. "I'm glad you're here, little one," he murmured before his lips touched hers. He felt her body tense beneath his chest.

But the kiss was sweet and tender, and Maggie found her eyelids fluttering as he softly teased her lips, then kissed the scar below her cheek. She found she was becoming accustomed to his touching her like this, found that his warmth enveloped her when he was close. For a moment, just one moment, he made her forget that she hadn't wanted to come here, that she hadn't wanted to be a wife. For just a moment . . .

Hunter propped himself up on one elbow. "Do you like the house?" he asked, his hand resting lightly on her arm.

"It's a nice house," she said truthfully.

"Tomorrow I'll take you out and show you the rest of the place," he said as his fingertips began to lightly stroke her inner wrist. "I have a little mare I'd like you to see, also. I'm thinking of breeding her with Pride."

Maggie nodded dumbly. The strangest sensations were traveling the length of her arm, and she found the feeling distracting.

"Your skin is so soft," he murmured, looking briefly at the delicate spot he was caressing. "Do you like that?" he asked.

Startled, Maggie's eyes dropped away from his and stared at his shoulder. The muscles there and along his arm were bunched and contoured, reminding her of hills and valleys. He was strongly built, and yet he could be so gentle.

"I think you like that," Hunter said softly as he watched her eyes roam across his shoulder and arm. Was she just a little curious? "I like to be touched, too, Maggie," he said.

She raised her eyes to his for a brief moment, then lowered them again as she hesitantly placed her hand on his shoulder.

Her palm was soft and warm as she ran it slowly down his arm, testing. Hunter dropped his head, closing his eyes as he rested his cheek next to hers. "Your touch is good," he breathed.

Maggie tore her hand away as if she had been scalded, dropping it across her waist. "I'd like to sleep now," she said softly, closing her eyes and turning her head away. Being this close to him was very confusing. It was time to retreat.

Hunter raised his head and smiled as she turned away from him. He was not displeased. In fact, he was much encouraged. One brief touch could lead to many others. And he thought it a good thing that she had withdrawn, for her touch *had* been good and it did not take much for him to react to her. He dropped a light kiss on her temple and lay down on his back as he silently laughed at himself. It was getting so that all he had to do was think of her and his body would respond. If she knew how many times he'd had to turn away so as not to frighten her with the tight fit of his trousers, Margaret would have gone running back to Treemont on her own.

Smiling into the darkness, ridiculing his own plight, Hunter placed his hand over the much smaller one that rested on the bed near his hip.

CHAPTER
❧18❧

Margaret awoke the following morning to find the other half of the bed empty, with only a rumpled pillow as evidence that there had been another occupant during the night. Somehow not seeing him beside her when she awoke was disturbing.

She turned her mind from it, however, noting that the sun was high and she had much to do in addition to becoming acquainted with her new home. She washed quickly and dressed in a plain high-necked white cotton blouse and a dark blue skirt. Braiding her hair into a single thick plait as she went, Maggie hurried down the steps and into the kitchen, following enticing aromas and the sound of someone humming off key. Pushing open the swinging door, Maggie entered the sunshine-brightened room.

"Good morning!" Marie-Louise called brightly, greeting her with a warm smile. She had suspended a board on the backs of two straight-backed chairs and was ironing snow-white sheets.

"Good Morning," Maggie said. "Thank you for your

beautiful gift and the tasty supper you left us last night. That
was very kind.''

"Ah, it was nothing,'' she returned. "I just wanted to
welcome you, and I'd made another pie for Jason and
Jeffrey and me.'' She twisted toward the stove, exchanging
the cooling flatiron for a hot one. "There's coffee here, and
I kept a plate for you in the warming oven. Cups in the
cupboard.'' She pointed to the first door in the bank of
cupboards on her left.

"You've eaten?'' Maggie asked, collecting a cup and
looking about for utensils.

"On the table,'' Marie-Louise advised with insight.
"We ate ages ago. We always get an early start around
here.''

"I'm not usually so slow starting the day, myself,''
Maggie said without thinking.

Marie-Louise hooted with laughter. "They'll whack you
out every time! Leave it to a new bridegroom!''

Maggie blushed, even though she knew what Marie-
Louise was thinking had never happened. She wondered
how the young woman could speak so bluntly about the
very things that caused her so much discomfort. Ducking
behind Marie-Louise, Maggie removed the earthenware plate from the warming oven with the aid of a folded
towel.

"Jeffrey and I have been married for nearly seven months
now, and there are many mornings I'm slow in starting the
day. Not that I'm complaining,'' she added with a twinkle
in her eye.

Maggie had moved around to the far side of the table so
she could talk with the other woman, and now she sat there
looking aghast to think this behavior on the part of men
could continue with any frequency over such a long period
of time!

Marie-Louise mistook Maggie's shock and said, "Well,

if we can't tease each other about things like that . . . I mean, sometimes women need to confide in other women, don't you think?''

''I don't know . . . I—''

''I can talk to Jeffrey about anything,'' she went on with hardly a breath. ''But it's not the same as talking to another woman. You'd better eat those eggs before they get cold.'' She set the flatiron down on the next sheet. ''And as soon as you've got your strength up,'' she teased, ''we'll go upstairs and unpack your things.''

Blushing again, Maggie bowed her head and devoted her attention to her breakfast.

It took the two women a couple of hours to organize Maggie's belongings and tidy up the master bedroom, and Maggie thought she would die if Marie-Louise said one single word about the rumpled bed! There was none of that, however, as the other girl sensed Maggie's shyness about her new circumstance, and they got on famously.

Maggie then found herself caught up in a whirlwind created by Marie-Louise as she prepared lunch for three hardworking men. ''They like lots of cold lemonade and some sandwiches when it's hot outside, but I've got some soup here that I made yesterday, and that will disappear, too,'' she said as Maggie buttered bread to be crowned with hunks of cheese and lettuce from the kitchen garden.

The soup had no more than warmed when the thunder of booted feet announced the arrival of the three men on the porch outside the kitchen door. Marie-Louise immediately filled three large bowls with rich broth and noodles. ''Would you take them those towels?'' she asked, nodding to three folded flannels. ''They bring their own water up for washing.''

Maggie was a bit dumbfounded by all the bustle, but she took the towels to the door. It occurred to her in that instant that she would have to face Hunter for the first time that day.

The men were all shirtless, a daunting sight for a straitlaced young woman, and were bent over three identical enameled basins of water that had been lined up on a low bench.

Marie-Louise walked to the screen door and looked out as Maggie stood hesitantly by, waiting shyly. It was true, Maggie had seen many a naked chest, but she had always kept her distance. And it was not the sight of all that flesh that truly concerned her. It was her husband's reaction to her, in view of last night's events. She had wondered all morning if he would be angry because she had turned him away. She'd lain awake for hours, sorting through her thoughts and resolving little. She had, however, managed to acknowledge that she liked the feel of his hand on hers.

Hunter was the first to finish washing, water dripping from his face and neck, running in rivulets down the wide expanse of his chest. He turned and saw her look of apprehension and smiled, reaching out to take the towel she offered.

"Good morning, slugabed," he teased and took a step or two around Jeffrey, startling Maggie by dropping a quick kiss on her cheek.

"Dinner is ready," she mumbled inadequately.

Hunter laughed as she blushed at his kissing her in front of others.

Jason and Jeffrey took her attention then, greeting her for the first time that day and thanking her for the towels.

The meal was a noisy, hasty affair with the men catching Hunter up on the events that had taken place during his absence. The state was still recovering from the ravages of a war that had taken place some twenty years previously, but slowly, with patience and sacrifice, they were gaining ground. And this farm and these people seemed to be faring well, Maggie thought.

"Feddler fell off his roof and broke a lot of bones," Jeffrey was saying, taking time to smile up at his wife as Marie-Louise refilled his bowl for the second time. "Jason and me have been going over there and helping out in the afternoons. His wife's about due, too, and he's hollering from his bed in fits of temper most of the time. Marie-Louise goes over with us and gets the supper to give poor Janie a minute off her feet."

Hunter nodded, taking a bite of his sandwich. "We'll all go over for a bit today, then. The more hands, the more we get done."

Margaret wasn't certain she was ready to be thrust into local society, but she could hardly beg off when a family was in need.

"Janie has a toddler and one on the way any day," Marie-Louise explained as she returned to her chair. "And her husband's an old *boss*."

Jeffrey's spoon clattered against his bowl and he turned his head sharply in her direction. "Marie!"

"Well, he is," she said defensively. "He works her to death!"

Jason chuckled at their bickering, and Hunter said quietly, "We'll help her all we can."

"You could shoot the old bugger!" she said.

Jeffrey dropped his spoon. "Woman!" he bellowed.

Hunter raised both hands. "Peace, you two!" he commanded, and they both looked his way. "We can't change Janie's circumstances, Marie-Louise," he said quietly. "We can only lend a hand."

''You can't change what she doesn't want changed,'' Jeffrey stated firmly while Marie-Louise glared at him.

Maggie had remained silent through all of this, astonished by the heated argument. Hunter saw her frown and squeezed her hand briefly. ''They go on a bit, these two,'' he said as the others returned their attention to the meal.

The Feddler place was not nearly so grand a farm as Hunter's. The three-room hut suffered for lack of repairs, and the barn had great gaping holes where wallboards had sprung away and never been replaced.

Maggie rode to the small farm on a sprung buckboard seat, sandwiched between Hunter and Jason. Jeffrey and Marie-Louise sat or rolled around the wagon bed as they were jostled about on the rough road. Maggie realized rather quickly that the rolling around was mostly by design.

Hunter pulled the team and wagon up before the dilapidated house and handed the reins to Jason. ''I'll take the women in and pay my respects to Feddler,'' he said. ''I'll join you in the barn shortly.''

Not a question or comment stayed him as he jumped to the ground and turned to hold up his arms to Maggie. ''Come,'' he said simply, and she leaned forward, placing her hands on his shoulders as he bore her weight easily with his hands at her waist.

He released her, walked to the back of the wagon, and reached for Marie-Louise. But after he had set her on the ground, he teased, ''You're not getting a bit heavier, are you, girl?''

''Jeffrey and I will tell you when,'' she returned primly and winked at her husband as she turned toward the house.

Hunter took Maggie's hand and followed in the younger woman's wake as Jason drove the team off toward the outbuildings where they would feed the stock, clean stalls, and milk the cow.

"Feddler outlived his first wife," Hunter explained as he tucked Maggie's hand securely into the crook of his arm, "and they were childless all the years of their marriage. Her death left him bitter and disgruntled, but don't be afraid of him. Janie is much younger than he . . . younger even than you," he added, "but I don't think Feddler abuses her. He's simply a gruff old man, and his young wife tries very hard to please him. Don't let him upset you, my pet. He may howl like a wolf, but his bite is less than that of a mosquito."

Maggie was grateful for the warning, and her eyes told him so when she smiled up at him as he held the front door open for her to enter.

"I won't be far away," he added and he followed her into a room that was overstuffed with furniture from years gone by and a clutter of knickknacks on every surface. "His first wife was a collector of sorts," Hunter whispered lightly next to her ear, and Maggie coughed to cover a telltale giggle.

A very pregnant young woman turned away from Marie-Louise and came toward them then. She was dressed in a loose, flowing brown dress that boasted little shape except her burgeoning one. But her smile of greeting was sincere.

"Janie," Hunter said, taking the young woman's hand. "You're well?" he asked.

The girl, who appeared to be no more than sixteen, nodded happily. "Fine," she said simply and turned toward the woman at Hunter's side. "Your wife?" she asked, and Maggie began to suspect she was a woman of few words.

"This is Maggie," Hunter said in a way that made his new wife's head snap around in his direction; he had actually sounded *proud*! "I'll say hello to Feddler," Hunter announced after he had completed the introduction. "And leave you women to it," he added, squeezing Maggie's hand before he left.

Maggie turned her head slightly and spied a tiny, perfect blond creature riding the arm of a smiling Marie-Louise.

"Isn't she a sweet thing?" Marie-Louise asked, stepping closer to the two women. "This is Sarah," she announced and looked expectantly at Maggie.

The toddler was not yet two years old, Maggie guessed, but her alert blue eyes and smiling face would have captured the heart of anyone who came within sight of her. Sarah was a captivating little girl who played no favorites and sought the attention of any who would give it.

When her small arms reached out toward her, Maggie could not resist. She sat down and balanced the child on her forearm while her other hand steadied Sarah's back. Maggie was unfamiliar with very small children, but she took instantly to this one, keeping her occupied while Marie-Louise and Janie chatted and worked around the kitchen.

She was so engrossed with teasing and tickling the child, in fact, that she didn't notice Hunter's approach until he was beside her.

"Let me take her," he said, reaching out with both hands. The child immediately went to him. "Hello, Sarah my darling," he said softly, gently poking a finger into the rounded tummy. "Maggie, let me introduce you to Feddler before I leave to help the men." He balanced the child in the crook of one arm while he helped Maggie up from her chair. "How do you like this little mite?" he asked.

"I think she's wonderful," Maggie said happily, and then

a chill went through her as Hunter turned those intense, black eyes her way.

"Do you think we could share one of these someday?" he asked.

CHAPTER

❧ 19 ❧

That evening, after they had returned home, Maggie and Marie-Louise shared the kitchen duties, falling into an efficient routine. While Maggie set the table and cleaned up, the younger woman cooked. The two women talked quietly to each other as Maggie washed the supper dishes and Marie-Louise dried.

The men remained at the table, but Hunter found his attention drifting away from the talk of farming. Maggie was standing with her back to him, and Hunter caught only a glimpse of her face as occasionally she turned to her companion. He found himself wishing that they could be alone, that he could share the kitchen chores with her, just to have her turn her attention toward him. He was suddenly, selfishly, impatient to be alone with her.

When at last Maggie turned away from the sink to remove her apron, Hunter took a last sip of his coffee, ground out his cigar, and moved to her side. Taking her hand in his, he said to Marie-Louise, "You'll forgive me if I take her away for a while?" he asked.

Marie-Louise's eyes twinkled. "I don't know if I should let you," she said saucily.

Hunter laughed and pointedly ignored the remark as he pulled Maggie toward the door.

"Where are we going?" Maggie asked, as they stepped out into the sultry evening air.

"I want to show you that little mare," he said.

The moon lit their way as Hunter slowly led her toward the barn. He was in no hurry. It was pleasant to walk with her, her small hand tucked into his.

"The air is sweet," Maggie said, taking a deep breath. "Honeysuckle."

Maggie didn't know what to say after that. Hunter seemed to be in one of his quiet moods, and he was certainly taking his time in getting out to the barn.

"I like to walk," he said as he tipped his head back and searched the starlit sky. "Especially at night," he added softly. And then he smiled down at her. "Do you like to walk, little one?"

Maggie remembered walking with him years ago, when she was an innocent girl, falling madly into first love with the most handsome, the most considerate man she had ever known. They had not held hands then, as they did this night, but she could remember wanting to walk with him forever. "I like to walk sometimes," she said at last.

"And will you walk out with me?" he teased, lightly squeezing her hand.

Maggie looked up at him, puzzled. "As if we were courting?"

"Of course. Don't you think I'm courting you, Maggie?"

"But we're married," she returned, as if the idea of being courted now was outlandish.

"I think a beautiful woman deserves to be courted, even by her husband. *Particularly* by her husband."

Maggie turned slightly away. "Hunter, I wish you

wouldn't keep referring to me as a beautiful woman. We both know I'm not. It seems . . .''

Maggie stopped in mid-sentence when Hunter pulled up short and turned her to face him.

''That's another reason why I could kill that man from your past,'' he said evenly. ''He stole your confidence from you as well. You have no understanding of how truly lovely you are, Maggie.'' He cupped her face with his hands, his thumb lightly teasing the soft skin around the scar. ''I told you once before this doesn't detract from your rare beauty or what I see when I look at you,'' he added, his tone easing. ''I'm scarred, too, but I think I'm still beautiful,'' he teased.

Maggie stared, incredulous, before a slow smile crept across her lips. ''You're crazy!'' she said with a laugh. ''You're not scarred.''

''I am, too,'' he said, grinning at her. ''Remind me to show you my scar sometime when we're alone.''

He took her hand again, and they entered the dark barn. Maggie stood just inside the doors while Hunter lit the lantern hanging on the wall nearby.

''She's down here,'' he said, then led the way, holding the lamp high when he stopped at the door of a large box stall. ''This is her royal highness.''

Maggie peeked through the steel bars of the stall. ''Is that her name?'' she asked, her tutored eyes going over the filly.

''No,'' he said, hanging the lantern on a hook above their heads. ''I just like to think she'll eventually be the queen of my stables. Her name is Fancy That.''

Maggie laughed. ''Really?''

Hunter shook his head. ''Think we should change it?''

''No. I think it's cute. And she's a lovely mare, Hunter. She should do well for you.'' After a moment Maggie turned and pressed her back to the door of the stall. Hunter was standing very close, his dark eyes staring down at her.

''I think she'll do well,'' he said. And it was clear that he was not talking about the mare. His eyes moved upward, closely examining her hair before he touched a soft curl at her shoulder. "Do you know I *had* to bring you out here?" he asked, bracing his free hand against a bar near her shoulder. "I found myself sitting in that kitchen resenting the presence of my own friends, Maggie."

"Why?" she asked, her blue eyes searching his for an answer that should have been obvious.

He smiled. "You really don't understand, do you? I'm a grown man, but I feel like a lovesick boy. I want to be alone with you all the time. I find myself resenting my work and your work and anyone who takes you away from me." His hand caressed her face, her neck, and the length of her arm as he spoke. And Maggie found herself, not afraid, but awestruck by what he was saying. "I want to be with you, kissing you and touching you, and when I can't, I think about you."

He dipped his head, and Maggie knew she was about to be kissed. But she was so stunned by the things he'd said that she could offer no resistance. Did these things mean that he really did love her? she wondered. With her next thought, she dismissed the notion. He merely wanted her. He didn't know her well enough to love her, surely.

Hunter put his arms around her and pulled her lightly against him. "This will be a real kiss, little one," he breathed and slanted his lips across hers, pulling her close against his chest. "God, Maggie," he whispered, raising his head a fraction, only to return and trail velvety kisses over her face. Hunter carefully held his lower body away from her, but when he kissed her neck, he dared to place his hand just below her left breast.

Maggie could feel her heart thundering in her chest, but she did not think it was from fear. Rather, it was the warm and teasing things he was doing, and she could feel the heat of him even through their clothes. Something was happening within her that Maggie could not identify. It was similar to when she had shared the brandy with him . . . liquid fire running downward.

But then, without conscious effort, Maggie flinched away from him when he cupped her breast. Alarmed, she reached up and clamped her hand around his wrist, her pale blue eyes pleading with him.

"Don't," he whispered. "Just let me touch. Just let yourself *feel*, Maggie."

Her fingers remained around his wrist, but Maggie ceased her attempts to remove his hand from her. She was watching him as he stared down at her, his eyes watching the small circular motion of his thumb.

"You're lovely here, too," he whispered. "See how you respond to me, little one?" he asked. He raised his eyes to her and smiled the smile of one drunk on passion. "I think we had better stop now," he said huskily. "And I think I'd better head for the creek and a cold swim."

Maggie was chagrined having his hands on her and having to back out gracefully. What did one say after moments like these?

They went on for days and weeks. Hunter was relentless in his pursuit of her, sexually and otherwise. He teased, he cajoled, and he became bolder each time he touched her. Maggie soon became a quaking mass of nervous tension. A kind of tension that was completely foreign to her.

"What the devil is *wrong* with you?" Marie-Louise asked as they worked in the heat of a noonday sun over a steaming caldron of wash water.

Maggie straightened up from stirring the heavy clothes to brush a lock of hair back from her face.

"Have you got the curse or some other problem?"

Marie-Louise snapped. "I'd like to know so when you boss me around I can either sympathize with you or tell you to stow it!"

That caught Maggie's attention, and she seemed to wilt as she stroked her damp brow with the palm of one hand. "I'm sorry," she said softly. "I didn't mean to take it out on you."

"It?" Marie-Louise returned. "Do you want to talk about *it*?"

Margaret merely shook her head and stared at her new friend in such hopeless misery that Marie-Louise was forced to relent.

"I'm sorry," she sighed, dropping a dripping sheet back into the tub. "Let's get something cool to drink." She placed a damp hand on Maggie's shoulder and guided her toward the kitchen door.

A pitcher of chilled lemonade appeared magically from the root cellar, and Marie-Louise dampened two small cloths before they sat down at the table. "Now tell me what this is all about," she muttered around the cool cloth as she slowly stroked her face.

Maggie did likewise, feeling relieved of a great deal of grime as she took the cloth away. "There's nothing to tell," she said.

Her companion sat upright in the facing chair. "There is, too," Marie-Louise said forcefully. "And don't you lie, Maggie Maguire, or you'll turn into a toad!"

Maggie laughed at that. "Where do you get such notions?"

"Never you mind where I get them," Marie-Louise said sternly, reaching for her glass. "You'd best unload your mind before you pop a blood vessel."

Margaret stared at her candid friend, whom she had often secretly envied in the weeks past, and took a long sip of lemonade. Marie-Louise always seemed so free and easy with her Jeffrey, never concerned if others were around when they stared at each other or touched or even kissed quickly. Hunter stared and touched, but it only made Maggie want to jump right out of her skin.

"Do you mind making love with Jeffrey?" she asked, blushing at her own temerity and trying to hide behind her glass.

"Mind?" Marie-Louise laughed, obviously taken aback. "What a funny question."

"I mean,"—she hesitated, studying the grain in the wooden table—"do you *like* his lovemaking?"

Suddenly Marie-Louise sobered, sensing serious turmoil within the other woman, and it had nothing to do with the prowess of her man. Then again, perhaps it did. "I like it," she said softly. "Very much."

"Don't you ever resent the way you feel?" Maggie asked.

Marie-Louise reached out and covered Margaret's hand where it lay on the table. "How can I resent feeling special?" she asked.

Maggie's eyes met hers. "Special?"

"Every time," Marie-Louise answered candidly. "As many times as he wants me, I want him, too. And Jeffrey always makes me feel special."

Margaret frowned at that, staring down at the hand that covered hers. "But that's *all* men want," she said. "How can you not resent that?"

"Do you really believe that's all Mr. Maguire wants from you?"

Maggie nodded.

"I think you've lost your faculties," Marie-Louise said. "That man is crazy about you."

"That's what I mean," Maggie said fiercely.

"And I'll throw in *stupid!*" Marie-Louise added for good measure. "That man *loves* you!"

Maggie was clearly shocked by that revelation. "That's impossible!"

Marie-Louise frowned. "Why is that so impossible?" she asked reasonably and watched Maggie as a mixture of emotions flashed across her face. "So the problem isn't his," she said softly, taking a drink before studying a trickle of condensation running top to bottom on the glass. "It's yours."

Maggie darted an angry glance at the woman. "My problem is *him*."

"I don't think so," she returned thoughtfully. "The problem seems to be that you don't like what he does to you. Is that it?"

Maggie nodded. "I resent the control he has over me."

Marie-Louise thought that one statement contained more information than a grammar school textbook. "So you resent him, and you think all he wants from you is sex. You can't believe he loves you." She was warming to her topic now. "Well, I can set you straight on the last point, Maggie Maguire. That man is so much in love with you he's walking around bumping into doors. You know, I like you Maggie, but you can be a hard woman sometimes. Now, I figure you don't like being that way 'cause I've seen you moping around and thinking deep thoughts, and I guess you haven't been very happy. But if you resent him so much, you answer me this: How would you feel if something happened to Mr. Maguire? How would you feel if he got sick and died and you didn't have him anymore? How would you feel if he stopped loving you and he went looking for someone else? What would you do then? How would you feel? You answer me those questions, Maggie, and I'll tell you just how much you *resent* him."

The two women stared at each other, both troubled but for different reasons. When she could no longer hide her anxiety, Maggie covered her face with both hands. "What shall I do?" she choked.

"He's a fine man, Maggie."

"Yes."

"You like him?"

Maggie nodded her silver-blond head.

"You respect him?"

"Y-yes."

"And all this talk about resentment . . . ?"

Maggie lowered her hands to the table and worried the damp cloth with her fingers, bowing her head as she tried to express her feelings. "I didn't want to marry him, you see. I didn't want to leave my home. And then he and my father . . . well, they controlled my destiny. I didn't want to like Hunter, but my mind keeps playing tricks and I find myself looking to him for . . . I don't know . . . all kinds of things. I haven't wanted him to make love to me." She darted a glance at the other woman.

Stunned, Marie-Louise leaned forward and whispered, "You haven't *wanted* him to? You're not telling me that he *hasn't*, Maggie?"

Maggie nodded her head briefly and found she could not look into her friend's eyes.

"Oh, my God," Marie-Louise breathed. "I don't believe it. You're cheating yourself, Maggie. And him. All this because you resent him?" she asked. It seemed impossible to her that two people could live together and sleep together and care for each other and not make love.

"It's a little more involved than that," Maggie said. "But now I want . . . I mean . . . I don't know what to do."

"You know what I think, Maggie?" Marie-Louise asked quietly, taking her friend's hand again. "I think you just sort of slipped into loving him, and that's got you scared to death.'' She smiled patiently when Maggie looked up, wide-eyed. ''Don't you see? You didn't go off your food and get knots in your stomach and have your heart thumpin', because you didn't fall in love head first all of a sudden, like I did! But I think you love him, and you won't let yourself admit it because you're afraid he won't love you back. But that's bunk! Everyone around here can see he loves you except *you*! And I also think, whether you understand it or not, you're as frustrated as hell. You think about those questions I asked you,'' she pleaded, squeezing the hand that lay motionless under hers, ''because if you keep on this way, Maggie, you're going to lose him.''

A heavy silence fell between the two women as they stared at each other until Maggie became uncomfortable. She straightened in her chair, easing her hand free. ''I'll finish the washing,'' she said quietly.

Marie-Louise scowled. ''You take yourself out for a walk and do some thinking, my friend,'' she said, pushing Maggie toward the door. ''And don't you come back here until you've resolved this one way or another 'cause I'm sick of your moping.''

Maggie smiled at the chiding that should have sounded firm and didn't make it. ''Thank you,'' she said and darted toward the door.

She strolled past the kitchen garden toward a lane that led to the planted fields beyond the barn. The day was sultry; it hadn't rained for weeks. The dirt track had dried to dust, and she studied the small puffs that exploded around her sturdy black shoes as she took each step. It seemed to her that she was a lot like those puffs of dust much of the time, exploding and then settling, only to explode again. And Marie-Louise had been right: Her anger had resided with her for so long that she seldom had a thought that was not colored by it. Anger had channeled her thoughts into a narrow pattern, but she could see the wisdom of her friend's words. If she didn't change her ways she could lose Hunter. It was time to make up her mind.

The lane wandered to the left once she passed the barn, but Maggie could see all three men gathered at the fence of the large paddock off to her right. Pride was running free, striding in high form about the enclosure as the men watched. Jeffrey disappeared into the barn just as Hunter turned and saw her. He waved a greeting as he pushed off from the fence and walked her way.

Maggie clasped her hands behind her back and waited.

"Were you looking for me?" he asked as he wiped perspiration from his brow.

Maggie managed a timid smile. "I was just walking," she replied.

Hunter looked disappointed. His eyes darted toward the paddock and then returned to her. He was frowning slightly. "I should warn you, Maggie. We've got a mare in heat, and I want to put her in the paddock with Pride."

Maggie's eyes darted to where Jason stood at the fence, then rose to Hunter's again.

"I thought with the other men around . . ."

"Yes!" she said hurriedly. "I'll walk farther on." She turned quickly, hearing the mare trumpeting as she was being led from the barn.

Hunter's hand latched on to her arm, however, and he grinned when she looked back over her shoulder at him. "You could watch from the loft," he teased.

Maggie's brief frown of concentration disappeared. "You remember that!"

He nodded. "I remember everything about you, Maggie," he said softly, the intensity of his gaze making her decidedly uncomfortable. He watched her eyes dart away then, knowing he had frightened her off once again. ''You'd best go along, love.''

Maggie nodded, turning her attention to the winding of the lane. She'd best get along, she thought.

Love?

CHAPTER
20

Two hours later Maggie stormed into the kitchen and ran to the stove, halting at Marie-Louise's side. Her entrance was so thunderous that the other woman turned in alarm, holding a spoon, like a weapon, dripping gravy on the floor.

Staring at Maggie's red face, Marie-Louise looked quickly toward the door, saw nothing, and looked at her friend. "Is something chasing you?"

Maggie shook her head vigorously. "I need your help," she gulped, having left most of her breath out near the cornfield.

"Of course!" Marie-Louise cried, growing alarmed. "What on earth is wrong?"

"You have to teach me to cook before suppertime."

"What!"

"I need to make a special supper." Maggie took a deep cleansing breath and added, "For Hunter and me."

Marie-Louise narrowed her eyes, waving the spoon in agitation. "You mean you came charging in here like that because you want to cook supper?"

"You don't understand."

"No, I don't! I thought someone was hurt!"

"I'm sorry."

A slow knowing grin began to spread across the other woman's face. "Well, Lord love a duck!" she crowed. "We'd best get a move on!"

Maggie snatched up a cloth and began to wipe up the gravy from the floor while Marie-Louise planned coming events. "We'll start cooking supper, and then you'll need a bath. You're dripping wet from all that running." She clamped a lid on the iron pot on the stove. "This stew will do for Jeffrey and Jason and me." She giggled. "Jason will hate sleeping in the barn another night."

Maggie stood up, frowning. "Oh, no, he doesn't have to."

"Yes, he does, my friend. He prefers the barn to sharing the cottage with Jeff and me and you need this whole evening with your husband . . . alone." She stopped picking potatoes out of one of the wooden bins and turned with a small frown. "You do want him, don't you, Maggie? I mean . . . that's what this is all about?"

Maggie nodded. "I do want him," she said softly. "I only hope I know how to get him."

"Maggie," her friend drawled, "I have a feeling all you have to do is tell him." And then she threw back her head and laughed. "I *love it!*" she crowed again. "Let's get started!"

There was a bit of confusion when the men came up to supper that evening. Hunter had already bent over his basin of water and was washing vigorously, but Jason and Jeffrey were interrupted in the act of stripping off their shirts.

"Never mind that," Marie-Louise said to Jeffrey as she plopped a pie into Jason's hands. "You'll take this to the cottage for me, won't you, Jason?'' she asked and ducked back into the kitchen.

Hunter stood up, dripping water down his chest and frowning at the other men. ''What's this all about?''

Jeffrey shrugged, staring curiously at the kitchen door.

''Appears she's got a bee. . . '' Jason halted as Marie-Louise came toward her husband with a black pot still steaming from the stove. ''Watch your fingers, Jeffrey,'' she ordered as she held the stew out to him. ''Grab onto the cloths.''

''Marie-Louise, what the devil. . . ?''

''I just want you to carry this to the cottage,'' she said sweetly, smiling over her shoulder at Maggie, who had come to stand in the open doorway.

Jason's mind took hold of the situation as he was being ushered down the porch steps. ''Guess it's the barn for me again,'' he grumbled.

Hunter frowned at his three friends' backs for a moment before turning to his wife. ''What's going on?'' he asked at last.

Maggie lowered her eyes shyly. ''They're going to eat at the cottage tonight,'' she said quietly.

Hunter continued to study her face as he took the towel she offered. ''Now, why would they want to eat down at the cottage?'' he asked, cautiously keeping his mind blank in case it ran off in the wrong direction. Something was afoot, but it might not be what he was hoping.

''Don't you want to finish washing?'' she asked.

Hunter shook his head. ''No, I want to know why our friends aren't eating supper with us tonight.''

''I asked Marie-Louise to arrange for us to be alone,'' she admitted.

Hunter ran the towel over his face, afraid to ask his next question. ''Why would you do that, Maggie?''

She studied the floorboards as she answered. "I want us to have a special supper together. Just the two of us."

He could not help it; his mind shifted, the knot of fear left his stomach, and his heart began to pound with hope. He stepped closer to her, placed his forefinger under her chin, and raised her face. "Look at me," he commanded gently.

"I cooked for you!" she blurted and watched his frown turn to something that was not quite a smile but was infinitely tender.

"Did you, now." He looked down at the pale blue dress she was wearing. The collar was high on her slim neck, and the bodice was lacy. The tubular sleeves were made of the same lace, while the satin skirt hugged her waist and fell softly to the floor. His eyes roamed upward again; she had freed her hair of the braid and brushed it back softly from her face. His Maggie had taken pains with her appearance, it seemed. And she had plotted with Marie-Louise to be alone with her husband. Hunter smiled down at her. "I'll just finish washing up," he said simply and turned away to face the bench.

Maggie's heart had been thundering all through his long scrutiny of her, and now she didn't know what to say. As Marie-Louise had said earlier in the afternoon, she was as nervous as a hen around a hatchet.

And what had her most worried in this instant was the fear that her supper would not be edible. She dashed into the kitchen and peeked under the lids of several steaming pots as Hunter seemed to prolong his washing up.

He was, in fact, being extremely thorough, his mind running wild while he tried to persuade himself to settle down. He did not want to jump to any wrong conclusion and frighten her. Perhaps she merely wanted to talk alone with him.

As he dried his face, he noticed a clean white shirt hanging on a wall peg to his left.

One of the women must have left it there. . . . Maggie?

He set the towel aside, pulled the shirt on over his head, and walked into the kitchen to join his wife.

Maggie was bustling from stove to table and back again but managed a timid smile when she saw him enter. "Supper is ready," she said, taking the last of the serving dishes to the table. She stood anxiously beside her place, watching as Hunter came to stand beside her. His eyes fell to the table setting, noting the freshly cut flowers in the center. The earthenware pitcher that usually held the utensils had been removed, and knives and forks had been set beside each plate. Next to his place at the head of the table, she had left a tall bottle and crystal wine glasses accompanied their settings. She'd set out enough food for an army, he noticed, as he inspected a steaming platter of steak accompanied by rich gravy, buttered carrots, and tiny onions in white sauce.

He turned his head to look at her.

"The popovers almost burned" she said lamely.

"It looks wonderful, Maggie," he said quietly. "You did all this?"

"Well, Marie-Louise helped a lot."

"There's only one thing missing," he said, and her eyes darted around the table in alarm. "No, love," he said, reaching for her. "Everything is perfect." He took a small step closer, his hands going to her shoulders. "The one thing missing is my thanks," he said and pulled her into his arms and held her for a while.

"You'd best not thank me yet," she said anxiously.

But Hunter was not thinking of the meal she had prepared.

And neither was Maggie.

After a time he kissed her lightly on the cheek, pulled away from her, and held back her chair while she sat down.

"We should enjoy this before everything gets cold," he said and took his own place.

Maggie passed the platter of steak for him to serve. Beef was a rarity for them, but just the day before Feddler had repaid Hunter by slaughtering one of his animals and giving them the choicest cuts.

Hunter took ample of all she had prepared and poured them each a glass of wine while Maggie spooned some onions onto her own plate. And before she could take a bite, she felt his eyes on her and looked up to see him holding his glass aloft. Silently he toasted her, then raised the glass to his lips and sipped a small amount before setting it down beside his plate.

He propped his forearms on the table edge, staring down at his plate for a moment before he asked quietly, "Will you tell my why you've done this, Maggie?"

The silence grew until he glanced up to see her looking at him with concern and something else he could not identify. "I want to be a real wife to you, Hunter," she said at last, praying once again that she was not too late in reaching out for him. If he no longer wanted her . . . "I've been miserable for weeks, and I didn't understand why. And . . . I didn't know how to tell you. So I asked Marie-Louise to help me," she finished lamely.

He breathed again, raising his shoulders in relief as he reached out and squeezed her hand. "You simply had to say the words, Maggie. I've been waiting to hear them."

"That's what Marie-Louise said." As soon as the words were out of her mouth, Maggie wanted to snatch them back, but it was too late, of course.

He laughed at the dismayed expression in her eyes.

"You two must have had quite a talk today," he said as he cut into his steak.

"We . . . chatted," she admitted as her eyes followed the path of the meat to his mouth. Leaning forward a bit in her chair, Maggie awaited his reaction; and he gave it. The steak was wonderful, and the look he turned upon her told her so. Maggie sagged back in her chair in relief.

Seeing her droop like that made Hunter realize just how important this evening was to her. She was trying her best to make a statement and did not have the words at hand to make her meaning clear. And he understood that she might need more time—a lot must have happened within the space of one afternoon—but *he* had the words, and until this evening he had held them protectively within himself. The time for withholding was over, he decided.

She was smiling now, relieved that her meal was a success. Even though her wine remained untouched, Hunter passed his glass to her, and she sipped cautiously before returning it to his hand.

"Do you feel better now?" he asked and she smiled; she did. "You've made me a happy man tonight, Maggie," he said softly. "I want you to know that I care very much and I want you to be happy, too." His eyes continued to bore into hers as he added, "I want you to know that I love you," he said simply, "and there is no reason for you to be afraid of that."

"I'm not," she said in return.

"And I understand that you cannot say the same to me—not yet, at least—but that's all right, love. It's enough that you want to be my wife." Enough for now, he thought. "Do you understand what I'm trying to say?"

"I do *care* for you," she said shyly.

He smiled, reaching out to squeeze her hand again.

It was enough for now.

The entire meal was a tribute to the teaching abilities of Marie-Louise, and while Maggie found she could only poke at her food, Hunter did her efforts justice. They enjoyed some open, frank discussions and moved on to some lighter topics as, late in the evening, they cleared the table and washed up.

Hunter took a small portion of brandy with him as he followed her up the stairs to their room, wondering what she had thought about this aspect of their marriage during her busy day.

He did not have to wait long.

He entered the large bedroom a few paces behind her and found Maggie turning to watch him nervously again, just as she had when he had first tasted the steak. His eyes went instantly to the bed, finding that the covers had been turned back invitingly and the snowy white sheets boasted not one wrinkle. A vase of freshly cut flowers had been placed on the bedside table beside the lamp, which was glowing softly.

He turned to her and smiled again as Maggie clasped her hands tightly in front of her and smiled back. "I'm not certain I'll be as good at this as I am at cooking," she said.

He threw back his head and laughed. "Did your cohort instruct you to say that?" he teased.

Her smile slipped a little in confusion. "I mean it, Hunter," she said.

He nodded, reaching for her. "I know you do, Maggie, and you have nothing to worry about on that score." He tipped her head back and stared down at her. "You please me, woman," he breathed. "And you don't even have to lift a finger to try," he added as he lowered his head and slanted his lips across hers.

Maggie found this kiss intoxicating. They enjoyed the slight taste of wine on each other's lips, and she found herself growing breathless as the kiss deepened and all notion of time disappeared.

When Hunter pulled away, watching her as his hands dropped and spanned her small waist, Maggie's arms remained around his neck for a moment before she took her cue and started tugging his shirt out of the waistband of his trousers. Moments later the shirt sailed away into a shadowy corner, and Hunter turned her around without a word and unbuttoned the back of her dress. Maggie felt the shoulders and waist sag free seconds before he stepped around in front of her.

"I want to see you," he breathed and pulled the dress forward, letting it fall to her feet. He tugged at the drawstring of her petticoat, and it, too, fell to the floor. Next her lacy drawers were down around her ankles and he was reaching for the hem of the pretty camisole she wore, lifting it slowly upward, revealing her beauty a mere fraction at a time. "You're so lovely," he murmured and held one hand up for her to take as she stepped out of the puddle of material at her feet.

She stood shyly before him, uncomfortable with having someone see her this way. Still, Maggie was determined. She reached out hesitantly toward the waistband of his trousers, but Hunter caught her wrist.

"Let me do that tonight," he said, understanding that this was difficult for her. "One step at a time, my darling," he added and bent to scoop her up in his arms and hold her securely against his chest as he walked to the bed. He was reluctant to let go of her but laid her slowly in the center of the white sheets and then turned to sit on the edge of the bed to remove his boots.

Maggie watched him as he stood to unfasten his trousers. He hooked his thumbs in the waistband and quickly peeled the trousers down the length of his dark, muscular thighs. His flanks were tight and muscular as well, and it occurred to her that she had not realized how much dark hair covered his body. She then reminded herself quite ruefully that she had never allowed herself to look at him before.

Naked now, Hunter lay down beside her and drew the sheet up to his waist as he turned on his side to face her.

"Could I have my woman back now?" he teased and moved closer to her. "God, Maggie!" he breathed, as her arms went around him and he buried his face in her luxuriant hair. "You smell sweet and lemony," he said quietly, his hand roaming down her back. But he was careful to hold his lower body away from her for just a while longer while his hands and mouth roamed over her face and shoulders. His chest lightly teased her breasts as he bent over her, devoting considerable attention to the soft spot beneath her ear.

Maggie nervously searched her mind for what she should do or say now. Should she talk or touch? Should she kiss him?

"Did Pride take to the mare?" she whispered, and almost immediately Hunter's shoulders began to shake. "Hunter?" She frowned, her arms tightening around him briefly before she realized what was happening. . . . He was laughing!

Maggie punched his arm. "Hunter Maguire!" she chided, cursing him with his own name.

Hunter rolled away and fell onto his back. "God! Don't get me thinking about that!"

Maggie reared up and over him. "It's not funny!" she sputtered.

He nodded his head vigorously, tears of merriment pooling in the corners of his eyes. "It is!" he choked. "I'm fighting to control my ardor, and you have to put that picture in my mind!"

Maggie's confusion lasted for a moment longer as she stared down at her laughing husband, but then she, too, understood and began to laugh softly. "I'm sorry," she said.

Hunter hooked an arm around her neck and drew her down onto his chest. "You should be," he teased as his laughter began to subside. "You could have ended our evening before it had even begun."

She smiled down at him, making herself comfortable by propping her arms on his chest. ''Really, Hunter?'' she asked, and in spite of her light tone, he understood that she was genuinely curious about it all.

''Really,'' he said, pulling her up and over his body. ''I'm aching for you, my love, and that makes the situation tenuous at best.'' He drew her head down then, kissing her lightly as one hand began to roam the length of her body. ''I want you to find your pleasure and understand it before I seek mine,'' he breathed.

He slowly turned her onto her back then, propping himself up on his side. He kicked the sheet to the end of the bed and away, then took his time inspecting her body. She was long-legged despite her lack of height. She had a narrow waist and pleasingly full breasts. Her abdomen was flat, and it was here his hand fell first, spanning her pelvic bones with his hand as if carefully considering her capacity to carry his sons. He dropped a quick kiss on her belly as his hand continued down her thigh and his lips worked their way with painstaking slowness toward her breast. Once there, he teased a taut, dark nipple with his tongue and felt Maggie arch her back in reaction. ''Good,'' he breathed as he turned his attention to her other breast. ''You like that,'' he said with conviction.

Maggie found her eyes closing as she concentrated on the maddening tremors shooting through her body. She placed her hand on the back of his head, begging him with the slight pressure of her palm to continue this amazing agony. He had touched her there before, but always there had been clothing between them. She had felt teased and somehow cheated then. Now, she was beginning to understand why she had been tense and miserable all these weeks during his courting.

His hand had wandered high between her thighs, and Maggie's initial reaction was to reach down and grasp his wrist. He moved up along her side, teasing her chin as his lips traveled toward her mouth and his fingers stroked her hip. "I know, darling."

"I'm sorry." She raised her lips to his as he teased them. "I thought I had settled this in my mind. I just. . . Please don't stop." She closed her eyes, embarrassed that she had turned coward after promising herself she would not.

Hunter knew a few brief moments of angry frustration that she should be so apprehensive about something that should be so very special between them. He did not want her to feel afraid. He wanted her to feel only physical desire.

Maggie opened her eyes and watched her husband prop himself up, his elbow close to her shoulder. He raised a hand to lightly brush tiny wisps of hair back from her temple.

"Do you know about finding release?" he whispered.

Maggie shook her head. "No."

He ducked down his head, and his tongue outlined the ridge of her ear.

Maggie shivered in response.

"Then I must tell you that what happens here between us will be a mutual thing, little one." His lips moved slowly along her jawline and he kissed her between words, his hand returning to her breast. "You must not fear anything you feel, Maggie," he breathed. "Only good will come of it."

Maggie had closed her eyes again, totally abandoning herself to the feel of his hands on her. The finest brandy in the world could not duplicate these feelings of hot liquid coursing through her. Her breathing became labored, as did Hunter's, and she feared they would both expire on the spot.

Hunter felt the tension building within her as her body strained and twisted toward him. His hand sought that most intimate part of her then, his fingers teasing her determinedly. He smiled at Maggie's chagrin. "It's fine, my love. It means you're ready for me. It's natural." He felt her body tense slightly as his words trailed off.

Hunter put his other arm under her back, pulling her close into the security of his body as he continued to play with her, whisper to her, and lave her taut nipples. And then he received his reward. Maggie groaned and arched up hard against him, crying out his name as her fingers dug into the muscles of his shoulder.

"Little one," he whispered as she wrapped her arms around his back and pressed her face against his shoulder. "Maggie," he breathed as he pulled away slightly, hovering over her a moment before slowly lowering his body between her open thighs. He rested there, gathering control in order to prolong the moment. But Hunter had wanted her for *so* long.

Stunned, Maggie turned fully onto her back as he directed and lay staring up at him as she felt him shift upward and slowly fill her body. "Oh, Maggie," he breathed as he nuzzled her ear. He seemed to want to rest within her, and Maggie raised her arms, inviting him to lower his weight upon her as she welcomed him into her embrace. This, too, was a curious experience—no fear, no pain, just a rush of feelings.

Her embrace was about all that Hunter could endure, however, and he made several long slow movements with his hips before he drew back and quickly pressed forward, shuddering with an intensity that frightened Maggie as he gained his own release.

They clung to each other for a time, Hunter conscious of his weight on her but knowing instinctively that she was not ready to let him go.

"Are you all right?" she whispered.

Hunter smiled against her hair. "I think I'm supposed to ask that of you, love."

"It's just . . . It seemed . . . so violent."

Hunter raised his head and frowned down at her. "For whom?"

"You," she said shyly.

His smile returned with that. "I think it will always be like that between us, Maggie."

Maggie's mind was a mass of tender thoughts, but she could not bring herself to utter them and sound any more foolishly unsophisticated than she already had. The tender words would wait until she felt more sure of herself. Instead she teased, "Well, it was quick, Hunter Maguire," and he laughed against her shoulder.

"I'm not finished with you yet, woman, so don't get too cocky."

She smiled up at the ceiling and stroked his back in slow, wide circles; he had stated a fact and she was the holder of the evidence. And most amazing of all, she was content!

Hunter planted his elbows on either side of her and raised himself up. Smiling down at her, he said, "You didn't waste much time yourself," and he raised a hand to stroke her cheek. "You're all right, aren't you, love?" he asked, his dark eyes staring into her smiling blue ones. He wasn't asking after the state of her health; he was worried about the state of her mind.

"I'm perfectly fine," she said quietly, and he ducked his head down to suck lightly on her lower lip.

Maggie felt him move lightly, easing upward and rotating his hips until a tiny flashing tremor surprised her. She arched back, pressing her head into the pillow as she said his name with obvious surprise.

He became alert then, realizing the swiftness of her arousal. "Move your hips," he whispered and placed a hand at her waist to guide her movements.

Within moments Maggie's body exploded into furious shudders as he held her tight against him.

After a moment she went limp in his arms, and he

lowered her down onto the pillow while he continued to smile at her. "That was something," he said, and a heated blush rose up from her bosom to the roots of her hair.

He laughed softly at her consternation and lightly caressed her cheek, using the brief interval to regain control over his own desires. Then he eased himself away from her. "I think I'd best leave you alone for a bit," he murmured. "I don't want you to be sore."

"Where are you going?" she asked quickly, betraying her need to keep him close.

"Across the room, silly girl," and he looked down at his body. "Where else would I go in this condition?"

Maggie's eyes followed his and then flew to his face again. "Oh," she said quietly.

He laughed, bending to peck her cheek before he bounded up from the bed.

When he moved beyond her sight, Maggie was too exhausted to turn over and see what he was doing. Instead she just lay where he had left her and curled up like a weary kitten.

Her eyes snapped open the instant she felt his weight on the bed, however, and she stared curiously at the damp cloth in his hand.

"This is for you," he said and shook his head when she reached up for it. "Roll onto your back," he ordered and pushed her back before she could imagine his intent.

When he lowered his hand, she understood. "You can't do that!" she said and quickly clamped a hand onto his wrist.

Hunter's eyes returned to her then. "Why not?" he asked reasonably. "I've touched you there."

"But . . . it seems so. . . ." Her frown grew with her confusion.

"Intimate?" He eased her hand from his arm, ignoring

her protest. "Wait until we share a bath," he teased, darting a smiling glance at her.

"We won't be sharing a bath," she returned. The very idea!

"Why not?" he asked again and Maggie thought about it for a moment.

"Did Pride take to the mare, Hunter?"

CHAPTER
❧21❧

Maggie and Hunter alternately made love and talked with each other all night, with the result that they were both sound asleep long after the cock crowed. And they took a bit of good-natured chiding later on—Marie-Louise to Maggie and Jason and Jeffrey to Hunter—but on the whole everyone was pleased at the newfound closeness between the two.

Maggie felt that her life had begun again; she was reborn through the eyes of Hunter Maguire. He had taken to wife a woman who had thought to remain always alone, and he had rebuilt her confidence and her desire to live life to the fullest. He told her she was special, and she felt special. He told her she was loved, and she felt loved. He told her she was a sweet innocent, and she believed him. And, wonder of wonders, he told her she was beautiful, and she felt beautiful. The small scar below her cheek and the much larger, more worrisome scars inside her began to fade under his persistence.

Margaret Downing Maguire began to break free. She set her anger and resentment aside and began to learn from others the way to truly live and share.

And all because of one stubborn half-Cherokee who remembered an engaging child and coaxed her into being a woman.

A celebration of sorts took place in late September when Marie-Louise announced, much to the chagrin of her red-faced husband, that she was expecting their first child.

"A baby!" Marie-Louise cried, falling into her friend's arms when she and Maggie were alone.

"You can't believe it?" Maggie asked, joining in the exultation of the younger woman.

"It seems we've waited forever!"

Maggie looked around the yard, well beyond the point where the two women sat on the porch. Satisfied that they were alone, she asked, "How did you know?"

"What?" her friend asked, disbelieving.

"What were the signs?"

Marie-Louise told her.

There came a chill day in late October when Maggie and Marie-Louise worked for endless hours salting and dressing a pig and a deer for winter. The men had built substantial fires in the yard near the house and hung two giant black caldrons low over the flames so that the women could cook every last piece of edible meat.

Maggie was stirring brine in a deep barrel while Marie-Louise cleaned sausage casings. Maggie spied her husband forking hay from a flat wagon near the barn. He had removed his light jacket and rolled his shirtsleeves high up on his arms; his skin would be scratched and pricked raw by evening, she knew. She would have the tin of salve waiting that night in their room. Standing on her toes, Maggie waved, smiling when he returned the greeting.

"I'm waiting for another celebration," Marie-Louise said slyly, and Maggie turned a curious frown her way. "You two are almost as bad as Jeffrey and I are," she teased. "The way you're going, you're bound to get caught soon."

Maggie laughed a little and then grew strangely serious. "Do you think I'm barren, Marie-Louise?" she asked quietly. "I had to turn him away just this week."

"Piddle pups!" the younger woman announced and moved to Maggie's side, placing a reassuring hand on her shoulder. "You've only been married a few months. And you got a late start, as I remember. Besides, I was *forever* getting around to this, and it wasn't for lack of tryin'."

Maggie smiled thankfully. Then, as she turned her head toward the other woman, she spied a single rider storming toward the barn. "Who could that be?" she asked.

Marie-Louise turned to see a man jumping from a lathered horse, handing something to Hunter.

"Somebody from town, maybe," she mumbled. "About the auction, do you think?"

Maggie shook her head, not knowing why a man would rush so to their home. He spoke only briefly to her husband, and then Hunter was shaking hands before the man mounted his horse and rode off at a slower pace.

Maggie let go of the wooden paddle she had been using and watched across the distance, lifting her apron and wiping her hands as Hunter studied a piece of paper and then raised his head in their direction.

"It's a letter," Maggie whispered and broke into a smile. "From my father and sisters perhaps!"

Maggie broke into a run then, lifting her plain woven skirt to her knees as she made a path toward him. Only when she realized he was not hurrying to show her the letter did Maggie stop in confusion. "Is it from Papa?" she called.

Hunter shook his head, quickening his pace to reach her, wondering why God had set *him* to tell her.

"Let's go inside the house," he said when he stood before her.

Maggie shook her head, looking down at the crumpled paper in his hand. "I want to see the letter, Hunter," she said reasonably. She did not like the way he was behaving, and she began backing away from him.

"Maggie," he said softly, reaching out toward her and staring into her troubled eyes. "It isn't a letter, pet," he said quietly. "It's a message from Denise . . . about your father."

Maggie avoided his hand, knowing instinctively that he was conveying bad news. "Let me see it!"

"I'll tell you," he said softly, the pain in his gut growing as he watched a worried frown creep across her pretty face. "Your father—"

Maggie instinctively knew what he was about to say before the words could leave his mouth. "No!" she cried and turned to run from him.

Hunter caught her with little effort, his long legs taking only seconds to gain her side. And then he grasped both of her upper arms. "Maggie . . ."

"He's dead!" she cried. "Don't tell me that!"

"I'm sorry, darling," he said and pulled upward on her arms as her knees seemed no longer able to support her. "Oh, Maggie," he whispered, pulling her up against his chest. "I'm so sorry."

Marie-Louise had run the length of the yard by now and stood staring at them in alarm.

Hunter looked at her with a worried frown. "It's Maggie's father," he explained and stooped to pick Maggie up in his arms. "Come with us to the house," he said, and Marie-Louise fell into step beside him.

"Tell me you're lying," Maggie cried against his neck, but she knew he wouldn't lie to her, and her arms tightened around him. "How can it be?" she asked.

Hunter's arms tightened around her. "I don't know, my

love,'' he breathed against her ear. He wanted to absorb her pain, and yet he knew he could not.

Maggie continued to cry, drenching his shirt with her tears, as Marie-Louise darted ahead and held open the door for him.

''If you want to take her into the parlor,'' she said, ''I'll fetch some water.''

Marie-Louise sped into the room while Hunter sat in a large chair before the cold fire, his weeping wife held firmly against his chest. He nodded and smiled when Marie-Louise held up his precious bottle of fine brandy.

''I want to go home, Hunter,'' Maggie whispered brokenly against his shoulder.

Hunter accepted a plain glass half filled with brandy. ''I know, love,'' he said softly, ''and I'll take you there. Drink some of this now.'' He held the glass close to her mouth, but she would not lift her head to drink. ''Come, now,'' he ordered, and Maggie automatically obeyed the tone of command.

Marie-Louise, not knowing what to do, began to build a fire against the late afternoon chill. She felt bad for her dear friend, and her eyes kept darting back over her shoulder, seeing Hunter's strong hand stroking his wife's back. And then he seemed to notice her own despair and held out a hand to her.

''Come along,'' he said softly, and Marie-Louise moved quickly across the few paces between them, dropping to her knees, her side against Hunter's thigh.

''I'm sorry, Maggie,'' she whispered.

CHAPTER

❧22❧

"It looks tired and care-ridden," Maggie murmured.

Hunter ducked his head toward her. "Pardon, darling?" he asked, and she repeated her comment. Hunter had her tucked close against his side as the rented hack drove them from the train depot to Treemont. They were entering the grounds now, and Hunter tried to view her home as Maggie was seeing it.

"I hadn't noticed before," she continued softly as her eyes roamed her beloved home. "Being away . . . coming back . . . I hadn't realized until now."

In fact he had noticed last summer that the place could use a bit of refurbishing, but times had been hard for most southerners and he had thought nothing of it.

Maggie had not slept properly or taken much food for the past forty-eight hours. She was worried about her sisters and about Treemont, but she had not yet begun to miss her father; that would come later.

"You mustn't worry about the farm, Maggie," he said softly. "Leave that to me. Right now there is something of greater importance we must discuss."

She turned her face up to him then.

He smiled and kissed the tip of her nose, the most aggressive action he had offered for two days. He had simply held her when she needed holding and listened when she chose to talk. "I love you," he said softly. "Remember that."

"Is that what you want to discuss?" she asked, and he shook his head. She was serious; not a laugh line crinkled around her eyes.

"I want to discuss your sisters, little one," he said. "Denise will soon be off and married, but Florence and Jennifer will have certain fears."

"Denise cannot marry now," she returned quickly.

He silenced her with a forefinger against her lips. "We'll discuss Denise's and Timothy's situation with them in due course. For now I think we must reassure Jennifer and Florence that they will always have a home with us."

Margaret Downing Maguire stared intently at her husband, her blue eyes moist, purple circles of fatigue outstanding below her fair lashes, and then she reached up and put both arms around his neck. "You would take them in?" she asked.

He wrapped his arms around her and squeezed gently. "Of course, we will," he said lightly. "They are sweet innocents, and they're your sisters. Of course they'll live with us."

"I thought you might expect Denise—"

"Denise is not much more than a girl, and she has a new life to start. She cannot care for two younger sisters, and I would never dream of asking it. You and I are much more suited and much more established. We'll care for them and love them, Maggie."

Maggie dropped her arms from around his neck and wrapped them around his back as she settled herself comfortably, her cheek against his chest. He was large and warm and secure. He was becoming day and night, and all seasons. He was a man to be reckoned with when he set his mind to something, but he was, above all else, a man of gentle, loving ways. He was her husband.

"You are a remarkable man, Hunter Maguire," she said.

"I am a simple man," he returned.

"A loving man," she breathed. "A man a woman could love."

He waited, holding his breath as he prayed for her to continue.

"I think I do," she said in a voice that was so soft he could barely hear it, a voice that quavered with fatigue.

He waited another long moment before smiling his understanding, his right hand coming up to stroke her cheek softly. "You'll let me know when you've come to a decision?" he teased, knowing she was too weary to jest in return. He knew only that he'd had to lighten the moment, for his heart's sake.

Maggie knew only that her feelings toward him had changed greatly. She did not know if these feelings could be called love, but she thought so. Hunter had become important to her. His happiness and comfort had become important to her. Yes, she supposed she was in love. Quite desperately in love.

Hunter felt Maggie stiffen against him as she raised her head and realized they were approaching the house now. She pushed away from him, smoothed the skirt of her traveling suit, and turned her head his way after she had surveyed the people who had emerged from the front door of the stately old homestead. She looked sad and devastated in that moment, and Hunter reached out and gripped her hand while he silently wished again that he could save her from this pain of loss.

"It . . . won't be the same," she murmured.

He smiled reassuringly. "No, it won't, my darling."

There were no words of wisdom to offer her, and they both understood that.

All three sisters were waiting for the approach of the hack. Timothy Fletcher, Denise's fiancé, stood behind them. Hunter had met the younger man only once and had been impressed with this quiet doctor who was so obviously devoted to Denise. That was just as well, he thought now, for they would soon be related by marriage, and he and Timothy would no doubt have many long discussions about the care of the Downing girls and the fate of Treemont.

Hunter alighted first from the carriage and turned to help his wife, who was quickly surrounded by three weeping young women. Over Maggie's head, he nodded to Tim, who had chosen to stay back a pace or two, and then placed a hand lightly on Maggie's shoulder.

Young Jennifer broke away first and ran toward him, tears flowing freely down her ivory cheeks.

Hunter's heart twisted as he held out his arms to her. "Hello, monkey," he said softly as she ran hard against him, her cheek against his waist as she wrapped her thin arms around him.

"We lost our papa," she cried.

Hunter bent and picked her up, and Jennifer's head dropped trustingly to his shoulder. "I know, sweetheart," he said.

Maggie watched him holding her sister. Jennifer was too big to be held like that, but against Hunter's size she seemed small and vulnerable. And, with Florence under one arm, Maggie found herself stepping next to him, tucking her small hand around his arm; she *needed* him.

Tim saw to the unloading of the luggage from the hack and then stepped forward. "Let's go into the house," he said as he put his arm around Denise's shoulders. "Everyone here is exhausted," he told Hunter. "And I'm sure you are as well."

It was true. Tim's mother had come to stay and help in any way she could, but the kindly woman could not assuage the grief within the household. They had slept little.

"I'll take your suitcases in once I've introduced you to everyone," Tim added as he and Denise led the way inside.

Friends and neighbors, he said, had come to express their sympathy and their concern over the fate of three young women who were now without parents. The girls had been inundated with questions about their future, and while everyone was well-meaning, Timothy told Hunter that the attention had only added to the distress the girls already felt.

The two men stared silently at each other as they stood inside Treemont's entrance. The next few days would be a test of everyone's emotional endurance.

In fact, the four young women presented a brave front to the world. Only when they were alone did they share their heartaches. Hunter and Tim stood quietly by, just being there.

The funeral was an ordeal in which Maggie and Denise stood stiffly, holding the hands of their younger sisters.

They returned to the house in the late afternoon. Early in the evening Mrs. Fletcher decided that the interval of visiting with friends and neighbors had gone on long enough. She encouraged Florence and Jennifer to go to bed, and Maggie insisted on seeing them to their rooms.

"I want to sleep in Florence's bed," Jennifer whined tiredly as she pulled a white, cotton nightgown over her head.

"All right, Jen," Maggie said quietly as she smoothed the thick braids back over Jennifer's slim shoulders. "But you must *sleep*," she added firmly.

The two younger girls shared a room that was cluttered with collections of their favorite things—dolls that had been given up by their maturing sisters and an abundance of junk, from rocks to ribbons, that Jennifer was fond of saving. Twin beds dominated the room, and a small table stood between.

Maggie sat on a chair in a corner of the room while Jennifer stood before her.

"What will we do, Maggie?" Jennifer asked. "I don't think Florence and I can look after Treemont."

Maggie smiled sadly at the thought and reached out to stroke her sister's slim arms. "Don't you worry about Treemont," she said quietly. "Hunter told me not to worry, and you mustn't, either."

Jennifer's brows crinkled with another worried thought. "But Denise will move to town, and—"

"You are not to worry, Jen," Maggie said again. She noticed that Florence had changed into her nightclothes and was sitting on the side of her bed, listening intently. "Hunter and I will look after you both. You mustn't worry about being alone."

"But you live far away," Jennifer returned, growing teary-eyed again.

Maggie pulled her up against her. "We'll be together, Jen," she whispered. "All of us."

A large shadow fell across them then, and Maggie looked up to see Hunter staring down at them. "All of us, monkey," he said. When Jennifer raised her head from Maggie's shoulder, he shooed her toward the bed. "You must get some sleep now. Both of you," he said, smiling at Florence, who had scrambled under the covers on her bed. The girl looked frail and thin, and the dark circles under her eyes worried him.

"I'm going to sleep with Florence," Jennifer said.

Hunter nodded and watched her lie down beside her sister. He pulled the blankets over them both and sat on the edge of the bed, smiling down gently as they stared at him. "Your sister and I have already discussed this," he said quietly. "We love you both, and we want you to live with us. Now, is that all right with you?" He looked from one to the other, and they both nodded, sleepy-eyed. "Good. And if you are worried about something, you'll tell us?" He smiled at their whispers of agreement. He reached out and touched their hands. "Will you sleep now?" he asked, and they nodded once again. "Good." He bent to kiss them each lightly on the forehead, then straightened and waited for Maggie to do likewise.

Maggie whispered good night and something else he couldn't hear. Then she walked toward the door and out into the hall before Hunter had even lowered the wick of the lamp.

He closed the door and stepped up behind her; Maggie was leaning heavily against the wall, her head lowered. Without a word, Hunter turned her into his arms and held her while she wept. She cried silently, her heart breaking for the two young girls who seemed so alone and bewildered. And she cried for her own loss and for the father she would never see again.

"They're so afraid," she whispered.

"We'll find a way to reassure them," he said quietly. "Come to our room now," he added. "I know it's early, but I think you could use a little sleep."

She shook her head and pulled away from him, trying to regain her composure, but it was easier to melt against him and let him be her strength. "We have a houseful of people," she said at last.

"I'll make your excuses. You need some rest, and they'll understand that."

"Denise is alone down there."

"Denise is with Tim. I saw him take her outside for some air. You have to worry about yourself now, Maggie," he said firmly. "Your sisters will need you, and you'll be of little help to them if you're exhausted."

Maggie hadn't allowed herself the luxury of thinking about being tired; there were simply too many other things to think about and too much to do. She had functioned under nervous tension for days now, and she knew that was why she was so weepy. Hunter must be truly sick of seeing her cry.

Nodding in agreement to his suggestion, Maggie lowered her eyes as she took a first mechanical step toward the room that had been hers and that she would now share with her husband.

Seeing the weary droop to her shoulders, Hunter hesitated not one moment. He swept her up in his arms and carried her down the dark corridor.

"I can walk," she murmured, lowering her head and pressing her lips against his neck.

"Tonight I'm not so certain about that," he said quietly as he entered a room that looked much like the bedroom of a very young girl. The bed was too short for him, and he scowled as he eyed the thing.

He laid her gently on the bed and removed her black shoes. Then, raising the skirt of the simple black dress, he reached under its hem and drew off one stocking at a time.

"I can get undressed," Maggie said softly as she watched him.

He reached for the buttons of her dress. "I've seen you undress," he said lightly. "Tonight, allow me."

"Why are you so good to me?" she asked.

His hands grew still just below her breasts. "I thought you understood that, pet," he said simply. "I love you."

"I've given you a lot of trouble."

He continued with his task, his eyes moving away from her face to watch his progress. "I happen to think you're worth it."

"I haven't been very . . . loving," she said in a small voice, propping herself up on both elbows. "I mean . . .

other than when . . . I don't mean when we're . . . together.''

Hunter frowned, trying to follow her, then sat on the bed beside her hip. "Together?" he asked.

She allowed her head to drop back onto the pillow, and her eyes moved away to stare at the curtained windows. "I mean . . . I think I'm loving when we're together. You know.''

"When we're making love, Maggie?" He gently took the hand that rested at her waist. "You *are*, pet. What's this about?" he asked, seeing her struggle with whatever was on her weary mind.

"All that has happened these past few days . . ." she whispered, rolling away from him. "I can remember when was very small and my mother and father would laugh and touch each other. My father's eyes would always go to her whenever she entered a room. I think they must have been very much in love. And . . . I remember the way they were together. I haven't been able to offer that to you." Her soft voice trailed off.

Hunter placed one hand on the mattress in front of her, leaning forward. Her eyes had closed. Sleep had stealthily enveloped her and eased her thoughts, at least for the moment.

"You've given me more than you know," he whispered, having gained more knowledge from those words uttered in half-sleep than she would ever suspect. There had been times, occasionally, when his courage had almost failed him and he had feared he was walking a fool's path with her. It would have been so easy for her to hurt him that once or twice he had almost felt the urge to withdraw in order to protect himself. But then he would look at her or smell the subtle distinctive fragrance of her or hear her laugh, and he would again realize that he would never leave her simply because she could not offer what he needed most. He would be with her until the end of his days regardless of whether or not she ever came to love him as deeply as he loved her.

But there had also been occasions when he had been greatly encouraged. And as he eased her out of her clothing, leaving only her lacy drawers, he understood that she had gone beyond merely wanting him, beyond needing a husband and companion, beyond feeling protected by him. Maggie had offered a first tantalizing hope that she was well beyond merely caring for him.

. Maggie had not so much as stirred during the time it took to get her settled, so deep was her sleep. Now Hunter drew the crisp white sheet and warm quilt up over her as he bent and kissed her softly parted lips. Their path had not yet been cleared of all the vines and thorns that could entrap them, but somehow Hunter knew they would survive together and emerge beyond it all to find some peaceful meadow.

CHAPTER

❧23❧

Timothy had seen the last of the guests depart, including his own family. He had sent Denise up to her bed even though evening had barely fallen and he was loath to have her leave his side. He could never have enough time with her, it seemed, but tonight she could barely converse, and he knew he must let her go.

Hunter appreciated the quietness of the house when he returned to the main floor, although he felt bad about not fulfilling his duties as host.

"I had planned to explain Maggie's absence," he said, walking across the room and sitting before the fire, opposite the younger man.

"I made your apologies, and everyone understood," Tim said, getting to his feet. "I don't know about you, but I could use something stronger than the coffee we've been drowning ourselves in all day." He waited until Hunter nodded his agreement before turning toward the small table in the corner of the room that held several crystal decanters.

Hunter sat back, crossing his long legs and resting one arm along the back of the settee. He watched Tim pour two generous amounts of Alastair's fine brandy into snifters. He rubbed his tired eyes, then noticed the solemn Anna clearing the remains of food and platters in the dining room.

"Thank you," he said as Tim extended a glass to him. He silently toasted the man before sipping. "I never hoped to have need of a drink," he said smiling. "But I need this one."

"Agreed."

The two men stared into the blazing fire that warmed the room against the chill of the fall evening and simply enjoyed the silence after the long days of people coming and going and the strain of seeing their loved ones suffer.

"Your family returned to town?" Hunter asked, for want of another opening to the conversation.

"Mother felt the girls would be in need of some privacy for a few days, and she's done all she can here for now."

"You'll stay?" Hunter asked. He suspected Tim would not leave Denise.

"I'll be comfortable enough in the guest room."

"Had Alastair been ill, Tim?" Hunter asked after a time, looking thoughtfully into the dancing flames. "I can hardly believe that a man his age just didn't wake up."

"I think he had, but when I suggested as much he brushed off my concerns," Tim said. "There's been some talk that Treemont isn't doing well." He leaned forward to rest his elbows on his knees and study the glass in his hands. "I suppose that's fairly obvious. Some of the fields have been left untended, and there isn't much help around the place. This farm once employed a number of full-time hands. Now I think only Anna and two boys are left to do the bulk of the work. But Alastair would never confide in me." He raised his head and smiled. "Not that we didn't get along, mind you. I don't believe Alastair confided in anyone after Margaret died.

"He took his worries to his grave, and I'm concerned

about what you will find here." Tim was astute enough to realize that Hunter would assume responsibility for Treemont, and he would bow to his greater experience. "I'll do whatever I can to help, whatever you ask. I only hope I'm wrong about the financial state of the farm."

Hunter's eyes returned to the fire. He frowned as he mulled over the information Tim had provided. "You have a great many patients who need your attention," he said quietly. "I'll take a look at Alastair's books, and in a few days we'll talk again."

"If Treemont is threatened"—Timothy seemed uncertain about how to word his concern—"Florence and Jennifer . . ."

Hunter tried to reassure the young doctor. "They will live with Maggie and me," he said.

Tim nodded, obviously relieved. "They are fine girls but . . ."

"You needn't feel guilty, Tim," he said kindly. "I'm very fond of those girls, and you and Denise have yet to establish your own lives. There is not a doubt or a concern in my mind over the matter."

There was, however, a concern that Tim wished to address. "About Denise," he said quietly, lounging back and taking a substantial drink before he spoke. "We were to be married next month, but of course that's out of the question."

"Why?"

Tim looked surprised. "She'll be in mourning."

"That's true, and a large wedding would certainly not be acceptable," Hunter said reasonably. "But perhaps we should discuss the possibility of a small, private ceremony—that is, if you are of a mind to wed her soon."

"The sooner the better," Tim breathed.

Hunter laughed for the first time in several days. "The anxious groom," he teased, and the doctor actually colored.

"I don't blame you. I was feeling that way myself not too long ago."

"I'm glad someone understands," Tim said quietly.

"We'll hold a family conference in a few days," Hunter said, "and discuss the matter. And a year from now we could have a celebration of sorts. Maggie and I haven't observed our own marriage with any of the usual festivities. Perhaps we can make it a joint effort then."

It was agreed and the two men downed the last of their brandy and parted company for the night.

Hunter crept silently into the room. He could hear the soft whisper of Maggie's deep breathing as she slept on while he removed his clothes and draped them over a chair.

Moving cautiously so as not to disturb her, he lay down, pulled the blankets up, and stretched his tired body as best he could in the short bed. Rolling onto his side then, Hunter wrapped his arms around his young wife and drew her against him as his eyes drifted closed and sleep overtook him.

Dawn was about to burst upon the fields of Treemont when Maggie opened her eyes. Hunter was sleeping on his back beside her, one arm holding her against his side. He was warm and strong and breathing deeply as she snuggled against him and closed her eyes once again.

Hunter drifted slowly up from sleep to near awareness as he felt a small hand and delicate fingers trail slowly across his chest. He opened his eyes to find Maggie gazing intently at the path her hand was making, and he lay quietly, allowing her the freedom to touch and feel as she would.

Maggie knew she had awakened him, but could not bring herself to look at his eyes. It was bold, this thing she was doing, but she had watched him sleep for long moments before daring to fulfill her need to touch the living strength that lay beside her. Something within her was driving her to touch and, ultimately, to encourage him to touch her.

Her hand strayed up his chest, feeling the hard muscles there before sweeping across one shoulder and down one arm that was easily as wide as both of hers together. His muscles twitched at times, she noticed, and then her hand was on the warm firmness of his belly. She hesitated there, finally raising her eyes shyly as if to ask permission to continue her quest.

Hunter had turned his head to stare down at her with a tender dark heat that would have encouraged her if his whispered words had not. "Touch me, love," he said, and when she failed to react, he placed his large hand over hers and guided her palm downward. "Hold me," he prompted and breathed in deeply when she did as instructed. "Do you want me, Maggie?" he breathed after several long moments.

She nodded. She did.

And together they celebrated living.

The morning was a series of chaotic events that made Maggie's head reel. The day had started out with everyone feeling as taut as any bowstring over the tensions of the previous days. Florence had completely withdrawn into herself, and Denise was having a difficult time looking at Tim as she worried over her duty to her sisters and her devotion to him. Jennifer continuously chattered or, alternately, spilled things. Tim was quietly trying to determine what was on Denise's mind that she should avoid him so, and Anna muttered and glared at everyone who came near her.

And, in the midst of all this, Maggie was having difficulty looking Hunter in the eye. She was suffering acute embarrassment at having engaged in what she considered as her first seduction.

They all felt the absence of Alastair, but Maggie felt duty-bound to help everyone return to some semblance of a normal life. She easily took control over the running of the household and the disciplining of two little girls who had easily slipped out of their routine of chores and school.

Hunter sat back proudly and watched her.

No longer was Maggie taking charge to fill some void in her life. Her control over Treemont and the people who lived there had become a caring thing. It was something she *wanted* to do, not something she was *driven* to do. She possessed a new confidence that surprised even her husband.

And there was something else about Maggie . . . her newly acquired understanding of what it was like to be in love.

Hunter had closeted himself in Alastair's study for most of the day, poring over books that outlined a fairly bleak picture. And it was with some relief that he looked up from his place behind the massive desk, to see Maggie in the doorway with a tray. Hunter quickly closed the account book he had been examining and sat back as she stepped into the room.

"I've brought coffee and cake," she said simply and placed the tray on the round table before the fire. "You've been locked in here by yourself long enough."

Hunter left his chair and skirted the desk. His gaze remained locked with hers as he pulled her easily against his chest. "And you, my love, are the perfect diversion."

Maggie tipped her head back, waiting for a kiss. She understood how much she had changed. She now waited expectantly for a kiss or a touch or a teasing caress each time he was near. She had grown comfortable with his frequent touching, and she would have been sorely disappointed if he'd failed to do so.

When he raised his head, she tightened her hands on the back of his shirt. "I need to speak with you," she said. "I could come back later. . . ."

"Absolutely not." He drew her down on his lap as he sat in the wing chair before the fire. "Now that I have you in here," he teased, "I'm not letting you go."

Maggie adjusted her bottom on his thighs and rested a forearm on his shoulder. "It's about Denise," she said, watching his eyes closely for reaction. "I think she needs to be with Tim."

Hunter's smile melted into something more tender. "Do you, little one?"

Maggie nodded determinedly. "I think she's torn about what to do. But I think they should be together."

"I agree."

Maggie's brows arched in surprise. "You do?"

"What brought you to this conclusion, Maggie?" he asked softly, but daring to answer the question in his own heart.

Maggie blushed lightly, and her eyes darted away from his as she began to toy with a button on his shirt.

"Can't you tell me?" he coaxed, cupping her cheek and turning her to face him. "Tell me."

"Sometimes I watch them looking at each other, and I see *us.*"

Hunter's eyes turned curious.

"Denise watches him all the time, and she looks at Tim the way I like to look at you," she said hesitantly. "I mean to say . . . I used to look at you and feel so many things I didn't understand. And I would watch you and feel a need for something I knew nothing about."

"You *used* to, pet?" he asked.

"Oh, it's much worse now!" she blurted.

Hunter wasn't certain if he should laugh or cry; he wasn't exactly catching her meaning. "How is it worse, Maggie?"

"Now I look at you and I understand all those feelings," she murmured. "And I want you all the time."

Hunter's smile returned and his hand roamed up from her waist to lightly cup one breast. "Now you understand my feelings as well, my love."

Margaret captured the back of his hand and stilled it, pressing it firmly against her breast as she buried her face against his neck. "Now I understand what it's like to love and be loved," she murmured. "And I want Denise to be as happy as I am."

"Oh, Maggie," Hunter breathed, as he wrapped his arms firmly around her and cradled her tightly against his chest. "I do love you, little one."

"And I think Denise and Tim must be going through hell," she returned bluntly.

Hunter laughed and then buried his smile in the soft silken curls he loved.

CHAPTER
❦24❦

Maggie charged headlong up the stairs to the second floor as if she were a girl again. But before entering Denise's room, she paused, patted her hair into place, and caught her breath.

Coolly she swung the door open and stared across the room at her unhappy sister. "I've come to talk with you," she said, entering the room and closing the door. "I believe I know what's causing these doldrums of yours, Denise, and it is most unlike you." She sat primly on the side of the bed and waited.

Denise raised tired eyes and left her chair by the window. "I miss Papa," she said. "Everyone does."

Her sister nodded as Denise paced toward her. "And . . . ?" Maggie prodded.

Denise stood before her, eyeing her warily. If she mentioned her problem—one that Maggie would surely not understand—she would sound selfish. On the other hand, her heart was heavy and her thoughts confused. "I don't know what to do," she said fretfully.

Maggie stood and clasped both of the younger woman's upper arms. "I think you should get married."

Denise could only stare, mouth agape.

"I've talked it over with Hunter, and he agrees."

"You have?" she stammered. "He does?"

"Of course." She hugged Denise. "I want you to be happy, Dennie," she whispered. "Just as I am."

The two women stepped away from each other, and Denise looked at Maggie as if the wrong person had returned home to Treemont. "*Are* you happy with him, Mag?"

"Very."

Denise began to grin. "I don't believe it!"

But obviously she did.

"He's been very patient," Maggie said. "And *very* persistent. Now," she said, looking around the room, "we must plan a small supper." She stared at the white gown on the dress form and added solemnly, "I'm afraid we'll have to choose a simple dress, Dennie."

Denise understood. They could not hold a gala affair when the household was in mourning.

The dress didn't matter.

She would have Tim.

It was very late in the afternoon by the time Maggie left Denise's room. They had started sewing another, simpler, dress while Maggie assured her sister that a private ceremony and a family dinner would be suitable. After all, she and Tim had already waited for over a year to marry. And Maggie understood now how passions could run high.

At the bottom of the steps, Maggie turned toward the kitchen. It was time to set the table for supper, and Anna would need help serving the meal.

Before she could swing the door open and enter the room,

however, Maggie was jolted to a halt by the sound of china breaking, followed by a heavy thud.

Alarmed by the noise, Hunter darted out of Alastair's study and came up behind Maggie. "What on earth was that?"

"I don't know." Maggie sprang into action, quickly entering the kitchen.

The sight that greeted her there almost defied belief. Florence had fallen and lay on the floor with her head perilously close to the heavy lion's-claw base of the table. She was half under the table, surrounded by broken china and globs of food. Anna was pulling furiously on the child's arm in an attempt to drag Florence out from under her shelter. And, unbelievably, the woman was poised to strike.

Maggie's immediate reaction was to race forward and clutch the woman's arm with both hands. "What are you doing?" she cried.

Anna turned enraged dark eyes on her. "I'm sick of this," she hissed. "The girl will never do as she is told. And she sassed me."

"Florence?" Maggie asked, astounded. "Florence is the most amenable person I know. What could she have done?"

"She refused to take the supper to those stableboys again!" the woman said belligerently. "I've had this problem with her before. I can't do everything in this house!"

Maggie's complexion had turned to angry purple by this time. "And for this you struck her?" she asked evenly, with deceptive calm. "You struck her when you know she is shy of those boys?" She jerked the woman's hand down and took a threatening step forward. "How could you strike her for refusing to do something that makes her uncomfortable? How could you strike her at all?"

"The girl is lazy!"

Maggie flung Anna's arm away. "Stay away, Anna," she ordered harshly. "Just get away from me for a moment."

Hunter had followed his wife into the room and had gone to Florence's side, once he'd determined that Maggie was dealing well enough on her own. He was kneeling among the food and the broken china with the girl clinging to his shirtfront.

Maggie knelt beside him. "Florence, let me see, darling," she said softly, although anger made it difficult for her to control her voice. The shy girl of thirteen turned a livid cheek toward her sister. Maggie winced when she saw the clear mark of a handprint and raised her eyes to her husband. "Did she hit her head?" she asked, raising a gentle hand to search for signs.

"Apparently not," he said grimly. "Fortunately."

And then, before Hunter could blink, his small wife had stood and whirled toward the housekeeper. Clearly she wasn't through with the woman as yet. Once again he felt pride swelling in his chest as he watched her.

Maggie clenched both hands at her sides in an attempt to control her rage. "Has this happened before?" she asked tightly.

Anna stared defiantly. "I told you . . . the girl does not do as she is told."

"I mean, have you struck her before?" Maggie asked bluntly.

Anna chose to remain mute on the point and crossed her arms over her ample bosom.

Maggie examined the older woman from head to toe and then, with a squaring of her shoulders, came to a decision.

Stepping forward, she extended one hand, palm up. "Give me your keys," she said quietly.

"What for?"

"I want your keys, and I want you packed and out of this house within the hour."

Anna was obviously stunned. "You can't—"

"I just did, Anna," she said evenly. "Out . . . within the hour."

The woman ungraciously flung her small ring of keys toward the stove and stormed out of the room.

Maggie sighed and bowed her head momentarily before turning to meet the eyes of her husband.

He was smiling!

Jennifer chose that moment to storm the bastille. The outer kitchen door banged against the wall as she entered. Executing an abrupt stop, the girl stared down at the sight of Hunter and Florence wallowing in food. "What on earth—"

Hunter gained his feet and helped Florence up.

Jennifer, still looking dumbfounded, caught sight of her sister's bruised face. "What happened, Flo?" she asked, frowning.

"I fell," the girl mumbled.

"Before or after Anna hit you?" Jennifer asked bluntly.

Maggie turned toward her. "This has happened before?"

Jennifer shrugged her slim shoulders. "A few times."

"But why didn't Papa do something about it?" she asked, perplexed.

"Florence would never tell, and she wouldn't let me tell, either. She said we needed somebody to cook."

Florence was straightening her skirt while trying to gain control over her emotions. But, before she could find the courage to hold her head up, Maggie lifted her chin high.

"You must never allow this to happen to you again, Florence," she said quietly. "We'll teach you," she said as she raised her ice-blue eyes to Hunter. "We'll teach you, Hunter and I. I won't let you become a victim, too."

• • •

Hunter Maguire trudged wearily up the stairs to join his wife in their room. For the past four hours he had been looking forward to some quiet moments alone with her.

Hunter felt as if he had aged a score of years in the short time they had been at Treemont. Emotions had been running high.

He entered the room quietly and closed the door behind him, then crossed the room to where she sat on the edge of the bed, brushing her hair. "Hello," he said quietly, placing the palm of one hand on her cheek before he bent to lightly kiss her lips.

He straightened then, tugging his shirt out of the waistband of his trousers as he walked to a chair and sat down to remove his boots.

Maggie's eyes followed him with sympathy; she could almost feel his fatigue. "It's been a terrible day," she offered softly.

He turned, smiling at her as he dropped one boot to the floor. "Not *all* of it, Maggie," he said, in what she deemed a most lecherous tone.

Her face colored and she turned her head away from him, raising the hairbrush once again, as she thought of their morning lovemaking.

Hunter laughed. "I was referring to the fact that you told me you loved me," he teased, and she turned back to him, laughing softly at her own stupidity. "Well . . . the lovemaking was a tiny ray of sunshine in an otherwise stormy day," he added.

She threw the hairbrush at him.

He laughed again and ducked as the thing sailed past his shoulder, then got him on the rebound as it bounced off the wall and hit him squarely between the shoulder blades.

Maggie raced across the room and fell to her knees beside

him. "Oh, Hunter, I'm sorry!" she cried, running her hand down his back and looking for damage.

"I'm all right, love," he said, continuing to laugh lightly.

"I didn't mean to hit you! I threw it wide!"

"God help me if you ever take *aim*!" he teased. Her eyes turned to his, and when he saw her honest remorse, he touched her cheek again. "Don't be a goose," he whispered. "I know you were playing." He kissed the tip of her nose and turned his attention to the removal of his other boot.

Maggie's chin dropped down to rest on her hand, which gripped the wooden arm of the chair; she and Denise had removed the two small boudoir chairs earlier in the day and replaced them with this far sturdier one for Hunter.

"Is Anna gone?" she asked, watching the play of muscles across his shoulders and down his arm as he moved.

"Well and truly," he muttered with feeling.

"I just can't believe she was mistreating my sister and my father didn't know about it."

"Florence allowed it to happen, pet, and that's a sad state of affairs," he said gently and sat back, his chest and feet now bare. He rested an arm on her shoulder while his fingers toyed with her silky hair. "We shall have to give Florence a good deal of coaching. She needs confidence."

"If she gets attention from you," Maggie said sincerely, "she'll be all right."

His hand stilled, and he stared at her for a long, breathless moment. "You mean that, don't you?" he asked, obviously taken aback.

"I'm a lucky girl," she said emotionally, her forehead dropping to his ribs. "I'm grateful for whatever made you come back for me."

He tugged gently on a handful of hair until she raised her

eyes to his. "It was pure selfishness, pure greed, that made me come back. I wanted the loveliest, liveliest, and sweetest woman any man could imagine taking to wife." Maggie rose up and threw her arms around his neck. "And she's a hussy, too," he teased softly. Maggie laughed, and he realized how much he enjoyed the sound of her doing that.

It was an honest and earnest few moments between them, a time of expressing by sight and touch and sound those things that were difficult to put into words. It was as if each could see beyond the flesh and bone of the other's chest and say, See, this heart beats only for you. It was a moment of profound emotion, of extreme sensation, without the passion of physical loving. It was something that neither had ever before experienced, something that neither had ever envisioned possessing.

It was *something*.

And then Maggie was standing before him, pulling on his hands and forcing him to stand. "You said you would teach me to *love* you." She dropped her hands to the waistband of his trousers.

"I have the distinct feeling that you already know how, my darling," he breathed as she made him naked.

She stood back from him then, her eyes slowly perusing his fine, muscular body, and enjoying the fact that she was feeling absolutely no shame as she gazed at him. He was hers, after all, and she was proud of that.

She gave a quick tug on the small pink ribbon on her bodice, shrugged with an exaggerated movement, and stood before him in an equal state of undress.

"Is this terribly wicked?" she asked, watching his eyes glow in the meager light of the single lamp.

"Perfectly," he murmured. "Beautifully," he added as he took his time admiring her body.

Maggie was not certain how to initiate the lovemaking. There seemed to be a difference between lying naked beneath the sheets with him and having him stand so boldly before her. But she eventually found her courage. She stepped carefully out of the gown pooled at her feet and took the few steps remaining between them. When she stood close enough to feel his body heat, she raised her hands and let them rest on his narrow hips. When he failed to touch her in return, she smiled up at him. "You aren't going to help me at all with this, are you?"

He shook his head, his gaze gentle but serious in his growing anticipation of what they were about to share. "You've touched me before," he said quietly. "You mustn't feel shy about touching me now."

"It's different, now that I understand how much I love you," she murmured.

"How is it different, little one?" he asked.

"It's suddenly very important that I make you happy," she said shyly, adding almost inaudibly, "that I please you."

"Don't you understand that I feel the same way?" he whispered.

She looked momentarily stunned by that revelation, but as she reasoned it out, she understood.

"It's all curious and frightening and magical," she whispered as her hand roamed up his chest. And she was pulling his head down, slowly down toward her parted lips.

Hunter groaned as his arms went around her, pulling her close against his rigid lower body. He was aching for her, but he sought to control the urge to enter her even before she had fully exercised her powers. This was Maggie's moment.

She guided him to the bed, and what took place there was a true test of two bodies straining to be together while they tortured each other by remaining apart.

And eventually the test had gone too far. Maggie could barely breathe as she looked down at him, her ample breasts pressed against his massive chest. "I want you now," she said.

Hunter lay on his back, groaning with the heat in those ice-blue eyes. "Then take me," he whispered and smiled at her puzzlement. "I'll show you how, love," he breathed and guided her hips up. "Easy now," he instructed, and her eyes widened with the pure, sweet sensation of taking him into herself this way. Then he touched her, and coached her into moving freely. Soon Maggie exploded into a thousand shards of color as her spine stiffened and her head fell back.

Watching her and feeling her body tighten around him was more than Hunter could bear, and he lowered his hips into the mattress before thrusting upward a time or two before finding his own exquisite release. His body continued to vibrate even as Maggie fell upon his chest.

It was several moments before their harsh breathing returned to normal. Maggie, her cheek pressed to his, murmured, "It's a good thing I don't discover I'm in love every day. I don't think I would survive."

He laughed softly, and the palm of his hand connected with her backside. "You will discover love every day . . . with me!"

"You're arrogant," she teased.

"Damn right!"

She eased off him then, but Hunter did not remove his arms from around her and Maggie fell on her side close against him. "How can this be, do you suppose?" she murmured. "This special thing between us?"

"I suppose all lovers feel this way," he returned philosophically.

That wasn't what Maggie wanted to hear. "Don't you believe this is special?" she asked, raising herself up on one elbow to better see his eyes.

"I think it's very special, my darling. But others have probably gone before us."

"Oh, pooh!" she scoffed.

He laughed. "I'm sorry," he said. "That wasn't very romantic of me, was it?"

"No."

"I'll try to do better," he teased, his hand lightly stroking her arm. "Perhaps you could teach me?"

She laughed. "I would throw something at you again, but I'm afraid of a catastrophe."

"So am I," he admitted, and she settled down against him, her fingers stroking slow, small circles on his chest as they both drifted into their own private thoughts.

"I suppose I've done a foolish thing, firing Anna that way?" she reflected after a time. Maggie could feel Hunter's head moving on the pillow before he replied.

"You did exactly the right thing, as far as I'm concerned," he said. "And you know you were right. I thought you were magnificent." He lifted his head a fraction and smiled down at her. "Did I tell you that?"

Maggie propped herself up on an elbow and frowned. "No you didn't, but it makes me feel better to hear it," she said. "However, we're now in a real pickle." She settled down against his side, making herself comfortable by using him as a pillow. "You know the limit of my cooking skills, and we have to have a nice supper for Denise and Tim." Maggie enjoyed the feel of his hand roaming up and down her back for a moment before asking, "Do you think we should advertise in town for a new housekeeper?"

When he didn't respond to her question after several moments, Maggie raised her head to look at him. "Hunter?" she whispered, wondering if he had fallen asleep.

But his eyes were open, and he turned his head toward her, his face a mask of such misery and sorrow that it made her afraid.

"Hunter?" she said in alarm.

He pulled her head back down onto his shoulder. "I hadn't planned to tell you just yet," he said. "But I think you need to know."

"Hunter, you're frightening me," she said, tightening her arm around his chest.

"We won't be replacing Anna," he said simply.

Maggie breathed the momentary relief of the uninformed. "Is that all?" she said before asking another question: "Who will look after this house after we leave?"

"Maggie, Treemont has some financial difficulties. There are no funds to hire a new housekeeper," he said quietly.

She was up and leaning over him. "What did you do with the money?" she blurted.

He stared at her for a long, painful moment. "I hope you don't mean that the way it sounded," he said slowly.

Her eyes widened, darting around the shadows beyond him until she realized fully what she had said. "Of course not!" she returned in alarm. "I only meant . . ." She stopped, confused, and turned away from him to sit up and pound the mattress with a small fist. "What the devil *did* I mean?"

"I think perhaps *you* should tell *me*," he said quietly.

Maggie turned frantically toward him, now fully understanding his tone. "Oh, no, Hunter!" she cried. "I would never dream of accusing you. I trust you completely. But I don't understand!"

He forgave her instantly; the financial problem was his alone. He had reacted defensively in an attempt to protect the very one he knew would suffer the most—his Maggie. How was he to explain what he had found in Alastair's ledgers? How was he to explain that her childhood home, her haven, was threatened almost beyond hope? How could he explain that he had no cure for what ailed Treemont?

Especially tonight when, in his own despondency, he feared he could not solve the numerous problems? How could he explain that to a wife who loved this place beyond all others?

Hunter propped a pillow or two behind his back and sat up, bending a knee and lightly pulling Maggie closer to him. "I didn't want to tell you at first," he said, holding her hand against his belly. "But I quickly realized that would be unfair. After all, Treemont is yours . . . yours and your sisters'." He raised his weary eyes to her, eyes filled with apologies that were not his to give. "I intended to pay the bills, but when I examined the accounts I found some disturbing entries. Maggie," he said softly, raising a palm briefly to stroke her cheek, "I've spent three days looking over your father's records, and what I have found is alarming. Treemont is heavily mortgaged . . . probably beyond its worth. I'm sorry, my darling, but without a large influx of funds we can't keep this farm afloat."

Maggie's eyes grew rounder and more troubled with each word he spoke, until her weary, overburdened mind could only rebel. "Papa was a good businessman!" she cried, drawing her hand away from the warmth of his.

"He was, Maggie."

"He would not have let Treemont fall into debt! You must be wrong!"

"Maggie, listen to me," he returned firmly, gripping both of her hands and holding them firmly against his chest. "This is not an indictment of your father. You must understand, pet, that many farms and other businesses are still struggling to regain what they had before the war. The South suffered great losses of many kinds, Maggie, financial losses among them. Families all over this state are still recovering even after twenty years. Treemont has done well, consid—"

"*You* didn't suffer!"

Hunter shook his head in dismay, continuing to be patient, understanding the confusion and the beginnings of resentment that were building within her.

"I was fortunate, love. I had a small inheritance given me by my father, English funds he chose not to withhold until his death, darling. That saved me. But Treemont has had to struggle up from the ashes of war. Its losses have been considerable."

"What can we do?" she asked, accepting the truth as he presented it, for she knew in every fiber of her being that he would not have told her these things unless he'd had absolutely no choice in the matter. They had been through so much, the girls and she, and Hunter had stood beside them . . . and now there was more.

He hugged her then, pulling her close to his chest and murmuring against her hair. "We'll find a way, Maggie," he said. "I'll go into town and see the bankers. Together we'll determine the exact amount of the debt, and from there we'll see what must be done."

"Hunter, will we have to leave soon?"

"No. We have time," he said hurriedly, trying to reassure her. "Jason will mind the place for us while we decide what our next steps should be. But, Maggie," he said softly, lowering his head and pressing his cheek against her hair, "I don't think we should tell the others. Florence and Jennifer have enough concerns, and this will be completely beyond them in any event. And Denise deserves as many happy moments as we can give her under the circumstances. Let's keep this between us for now, shall we?"

Maggie knew he was right. Her sisters were younger and did not deserve any further burdens . . . and she didn't, either, she thought, as she gripped his arm harder and pressed it into her midriff. Hadn't there been enough trouble? Where was it all to end? Would Treemont be lost to them forever? "I want to go with you when you see the bankers," she said quietly.

He did not hesitate in responding. "All right, pet," he said.

CHAPTER
❧ 25 ❧

he wedding of Denise Downing and Tim Fletcher was a
uiet affair with only immediate families present.

Maggie did not cry, as Florence and Jennifer did, when
enise was preparing to ride away to her new home; she
eld her sister close and whispered, "Be as happy as I am."

And while the statement was not a total truth, it was
ertainly not a total lie. The only flaw in Maggie's life was
er concern over Treemont. Certainly she was happy being
e wife of Hunter Maguire. As each day passed she found
erself more deeply in love and more spellbound by him. He
ever failed to woo her at every turn, no matter who might
e present, within the realms of propriety, of course.
lorence and Jennifer frequently saw Hunter touching or
ghtly kissing their sister. Florence blushed furiously, but
ennifer merely wrinkled her nose.

"Don't you get sick of kissin' her?" she asked one
vening as she came upon them sitting together on a settee
the parlor.

Hunter smiled, folding Maggie back against his chest and
ithin his arms. "No," he said simply.

"But that's all you ever do," she accused, walking close and leaning both hands, elbows locked, on the carved wooden arm next to Hunter.

"That is not all we ever do," he said.

Jennifer made a sound like the grunt of a piglet. "Well, you do it a lot. And touching!"

Maggie had worried about this, but Hunter had insisted that the girls should not be deprived of a loving environment. And he was not about to peer around corners each time he wanted to demonstrate a little affection for his own wife.

"I touch *you*," he said quietly to Jennifer, as he looked into her lustrous brown eyes. "In a different way perhaps, but I touch you. Don't you like it?"

Jennifer thought about that, scraping a thumbnail along a groove in the wood beneath her hand until Hunter captured her fingers with his own.

"Don't you?" he prompted.

She raised her eyes slowly to his. "I guess."

"I touch people because I like them or love them. It's a good thing, don't you think?"

"I guess," she repeated, a bit shyly this time.

"I love your sister and she loves me. That's why we touch and kiss sometimes. One day you'll like it, too."

"No, I won't," she said.

He laughed. "I'll check back with you on that in about ten years."

Jennifer made a face of disbelief, and Hunter tugged her down next to them while Maggie smiled.

Yes, she was happy with the loving ways of her man.

But the fear of losing Treemont tortured her.

Hunter wrote to Jason with two requests. He explained the first request to Maggie, and although she objected strenuously at first, she eventually saw the merit of what he

as doing. Jason would send funds, which Hunter would
fuse into Treemont. That would buy them time into the
ew Year. At that point he knew, but did not state, they
ight be forced to make some hard decisions.

Maggie's appreciation was boundless, and her love seemed
grow daily.

Hunter did not tell her about his second request.

The early weeks of December provided much needed
straction for them all as they fell to work in preparation
r their first Christmas in town. Denise and Tim had
rsuaded Maggie and Hunter and the girls to spend
hristmas with them, away from Treemont and the memo-
es of the senior Downings who were no longer there to
are the season.

Maggie agreed for the sake of Florence and Jennifer.

Hunter agreed for the sake of Maggie.

She had been drawn and tired of late, working to keep the
ouse neat and clean with only the girls to help, when they
ere not in school. And cooking was a chore for them all,
though Hunter was slowly teaching them, and some
assable meals were coming out of the kitchen. Though not
any.

Maggie had set Florence and Jennifer to work making
fts for the Fletchers and, most particularly, for their
ostess. The four of them would be staying in the senior
etchers' guesthouse over the holiday. They would give
rs. Fletcher a gaily decorated pine wreath adorned with
bbons and berries and pinecones, and Hunter had helped
e girls build a pipe stand for Tim's father.

During the evenings Maggie fashioned and refashioned
ome of her cast-off clothing into new dresses for her
ounger sisters. One thing Hunter could not deny: His
Maggie was a wizard with needle and thread.

One blustery mid-December evening, after Florence and

Jennifer had disappeared to their rooms, Hunter and Maggie
sat before a roaring fire. Looking away from the book in his
hand, Hunter watched her slim fingers push and pull the
needle until finally he reached out and took her hand in his.
"Your fingers must ache with all of this sewing," he said,
turning her palm up.

"I get dents," she said not unhappily as he examined the
red ridges in the pads of her fingers.

His eyes moved up to her face, and he frowned. "You
look so tired, Maggie," he said. "Why not put your work
away for tonight."

"Soon," she said, withdrawing her hand reluctantly and
resuming her task.

"I've got a small gift for the girls," he said abruptly, and
Maggie's head snapped around.

"We said we wouldn't buy gifts, Hunter," she said
softly, accusing.

"Small and alive," he teased. "And I'm not at all certain
the Fletchers will appreciate having it around."

Maggie laughed. "What on earth did you get them?"

"I don't believe I'll tell you, either. I'll make it a family
surprise."

"Is it furry?" she asked, moving closer to his side.

"Well, it has hair, I suppose," he hedged and watched
her moving in.

"Most babies don't," she said.

He looked baffled. "Babies don't what?"

"Have hair."

"What's that got to do with anything?" His brows arched
upward in confusion as she leaned against him.

"Did you get them a kitten?" she asked.

Hunter cupped her chin in the palm of his hand, raising
her face so he could look into her eyes. "A pup," he said
abruptly, distracted. "What is this talk about babies?"

"Just an observation," Maggie said smiling. "Most are quite bald, don't you think?"

"I *think* you are toying with me. I *think* you might be trying to tell me something," he said. He raised his hand to lightly stroke the shell of her ear while the rate of his heartbeat increased frantically.

Maggie could see him mentally counting backward.

"I *think* you might be pregnant," he said at last.

"I think I might be," she returned softly.

Hunter's eyes lit up like a flash of sulfur. "Oh, Maggie," he breathed, ducking his head to offer a brief kiss. "It would be so wonderful . . . but it's too soon, isn't it? I mean . . . we can't be sure?"

One thing about being extremely intimate with one's husband, Maggie thought, he did not miss much. And she found she could still blush with him. "But we can hope, can't we? It has been quite a while, and there are other signs."

"Really?" he asked enthusiastically. "What?"

Maggie's color heightened a bit more, and he laughed at her.

"Foolish woman," he admonished. "What signs, Maggie?"

"I get a queasy feeling sometimes, and . . . my breasts feel different."

His eyes dropped quite naturally to the bodice of her dress and his hand moved down to touch her gently. "They don't hurt, do they, little one? I don't want you to hurt."

She laughed lightly and put her arms around his neck, hugging him and pressing her cheek against his. "I think I might be expecting your baby, Hunter Maguire!" she said in a small voice that was filled with hope and excitement. And for the first time, of all the times she had thought about having a child, she realized that their baby might never see the place where she'd been born and raised.

Perhaps Treemont could not be saved.

But Maggie had found another haven, and that haven was Hunter Maguire and the children he would give her. Treemont was a place she loved dearly, but Hunter and the love they shared was her very life's support.

CHAPTER

❧26❧

The holidays proved to be difficult despite the Fletchers' best efforts. This first Christmas celebration without Alastair was simply too painful, and Maggie found herself wishing the holidays behind her.

Right after New Year's Hunter forced himself and the two stable hands into long hours of hard labor. They began by erecting new paddocks, and he drew up plans for a second stable. Maggie watched all the activity with growing curiosity, but Hunter remained steadfastly closemouthed about what he was doing.

They were absolutely certain now that Maggie was pregnant, and as Hunter washed up for lunch one day in the warm, cozy kitchen, he broached the subject of telling Florence and Jennifer that they would be aunts come summer.

''It's hardly a subject one talks about openly,'' Maggie said primly.

Hunter turned toward her as he dried his hands. ''It's hardly a thing we have to hide in shame, Maggie,'' he said logically.

"Well, of course not!" she returned, her eyes widening at the very idea.

"Do you want to wait until the girls begin to eye your growing figure with curiosity? They are your sisters, love. Don't you think they have a right to know?"

"It's . . . just . . ."

He laughed, wrapping his arms loosely around her. "You're embarrassed!" He kissed the tip of her nose. "Silly chit. I do love you, Maggie," he said lightly.

Her brows arched worriedly as she frowned up at him. "They're very young."

"Not so young anymore, darling. And the mention of babies should not be all that strange to them."

Maggie rested her forehead on his chest. "Jen will ask a thousand questions," she groaned.

He laughed. "Then we shall answer them."

"*We?*" she asked, looking up at him again. "You mean *me*. I know you do."

He shook his head. "I won't abandon you when the time comes if you need me there," he said.

But the experience was relatively painless for Maggie; Florence smiled and blushed softly, and Jennifer grinned, kissed her sister's cheek, and went her merry way.

Over the next few weeks Maggie's condition began to show just a bit, and Hunter watched her carefully. He insisted she was not to lift anything heavier than her hairbrush, and he was forever getting in her way as his hands magically appeared to bear any greater loads. Frankly, it was beginning to drive her crazy. She could hardly object, however, for not too many months ago Maggie would never have thought to be the recipient of such loving. Hunter seemed to have boundless energy when it came to so many things.

Maggie's nature took on a decidedly domestic cast as she

discovered newfound pleasures in providing small comforts for those she loved.

Hunter was off working and Maggie was attempting to make an apple pie one day in March when she heard footfalls on the porch near the kitchen door. Turning, she opened her mouth in amazement when she saw a familiar face beyond the small window in the door.

"Jeffrey!" she called excitedly, smiling as she wiped her hands on her apron and rushed across the room to greet Jeffrey Winter. "Come in!" she said, hurriedly opening the door. "I'm so glad to see you!"

The man with the shy brown eyes ducked his head in greeting. "Wasn't sure I had the right place," he said. Maggie reached up to offer a hug whether he wanted one or not.

A yellow pup raced through the door, whined and then barked until finally Maggie tried to hush him.

"Who's this?" Jeffrey asked, bending down to make friends with the animal.

"Mr. Finnegan," Maggie said and laughed when Jeffrey's head snapped up. "My younger sisters named him."

"He's a cute one," he said shyly.

"Give me your coat," she said. "Sit while I get you some coffee. What are you doing here? How is Marie-Louise?"

"I'll be glad for some coffee in a minute or two. But first I need you to come outside with me for a minute." Jeffrey turned toward the door again.

Maggie stepped out onto the porch behind him, Mr. Finnegan running at her heels.

"You brought Pride?" she asked unnecessarily, as the stallion was standing before her. "Why?"

"That's what Mr. Maguire wanted." Jeffrey walked around to the far side of the wagon. "I've brought something else as well," he said.

Maggie's curiosity was growing to the point she could no longer remain on the porch. Following Jeffrey, she rounded one end of the wagon. There, knees bent and giggling into her hands, was Marie-Louise.

"I don't believe it!" Maggie crowed. "How could you come all this way in your condition?" But she couldn't wait for an answer. Maggie was upon the younger woman, and they were hugging each other fiercely, even as they laughed.

"It was easy," Marie-Louise said, stepping back and wiping her eyes. "Jeffrey took good care of me and it was snug and cozy sleeping together under canvas in this skinny wagon."

"You two had best get inside out of the cold," Jeffrey said sensibly. "I'll take the animals to the barn."

"You'll find Hunter there!" Maggie called as she led her friend up the steps and into the house. Then she turned on Marie-Louise again. "I'm so glad to see you!" she said happily. "I've thought about you often."

"Me too," the younger woman said as she struggled out of her heavy coat. And that was when she first looked down at Maggie. "Oh, my God," she breathed, her eyes widening. "Are you?"

Maggie nodded happily, her hands dropping to her stomach. "I'm only just beginning to show."

Marie-Louise laughed at that and dropped her coat on the floor. Maggie gaped at the size of her. "Wait until you catch up to me!" she said proudly, her hands smoothing her dress down over the enormous belly. "Mind you, I've only got a couple of months to go."

Mr. Finnegan was whining and sniffing around the coat on the floor, and Marie-Louise smiled down at the pup. "Cute," she said. "I'd scratch his ear, but bending over that far is impossible."

Maggie laughed and retrieved the coat. "Come in and sit," she said. "I'll make you some tea."

Maggie hung the coat on a peg near the door and then set the teakettle on the stove. She turned as her friend was easing onto a wooden chair. "Have you been well, Marie-Louise?" she asked. "You look wonderful."

The younger woman laughed. "I look like the cow that wandered into the alfalfa," she said. "Bloated. But I feel good."

"I'm glad." Maggie sat in a chair opposite. "But you came all this way just to bring Pride to us? That's too tiring trip. . . ."

Marie-Louise frowned and stared blankly at the other woman. "Don't you know?" she asked. "Mr. Maguire asked us to stay on here for a time."

Maggie straightened in her chair, obviously surprised but pleasantly so. "That's wonderful!" she cried.

"Maggie," Marie-Louise said softly, "if you don't want us here, you just have to say."

"Don't be a goose," she said. "I'm thrilled that you're here. Hunter's always full of surprises."

"Are you happy with him?" she asked softly.

"Yes, I'm very happy," Maggie said.

"I had my doubts there for a while."

"I was a foolish, frightened girl then, Marie-Louise." Maggie flashed another quick smile. "But he's made a new woman of me."

The younger woman eyed her belly and grinned. "Obviously!"

Maggie was still blushing when the men came up from the barn.

Jeffrey took one look at the women and marched over to his wife. "What have you been saying now?" he teased.

Marie-Louise grinned up at him. "Honestly, Jeffrey," she murmured, "sometimes I think that Maggie is permanently pink."

And then Hunter was standing beside her chair, waiting

patiently. "Hello, Marie-Louise," he said and reached f
her hand. "Jeffrey tells me you're well."

She flashed him one of her most beautiful smiles. "A
big as a house and twice as healthy."

Hunter bent and kissed her cheek. "I'm happy you'
both here."

"Well, you said we could help, and we're here an
ready," she said, looking expectantly from Maggie t
Hunter and back to Maggie.

Maggie looked confused and then exasperated.

Hunter looked chagrined and then concerned.

And Marie-Louise frowned as she realized there had bee
a lack of communication between her friends.

"I have a plan that I want to discuss with you," Hunte
said, taking Maggie's hands and resting them across he
middle. She was sitting with her back against his chest, he
legs stretched out on the sofa in Alastair's study.

"You've had this plan for a long time, it seems," sh
muttered. "And you didn't choose to discuss it with me."

Hunter sighed and lightly stroked the back of her wris
"The plan can be set aside if you're not in agreemen
Maggie. I just wanted to firm it in my mind before w
started tearing it apart."

"But you've already sent for help."

"Aren't you happy that they're here?" he asked.

"I am," she said, "but I think I should be miffed wit
you."

"All right," he said, sighing as he hugged her against hi
chest. "You can be miffed, but in all fairness, they're
week early. I had intended to tell you they were comin
And even if you don't like the plan, isn't it nice to have ou
friends here?"

"I hate it when you're rational and I'm not," sh
muttered.

He laughed. "I know."

There was a long, strained moment between them, and en Maggie tilted her head back, smiling. "I'm happy ou've brought them here," she said. "I've missed Marie-ouise."

Hunter smiled and planted a quick kiss on the tip of her se.

"But this scheme had better be good," she teased. "Or ll vote it down."

"The ultimate decision is yours," he said, laughing at her tempt to be severe. "I want to have a . . . show, of sorts. s soon as the weather turns fine. Possibly the end of April early May."

Maggie frowned. "A show?" she asked. "What sort of ow?"

"A showing of Passion's Pride," he said, smiling at her onfusion. "To introduce a stud service that will provide for e care of the mares as well."

Maggie thought about that for a moment.

"The stallion will be like black gold for us," Hunter said. What do you think?"

Maggie continued to look confused. "Could you explain is to me, please?" she asked, perturbed that she had not thomed his scheme quickly enough.

Hunter turned her until she was facing him squarely. People will bring their prize mares here to Treemont to be ut with Pride. The owners will pay a fee, a flat rate, for the rvicing of the mares until they are caught. They will also ay a monthly fee for us to care for the animals. Right up to e birthing, if they wish."

Maggie's eyes grew large and round as she listened to his lan. "Of course," she whispered. "Not every owner of ne animals can boast a stallion like Pride."

"That's right," Hunter said, pleased that she seemed to ink the scheme held merit.

"But Pride is yours, Hunter," she said.

"Pride is *ours*, pet. It's my hope that he will help us sav̄
Treemont."

Maggie's ice-blue eyes grew suspiciously moist as sh̄
looked at him. "Do you think it will work?"

"I do."

"How will we get people to come?"

"We're going to offer a Sunday afternoon outing," h̄
said. "We'll advertise in town and in local papers. Peopl̄
will come to see the stallion and the property, and ever̄
thing will be all spit and polish. We want the owners c̄
prospective mares to trust the cleanliness and care we cā
give their animals. The second stable must be complet̄
and the old one well cleaned and whitewashed. Your tasḵ
with the help of Florence and Jennifer—and Marie-Louis̄
if she's not too burdened by then—will be to entertain th̄
ladies with tea and cakes or whatever. Jeffrey and I wil̄
show the men around the place and convince them c̄
Pride's merits." He winked at her and teased lightly. "Ẉ
don't want to offend the tender sensibilities of all those fiṉ
ladies with such talk."

"And you don't think I have any tender sensibilities?"
she asked with well-feigned offense.

"Not the woman I know who once hid in the loft," h̄
returned and she laughed.

"I'm having legal contracts drawn up," Hunter ex̄
plained. "We don't want any disputes over the terms of ou
agreement with the owners. And once they sign and delivē
the mares, we're in business!" He feigned a small frowṉ
then. "I suppose Jeffrey and I had better practice oṉ
salesmanship between now and then."

"Jeffrey, perhaps," Maggie murmured fondly. "But ̄
believe you could persuade a peacock to shuck its feathers.̄

Despite her cumbersome state, Marie-Louise still kneẉ
her way around a kitchen. She and Maggie soon fell into

mfortable routine of shared duties and of knowing each
her's moves.

"It's as if we'd never stopped working together," Mag-
e said happily.

The younger woman smiled from her place at the stove.
Yup. Except one of us is bigger and the other one's getting
at way."

Maggie laughed as she set out empty bowls. "But you
ally don't mind," she said sagely.

"The only thing I mind is that Jeffrey has to sleep
mslength from me."

Maggie hadn't thought of that.

"Don't frown so." Her friend laughed. "You've got a
ays to go."

"What's so funny?" Maggie asked.

"I never thought I'd see the day you'd *mourn* his not
ing able to touch you."

Maggie blushed, as Marie-Louise knew she would.

"I'll tell you something," she said. "*That* is one pretty
ush. I love it!" she crowed.

Just as Maggie remembered she could.

Florence found Marie-Louise a bit much for her tender
nsibilities, although she seemed quietly drawn to the
oman and would often watch her from a quiet corner of
e kitchen.

Jennifer, however, had no such reserve. She thought
Marie-Louise was fun. "Wow!" she said, upon seeing the
oman for the first time. "Is there really a baby in there?"

"A baby or a buffalo," Marie-Louise muttered. And then
e smiled at the girl's curiosity. "We're not sure."

Jennifer dropped her lunch pail and approached the chair
here the young woman was sitting. "Doesn't that hurt?"
e asked, frowning at the enormous girth.

"Jen," Maggie warned softly.

But Marie-Louise waved her to silence. The women a▮ girls were alone in the kitchen and what harm could there ▮ in a child's inquisitiveness?

"Come and feel," she coaxed and Jennifer approach▮ her cautiously. "He twirls around in there," she said, taki▮ the girl's hand and placing it on her stomach.

Jennifer's eyes were round as she concentrated. And the she felt something. "Wow!" she crowed and Marie-Loui▮ laughed. The girl twisted toward her sister then. "Does o▮ baby do that, Mag?" she asked excitedly and Magg▮ nodded.

Our baby? "A little bit," she said as Jennifer dart▮ toward her.

"Can I feel?"

Maggie flashed a mock frown at her friend. "See wh▮ you've started?"

Marie-Louise laughed again.

Hunter had always loved to put his hands on her, but ▮ almost seemed there was no better time than now. He wou▮ watch her face, as he felt the tiny flutters, and his ow▮ expression would glow.

"Sometimes I think I can't wait for her to come out," ▮ said one night as they lay in their bed.

Maggie snuggled more comfortably within his arm▮ "So, today it is *her*?"

"Her today, Gowan tomorrow," he quipped.

Maggie slapped him lightly on his inner thigh, laughin▮

"Oh, that's dangerous," he teased.

"And *that* was really awful."

"I know," he admitted casually. "It just came out. ▮ promise I'll try to do better."

Maggie sighed contentedly and teasingly scratched at o▮ of his arms that lay across her middle. "I imagine once I a▮

e size of Marie-Louise, I'll be ready for this baby to come t, too.''

''You won't be nervous having her here, will you, pet?'' asked with sudden concern. ''Marie-Louise will deliver fore you and—''

''Don't worry, dear husband,'' she returned lightly. This is something about which I have no fear.''

''None?'' he asked, surprised and immediately in awe.

''Well,'' she drawled, ''I might be a tiny bit nervous, but ly because it is my first time, you understand?''

''Of course,'' he returned wryly.

''And, too, by the time Marie-Louise gets through with of us, there won't be a bashful bone in any of our bodies. he whole world could come in and watch my delivery, and won't even bat an eye.''

''Really?'' he said, unbelieving.

''Really,'' she returned. ''When Florence stops blushing, unter, we'll know we're in trouble.''

''You love Marie-Louise,'' he said.

Maggie giggled. ''She's a terrific friend. I only wish she eren't so shy and reserved.''

They both chuckled over that, and then Maggie became ddenly serious. Her fingers dug into both of his forearms , she pressed her cheek against his chest. ''Your plan will ork, Hunter. It has to work.''

Hunter held her for a long while that night. Her words had ly confirmed his thoughts of the past weeks: All the while e smiled at him and joked with him and made love with m, the thought of losing Treemont was plaguing her mind.

CHAPTER

❧27❧

Maggie ventured into the attic of the old house, moving cautiously up the steep steps.

The attic was dim and musty, and dust motes danced in the narrow beam of spring sunlight that came through the small round window. Maggie set her lamp on an old wooden table and looked around. They should clean up here one day, she thought; the room was filled with worn things and dust collectors.

In a darkened corner she spied the object that had brought her up here, a large shape covered over by an old sheet. Holding her skirt carefully away from the wooden boxes and dusty furniture, Maggie moved toward the thing and whisked off its covering. Jennifer had been the last to use the high cradle suspended between two carved posts. It was in need of polishing and a new mattress, but it was a perfect beginning for her preparations. Excited by her find, Maggie moved quickly toward the stairs and made her way to her father's study where Hunter was once again working.

"Could you help me please?" she asked.

He raised his head. "Of course, love. What's up?"

"There is something I need, but you will have to help me," she said evasively.

He stood and rounded the desk. "We're a bit mysterious, aren't we?" he teased, moving to her side and dropping an arm casually across her shoulders. "What do you need?"

"We'll find it upstairs."

Hunter's brows arched abruptly. "Really?"

"Not that!" She laughed.

"Now I'm hurt," he said, turning her toward the hallway. "And disappointed."

"You are incredible," she accused lightly.

He nodded. "It's called lust, my love."

"Hunter!" she said as they climbed the stairs.

"I can't seem to help myself," he said conversationally. "I love you, I long for you, and I lust after you." He grinned. "The three L's."

She laughed. "You're insane."

"Yup," he agreed, still smiling.

Maggie led him to a door at the end of the corridor, and he frowned in curiosity as she opened it and he spied the steep, winding staircase.

"Good God," he said. "You didn't go up there alone?"

"Of course I did," she said, starting upward again. "I'm not made of glass, my darling. You must stop worrying about me just because I leave the kitchen occasionally."

"I worry about you," he said sardonically, "when you leave our bedroom."

"That's just the lecher in you," she accused.

"No, ma'am," he drawled.

"It's over here." Maggie led the way to the dusty corner. "I need this taken downstairs, please."

Hunter stood beside her and examined the cradle. "What a lovely piece," he said. "But you won't need it for quite a time yet, pet."

Maggie shook her head vigorously. "It needs waxing and polishing, and I want to make a new mattress and—"

"All right!" He held up a hand in surrender. "I understand. But I'll need help getting it down the bend in those stairs. I'll ask Jeffrey to come and help me."

He turned, waiting for Maggie to pass in front of him in the narrow area. "This is quite a storage place," he muttered, skirting cobwebs hanging from the wooden rafters.

"There are a few good things up here," she said defensively, picking her way carefully down the steps.

"Really?" he drawled, giving the area one last disgusted look.

Maggie stopped at the last step and reached out to open the door. Her body suddenly went still when she pulled back . . . with the doorknob in her hand. She stared at the thing for a moment, her mouth falling open as the ramifications of what had just occurred registered in her mind.

Hunter stepped down beside her just as Maggie turned an incredulous look upon him. He saw what was in her hand, looked briefly at the closed door, and glanced back to her astonished face. Hunter suddenly felt the humor of the situation well up inside him, and he threw back his head and roared with laughter.

"This is not funny, Hunter," Maggie said quietly.

Hunter was wiping his eyes now.

"It is not funny," she said again.

"It is!" he croaked, striving for control.

"Hunter," she said, smiling now herself as she realized she must have looked very ridiculous. "We have to pull this door inward in order to open it."

He nodded his head.

"In order to get *out*," she stressed.

"I know, love," he said.

"We're trapped up here," she said, crossing her arms under her breasts. But he was enjoying the kind of laughter that, once started, could ripple through crowds, it was that contagious, and Maggie soon found herself laughing as well. "This is insane!" she choked as Hunter wrapped his arms around her and pulled her against his chest.

"I don't mind being locked up here with you," he said, containing his laughter at last. But his smile remained as she looked up at him. "There are too many people demanding your time or mine and much too often," he said and lowered his lips toward hers.

Maggie accepted the kiss, but she found laughter bubbling up within her and her lips began to twitch against his.

Hunter gave it up as a bad job.

He raised his head and smiled down at her as he stroked her cheek with his knuckles. "I *do* love you, Maggie. I don't think I tell you that often enough."

"I love you, too," she returned in a solemn moment.

He laughed briefly, then sat on one of the lower steps and pulled her down beside him. "Has it occurred to you how fortunate we are?" he asked, holding her close against his side while he stared at a door they could not open.

"To be locked up here?" she asked.

He smiled, shaking his head. "We have everything— each other, a baby soon to join us, your sisters, good friends . . ."

And Pride to help us save Treemont, she thought. . . .

"I've thought of it often," she said. "And it was you who gave it all to me."

"I?" he asked, taken aback.

"If you had not been such an insistent ogre, I would never have left this place, never have loved or been loved, never have known the joy of being pregnant," she added wryly.

Hunter's eyes dropped to her stomach, and his hand settled there, stroking lightly. "But you don't mind, do you?" he said, knowing it was true.

"How could I mind? I feel wonderful. I think I'm very lucky."

"I would have felt guilty if you'd been ill all the time," he said, raising his smiling eyes to hers.

"And I would have seen to it that you did," she teased.

"Well," he said, staring once again at the closed door. "I suppose we should devise a plan for getting out of here."

"I don't really think we need to escape," she said quietly.

His head swiveled around. "Don't you, now?" he asked quietly.

Maggie shook her head. "I think you should kiss me again," she said softly. "I mucked the last one up by laughing."

And he did—several times, in fact—and Maggie found herself praying that the magic would never go out of this, that there would always be this sweet, vibrant intensity between them that she found so drugging.

He raised his head and smiled at the sleepy-eyed gaze she cast his way. "You are a devilish temptress."

"I am?"

"You are," he said firmly. "As pregnant as you are, I could take you right here this very minute. Why is it I never stop wanting you all the time?" he asked quietly.

Maggie's smile was serene. "Why is it I want you never to stop wanting me?"

He laughed softly. "I think we'd better get out of here," he drawled, "or you'll seduce me right here among the dust motes."

"I?" she said innocently.

Hunter, studying the look in those ice-blue eyes, mumbled, "Oh, hell," and pressed his lips to hers again.

They were still uncomfortably sprawled on the steps when Marie-Louise swung the door open.

"Well," she drawled, resting her forearms on her swollen belly. "And I thought playing in the attic was reserved for rainy days."

Maggie sat upright, but Hunter lounged on the steps, shaking his head with wry disappointment.

"We were locked in here," Maggie said primly, in face of the other woman's knowing smile.

"Uh-huh."

"We were!" she returned indignantly. "There's the doorknob on the step."

"What were you doing up here anyway?" Marie-Louise asked suspiciously.

"We were fetching a cradle," Hunter put in.

Marie-Louise looked around the immediate area and shot him a laughing, questioning glance.

Hunter could deal with the woman's teasing, but Maggie still blushed nicely. "Jeffrey will have to help carry it down," Maggie said, hiding her face in the act of getting to her feet. Hunter pushed up on her back and then stood beside her. "I mean, really, Marie-Louise," she continued, stepping through the open door. "We're going to have two babies in this house soon, and it's time we started to prepare a nursery for them."

Marie-Louise winked wickedly at Hunter and drawled, "Uh-huh."

Maggie laughed then, giving in to the woman's penchant for good-natured fun. Raising her eyes toward the ceiling, she said, "I believe I hear rain."

CHAPTER
❧ 28 ❧

Spring was the most colorful and wonderful time of year at Treemont. Magnolias blossomed large and pink and white, and the sweet bouquet of honeysuckle seasoned the air in the early evening hours. The lawns and the fields Hunter had chosen to use as pasture turned a rich green, carpeting the earth for miles around. Trees blossomed and budded and shaded the house with new leaves.

It was Maggie's favorite time. When she could persuade Hunter to abandon his work for a short while, her slow gentle pace would inevitably lead them to the orchard. They would walk slowly among the trees, taking in the sweet scent of blossoms as they talked softly of private things, of hopes and dreams that had melded into mutual desires over the short span of their marriage.

"When I was very young I used to love walking here. Particularly during springtime," Maggie said one day as they skirted the apple trees. "Then for a while I stopped coming."

"Did you?" he asked. "Why?"

Maggie frowned as she considered his question. "I'm not

certain why," she said, tipping her head to look up at him. "But during the time I was most unhappy I avoided this place. Strange," she added thoughtfully, "because it would have reminded me of happier times and I might have felt better."

Hunter stopped walking and turned to her. "And does it remind you of happier times now?" he asked, gently stroking her cheek. The loving look she sent his way in that instant was one he would never forget.

"Hunter, I've had no happier times than those I've spent with you."

As March gave way to April, the days warmed and the sun shone between the soft showers that replenished the earth and all that grew. The new barn was complete now. The old one and the exterior of the house had received fresh coats of paint, and preparations for Pride's debut intensified.

Denise often came to help Maggie and Marie-Louise during this time. Tim frequently drove her to Treemont and left her there while he made his rounds. He had explained to his young wife the burden Hunter and Maggie were sharing over the fate of Treemont. Denise had denied the information out of hand, claiming Tim must be mistaken. But as they discussed the matter further, it became obvious to her that Hunter had taken her husband into his confidence. Everything Tim had told her was totally incredible, but true.

Denise joined ranks with her sister then, throwing herself into any task that gave the less-than-agile women difficulty.

"Have we done all that needs doing?" Denise asked on the Friday before the event.

Maggie sipped her tea and nodded. "We'll make some small cakes tomorrow, but everything else is ready." Her hand dropped back to her lap then, weaving a fine needle through a piece of delicate pale blue cloth.

"It's beautiful, Maggie," Denise said, her eyes roaming

over the high cradle at Maggie's side. "But how can you be so certain you're having a boy?"

"I want all boys," she said simply.

Denise frowned. "Why, for heaven's sake?"

"Because boys are better equipped to look after themselves," she said lightly. "Although Hunter knows a few tricks to help a girl fend for herself."

"That's silly, Mag," Denise admonished, her frown deepening when Maggie raised serious eyes to her sister. "Have you talked to Hunter about this?" Denise asked quietly.

"Hunter would understand," Maggie said and returned her attention to her sewing.

"You can't be sure you'll have boys," Denise said logically.

"I realize that."

Denise was clearly baffled by this attitude; it seemed extreme, to say the least, particularly for a woman who had been raised with three sisters.

Suddenly an old nagging question returned to the younger sister's mind—a question she had never been certain she wanted answered. But perhaps the answer was the reasoning behind Maggie's strange opinion. Denise dropped to her knees and placed her hands on Maggie's arm. "I've wondered, Mag," she whispered. "That man who struck you . . ."

Maggie looked directly into Denise's eyes. "I was wrong to leave you wondering. The man raped me, Dennie."

"Oh, God, Maggie," Denise breathed and dropped her head to her sister's lap.

Maggie raised a hand and lightly stroked the younger woman's fine hair as she looked into the understanding eyes of her husband as he entered the room. "Don't you see, Dennie?" she said calmly. "It doesn't matter anymore."

• • •

Sunday dawned bright and beautifully warm, and Maggie
suggested they set the wooden lawn chairs on the grass in
front of the house. A flock of small tables were also brought
out. Here the guests could mingle and chat before the men
strolled off to the paddock where Pride would be strutting
free for their scrutiny. The day was simply too perfect to
spend indoors.

Tim and Denise arrived early in the morning, bringing
with them some very good news.

"I've had two inquiries about this service of yours," Tim
said to Hunter.

Both Hunter and Maggie were thrilled by this. "Really?"
Hunter asked. "By whom?"

"Two of my patients who know we are related. They will
both be here this afternoon, apparently. I'll introduce you
once they arrive."

Hunter smiled down at his young wife. "That's an
encouraging start," he said, putting an arm around her
shoulders.

"I hope Pride lives up to his name," Maggie said, the words
slipping out innocently. She colored lightly as the men
laughed at her wide-eyed dismay. How could she have
alluded to *passion* within earshot of three men!

But then Jeffrey announced that he thought he heard the
wheels of a carriage approaching, and Maggie gave no more
thought to her indiscretion.

Treemont took on a festive air as the afternoon pro-
gressed. Looking exceptionally lovely in a high-waisted
dress of summer blue, white stockings, and soft, pale blue
shoes, Maggie wandered over the lawns, chatting with
ladies of old and new acquaintance. Jennifer seemed happy
running back and forth to fetch tea and lemonade for the
guests while Florence moved more quietly and at a much
more dignified pace.

Hunter passed close behind Florence, who had just

elebrated her fourteenth birthday and paused to take a andwich from the tray she carried. "You look beautiful oday, Florence," he said, and she smiled with barely a hint f a blush. "But don't let any of these young bucks turn our head just yet. We want to enjoy your company for a w more years." He touched her cheek lightly with his ngertips and moved away. Florence's smile became a bit righter as she passed among the women; she knew she was ecoming a more confident person because of Hunter and 1aggie, and she loved them both all the more for their nderstanding.

Carriages, phaetons, and other vehicles arrived and de-arted throughout the afternoon, and Maggie had no oppor-nity to question Hunter about the success of the day. He ould appear across the lawn talking with a group of men nd would then stroll off with them toward the paddock. ccasionally she caught his eye and he smiled or waved a reeting, but they were both caught up in their individual les.

Marie-Louise had chosen not to join the festivities, laiming she would be uncomfortable waddling among the uests. Besides, she knew that if she sat down in one of ose deep-seated lawn chairs, she would never be able to et up. Instead she spent a relatively quiet afternoon in the itchen, refilling trays with the cakes and small sandwiches ey had prepared.

Late in the afternoon Maggie returned to the kitchen earing two empty trays and found Marie-Louise leaning eavily on one of the counters. After quickly setting the ays down, she dashed to the other woman's side.

"Are you all right?" she asked.

Marie-Louise smiled grimly and nodded her head, but 1aggie understood instantly.

"Marie-Louise, don't you dare!" she said. "Not today!"

"You should have mentioned that about six hours ago Maggie," she suggested and straightened, gripping the small of her back with one hand.

"Oh, my God."

"Well," she said. "Let's look on the bright side of this. If you tell all those people what's going on, they'll think there's something prolific about Treemont, and Hunter will get more contracts signed."

Maggie could only laugh at the woman's wit. "You are *something*, Marie-Louise," she said. "I think we should get you upstairs to your room."

"Maggie, you're not strong enough to help me up those stairs. I think you'd best get my Jeff."

Maggie nodded as she helped the younger woman to chair before dashing back outside.

Jeffrey went into a flap and charged into the house leaving Maggie standing alone halfway between the new barn and the house.

Hunter had watched his friend leave on the run and approached Maggie quickly. "Don't tell me," he whispered.

Maggie grinned.

"Well, what should we do?" he asked helplessly.

Maggie laughed. "Darling, this is the first time you've failed to know exactly what to do."

"Well," he drawled, chagrined, "this doesn't happen every day."

"It will, one way or another, if your plan works," she teased and rose up on tiptoe to plant a kiss on his cheek. "Go sign those contracts, dear husband." And she left him standing there while she went in search of Tim.

Chaos seemed to rein supreme for hours after that.

Tim and Denise shooed Maggie away from the second floor.

"But I can help," Maggie said unhappily. "I'm her end. I should be with her."

Denise turned her sister by a shoulder. "She's got ffrey," she said. "Now scoot."

Maggie took one look at the nervous, perspiring man and ubted that anyone should rely upon Jeffrey at the moent. The brief, hesitant look she flashed over her shoulder ade Denise laugh.

"It's all right," she said. "Get on with you."

Maggie found Hunter in a condition similar to Jeffrey's— cing the parlor floor. "Not you, too," she said.

He turned at the sound of her voice. "How is she?" he ked.

"Are you going to be like this when our baby comes?" Hunter grinned. "Worse."

Maggie laughed and clutched his arm. "Have the last of e guests gone?" she asked.

Hunter nodded and somehow his foolish grin turned to e of triumph.

Maggie's heart bumped against her ribs, and the baby cked her solidly for her lack of consideration. "Tell me," e breathed.

Hunter reached inside his coat and withdrew five folded eces of paper. "And possibly two more will sign later this eek," he said.

Maggie's eyes widened as she stared at the contracts in s hands. And then she dared to ask the question that could ean the life or death of Treemont. "Will it be enough?"

Her eyes rose slowly to those of her husband, and he was dding. Smiling! "It's a damn good start, little one," he id. "I think we'll make it."

"It's a boy!" Jeffrey bellowed from the top of the stairs.

Hunter raised his eyes upward, and Maggie took a deep, lieved breath as she rose up on tiptoe and wrapped her ms around his neck.

"You did it!" she cried.

"I did not!"

"I meant you saved Treemont!" She laughed.

"*We* did it, little one," he said, hugging her close and setting humor aside. "All of us."

EPILOGUE

ᴉe evenings were close to perfect, Maggie thought as she
ᴉlked slowly beside her husband to the double wooden
ᴉng Hunter had suspended from the ceiling of the
ᴉrch. They liked to spend the warm clear evenings sit-
ᴉg there, watching the sunsets and the clouds drifting
ᴉoss the sky. The air was warm and fragrant in June,
ᴉore the burdensome heat of July descended, and often
ᴉaggie was loath to go inside even when it grew quite
ᴉ.

ᴉHunter held the swing in place with one hand and took
ᴉaggie's hand with the other. "You're not getting any
ᴉter at this, love," he teased.

ᴉShe shot him a mock glare. "Well, you should try sitting
something that moves when your body barely will."

ᴉ"Point taken," he said, smiling as he sat down and eased
ᴉ against his side.

ᴉ"It's such a beautiful night." She sighed, dropping her
ᴉd onto his shoulder.

ᴉ"And I think you're very tired."

ᴉ"But I don't want to go inside. Not yet," she said.

Hunter's hand slowly stroked her upper arm as the
enjoyed this peace of being alone together at the end of th
day.

"Hunter," she said softly after a time. "I've neve
thanked you."

"For what, little one?"

"For saving *me* as well as Treemont."

"I didn't save you, darling," he whispered. "I simpl
refused to let you live without me."

Maggie turned her head against his shoulder and smile
up at him. "I'm glad you did."

"Even now?" he teased as his hand stroked down he
swollen body.

"Even now."

Hunter nodded and lightly touched her cheek befor
raising a subject he had been mulling over for months. '
think we should stay on here, Maggie. Would you prefe
that?"

She would, of course, but, "You have your . . ."

"I've been thinking about it a lot lately. Treemont is you
home, and Florence and Jennifer might be unhappy if w
uproot them now. Pride has drawn a lot of attention here
and I think we'll make a go of the stud service. It onl
makes sense to stay."

"And Jeffrey and Marie-Louise?" she asked.

Hunter stared up at the clear, darkening sky and sai
thoughtfully, "I think they'd like to stay," he said.

Maggie nodded her agreement. "But what about you
home?" she asked quietly.

"It's only a house, love, if you're not in it."

Maggie twisted awkwardly and put her arms around hi
neck. "I do love you, Hunter Maguire," she whispered.

"Jason will manage the place for us," he said, as h
dipped his head and pressed his lips against her cheek

We'll hold it as a legacy for our sons." And then he
smiled as he thought more about it. "And daughters."

Confident and secure, Maggie put one final bit of her past
behind her, at last. "And daughters," she whispered.

Home is where the heart is . . .

If you enjoyed *Spring Blossom*,
don't miss the other stirring tales
of true and tender love from
DIAMOND HOMESPUN
ROMANCE . . .

*Please turn the page for an
exciting preview of* Golden Chances
*by Rebecca Hagan Lee.
Available now.*

Washington City
December 1869

Reese Jordan grimaced as he finished writing out the advertisement. He hoped it was right. If it was, it would change his life. He studied the lines for a moment, then scratched out a word here and there and inked in others. He smiled, satisfied with the results.

He'd done it. He'd found a way to gain his heart's desire without compromising his beliefs. Marriage was absolutely out of the question. A real marriage anyway. But this . . . it would work. This was the plan of a master strategist. His plan.

Reese handed the sheet of paper to the clerk, who placed it in the pile to be typeset.

"I want it in tomorrow's edition."

"That'll be an extra two bits."

"Fine." Reese produced the money, including a generous tip.

"I'll set it right away."

Reese nodded. Early in life he'd learned that cash gained him the respect and attention he would have preferred to garner on his own. Right now that was part of the problem. He swallowed hard. By tomorrow his plan would be set in motion. There would be no turning back.

He slapped his hat against his thigh. The sound seemed to echo in the room. The clerk looked up at him questioningly. Reese jammed his hat on and stalked out of the office.

A wagon rolled through a puddle near the boardwalk. Mud splattered Reese's boots and his carefully creased trousers. Reese cursed beneath his breath, damning Washington and its endless flood of traffic. The capital was readying itself for Christmas. People crowded into the city to see the sights. Greenery, red ribbons, and the sound of bells were everywhere, surrounding the inhabitants. Reese had little patience with the holiday. His mind was focused on his past and the important matter at hand. He sprinted across the muddy street to the telegraph office. It wouldn't hurt to send the same advertisement to the Richmond newspaper.

Reese scrawled the ad copy on a sheet of paper, then paid the telegraph clerk. The cards had all been dealt. Now all he had to do was play them carefully and wait for the results. Reese found himself whistling as he exited the telegraph office and walked back to his suite at the Madison Hotel, not some Christmas carol but a bawdy little tune he'd learned in the war. It suited his mood.

Plan and plan carefully. That was Reese Jordan's motto.

The clicking of the handset alerted the clerk in the telegraph office in Richmond. He quickly jotted down the words to the advertisement. The telegraph key quieted. The clerk hastily scanned the message.

WANTED: HEALTHY WOMAN BETWEEN THE
AGES OF 18 TO 23 TO PROVIDE HEIR TO
WEALTHY RANCHER. WIDOW WITH EXCEL-
LENT LINEAGE PREFERRED. ONE CHILD AC-
CEPTABLE. MUST TRAVEL TO WYOMING AND
REMAIN FOR ONE YEAR. EXCELLENT SALARY
AND BONUS. APPLY IN PERSON TO DAVID
ALEXANDER, MADISON HOTEL, WASHINGTON
CITY, DECEMBER 20.

He read the advertisement a second time. "That can't be
right," he said aloud. "I must have missed a word." He
carefully penciled in the word "for" in front of "heir,"
then read the whole thing aloud. " 'Wanted: Healthy woman
between the ages of eighteen to twenty-three to provide for
heir to wealthy rancher. Widow with excellent lineage preferred. One child acceptable. Must travel to Wyoming and
remain for one year. Excellent salary and bonus. Apply in
person to David Alexander, Madison Hotel, Washington City,
December twentieth.' "

The clerk nodded, silently congratulating himself for
catching his error. He placed his fingers on the handset,
telegraphed his receipt of the message back to Washington,
then handed the corrected copy to the errand boy.